I knew it was

love, but the

I took my lips from his. "What about Barbara?" I asked.

"Didn't you hear what she said?" he said urgently, almost whispering, and kissed me again. "'You two have fun. Don't worry about me.' She was giving us permission. She *wants* us to make love tonight."

I felt lightheaded, dizzy again. I took an enormous breath and let it out in a long sigh. Of course I had heard what she had said, and could not interpret it in any other way.

"Why?" I asked.

He gave me another small kiss on the lips. "Because she's not afraid. She loves us, and she knows that we love her."

A quiet voice in my mind told me that no matter what Barbara had said, I was courting disaster, but a much louder and persuasive voice in my chest and between my legs told me that I wanted this man at that moment more than anything else in the world. I put my hands on his shoulders and closed my eyes and drew him to me....

Also by J. P. KANSAS:
Andrea at the Center

THE HOUSE GUEST
and Other Stories

J. P. Kansas

The House Guest and Other Stories

First Masquerade Edition 1998
First Printing July 1998
ISBN 1-56333-638-3

First Top Shelf Edition 1998
ISBN 1-56333-924-2

Manufactured in the United States of America
Published by Masquerade Books, Inc.
801 Second Avenue
New York, N.Y. 10017

THE HOUSE GUEST AND OTHER STORIES

The House Guest	7
The Audition	143
Fantasies	163
Oh, Brother	173
Billie	179
Going Natural	189
Waking	201
Plaything	209
Toes	225
No Man's Land	233
Sex on the Beach	247
Vampire	257
Love Bites	275

Bloody Mary 289

First Looks:
The Mindcap Deluxe Version 1 307

The Art Lesson 317

THE HOUSE GUEST

One

It happened in another time, in the early seventies, when I was a young girl, just out of college.

My mother and father lived in San Francisco, I had gone to college in Michigan, and I was applying to a music school in New York. My transcript and my performance tape were good enough that the school had invited me to come to New York to audition—at my own expense, of course. I had saved enough money from my various part-time jobs—doing baby-sitting, tutoring, giving local kids music lessons, playing in a trio for weddings and parties, and waitressing—for the bus trip there (and enough for the bus trip back, if I didn't get in), but almost no money after that to live. I'm sure that my mother would have sent me a few dollars, had I asked, but the fact is that my mother was not at all well off, and she had used every spare penny to help me go to college, and I hated the thought of asking for more. Asking my father for money was completely out of the question: He never had any, and he never gave me any when he did. I told myself that I'd get myself to New York first and see how things worked out. I could always ask my mother for help later.

When I think back on it, I find it incredible that I got off the bus with nothing more than I could carry and the optimism and invulnerability and naiveté of youth. I had dozens of friends in a dozen cities, but none in New York. For that city, I only had the names of a few relatives I barely knew and friends-once-removed.

In some respects, I was impulsive and spontaneous. In other ways, I was organized and methodical. As I had prepared for my trip to New York, I had listed the names on a separate piece of paper, in alphabetical order, each with telephone number, address, and notes: Who had given me their names, what their situations were, whether they might help me find a place to stay or a job. If none of the names on the list worked out, I had the phone number and address of the YWCA, where I could stay until I got settled.

A few days before I actually left for New York, I sat down at the telephone with my list. The first names on the list were Barbara and Steve Andrews, and I called their number.

The phone was answered on the sixth ring, just as I was getting ready to hang up. "Hello?" It was a woman's voice, sounding somewhat distracted.

"Is this Barbara Andrews?" I asked. In the background I heard what sounded like a mewing cat.

"Yes?" she replied, impatiently.

"My name is Nona Williamson. I'm a friend of Bill Ganz."

"Oh, yes," she said, her tone of voice changing completely. "He called us a week or two ago. He told us you might call. You have to—" The crying sound in the background got louder. "Just a minute." She muffled the receiver, but I still heard her shout. "Steve! Do you need any help with her? Why is she crying?" I heard the sound of a man shouting in reply, but the words were unintelligible. When she unmuffled the receiver, the crying seemed to be subsiding. "Sorry."

"That's okay. If I caught you at a bad time—"

"No. That's okay. Bill said you need a place to stay for a little while?" She made it sound like a question.

"Well, I have an audition for a music school in New York and I don't really know anybody and I don't have a place to stay and Bill thought you might be able to help."

"He didn't speak to you after he called us? I told him we don't have a separate room for you or anything. We have a small loft that isn't air conditioned, and a three-month-old baby. But you're welcome to sleep on the couch for a few days, until you find something more permanent."

"I don't mean to put you out. I have a few more names, and I—"

"If you don't mind, we don't mind."

"Well, I really appreciate it. I promise not to stay more than a couple of days."

"When are you getting in?"

"Late Saturday afternoon. I'm taking the bus."

"We'll be around then. Give us a call when your bus gets in and we'll give you directions."

"Oh, great. I'll do that. Thanks a lot."

Two

Saturday

Now, after an endless bus trip, I was actually there. I was, of course, terrified—of the immensity of New York City; of the audition; of the prospect of being accepted by the school; of the prospect of not being accepted; of my complete aloneness; and, more than anything else, of the unknown of my entire life waiting to unfold before me. But my terror did not deter me. I had been terrified before and had persevered, and would persevere again this time.

I had been warned about the Port Authority Bus Terminal, so as I looked for a telephone I kept tight hold on my suitcase, my purse, and my flute case.

"Hey, sweetie! First time in New York?" asked a tall

man with long blond hair under a Beatles cap and the usual combination of tie-dye, denim, and army surplus. I glanced at his face. He wasn't bad-looking, with narrow gray eyes, and he needed a shave. He could have been anywhere from twenty to forty. He fell in step beside me, walking with that exaggerated bounce I called the hippie shuffle. "You know, New York can be a dangerous place for a such pretty girl." I could tell that I was smiling and blushing despite myself. "Can I help you with that? You got a place to stay?"

I pressed my lips together and shook my head, meaning to discourage him, but he misunderstood. "You got no place to go? Oh, sweetie! That's terrible! You wanna crash at my place?"

"No thank you."

"Hey, it's no problem. You can trust me. I'm Tim. What's your name?"

"I'm fine. Thank you. I have somewhere I'm going." I saw the bank of pay telephones across the vast lobby and headed toward them in what I hoped was a determined, purposeful manner.

"Oh yeah? You need a ride? My wheels are just outside. My chick Janey's waiting for me. You can ask her if it's okay."

Although I had never been to New York, I had had some experience being hit on before. Without stopping, I turned my head to look at him directly for the first time. "My husband is meeting me."

He was certain I was lying, but when he glanced down to my left hand, he saw a band on my ring finger. It was not a wedding band, but a ring my mother had given me. I had turned the small stone toward my palm automatically, as soon as I was aware of him approaching me.

"Where is he, then?"

"I have to call him," I said, nearing the telephone booths.

"If you were my wife, I'd be here waitin' for you." I could hear the smile in his voice. "Instead of letting her get hassled by guys at the bus station."

I stopped at an unoccupied telephone and put my suitcase on the floor between my legs. "That's enough," I said, no longer flattered and no longer amused. There was a man in a uniform about twenty yards away. I had no idea whether he was a New York City policeman or a private guard of some kind, but he had a gun belt. "If you don't leave me alone, I'll start screaming."

The hippie actually doffed his Beatles cap and bowed. "No need, sweetie. Welcome to the big city. I think you'll do just fine." Putting his hat back on his head, he turned and strolled back the way he had come, just as jauntily as if had just relieved me of my life savings, my hymen, and my self-respect. I lost sight of him in the crowd, and I turned toward the telephone, digging into my purse for my address book.

I put some money into the telephone and dialed the

Andrews' number. At first, the call did not go through, but then I realized I had dialed the area code for Manhattan. When I dialed without the code, it rang.

After nine rings, as I was debating with myself between waiting and trying again versus trying another name on my list, Barbara answered the phone.

"Hello?" she said, sounding hurried and distracted.

"This is Nona Williamson?" I said, afraid that she wouldn't remember me, or would regret her offer. "I spoke to you a few days ago?"

"Hi, Nona!" she said, her voice changing to one of great warmth, as if we were close friends. "How was your trip?"

"Long and tedious," I said with a laugh. "But at least now it's over."

She gave me directions to their apartment. As it turned out, they lived in Chelsea. It was only about a mile away, and I treated myself to a taxicab.

I felt nervous and shy and self-confident and brave at the same time. I didn't consider myself reckless or a thrill-seeker, but I liked the challenge of new situations. The feeling of fear and excitement didn't throw me.

I was still largely untried; I had experienced the usual share of disappointments but no tragedies as yet. I had had crushes and passions and heartbreaks, but nothing that had not healed. I was continually eager to fall in love and always told myself that I hoped one would be the real thing, but at some level I had always held myself in reserve, knowing that I was not really ready for the real thing, knowing that I wanted to pursue my career as a musician more than I wanted to lose myself to love. In music, I had shown early talent, and I had worked hard. I had not been a prodigy and was no virtuoso—at least not yet—but I had been winning recognition, prizes, and scholarships at the local level since junior high school. With my invitation to audition in New York, I was letting my dreams and hopes and confidence rise.

The Andrewses, turned out, lived in a six-story white apartment building off the Avenue, with large brown metal windows. It looked as if it had been recently converted from a factory. On the ground floor of the building was a fancy housewares store. When I rang their button in the vestibule of the lobby, a buzzer unlocking the inner door went off without anyone speaking to me.

They lived on the fifth floor. The elevator was modern but slow. I was impatient by the time it reached their floor and let me out.

Almost exactly opposite the elevators, an attractive, petite woman of about twenty-five was standing barefoot in a doorway, holding the brown metal door open. She had curly, wheat-straw blonde hair and pale blue eyes and was wearing a colorful, loose-fitting peasant dress. She gave me a warm, welcoming smile. I liked her immediately. "Hi. I'm Barbara," she said. "Come on in."

I dragged my suitcase out of the elevator and crossed the wide-planked wood hallway. Transferring my flute case to under my left arm, I offered my right hand. "Hi. I'm Nona."

She accepted my hand and gave it a brief, firm squeeze. "Come on in," she repeated, opening the door wider. "Honey!" she called back into the apartment.

"Just a minute! I've almost finished changing her!" came a man's voice from deeper inside.

Barbara motioned for me to enter, and after I had stepped past her, she closed and locked the door behind us. I walked down a fairly short, narrow entranceway and into a large, bright open room, with regularly spaced pillars and huge, floor-to-ceiling windows along one thirty-foot wall. The wood-plank floors looked newly polyurethaned, and were covered here and there with Oriental rugs. The walls and the pillars were white. The windows were the same brown metal I had seen from the street. Furniture, some modern and some antique, was scattered rather sparsely through the large room; the walls were hung with a few colorful framed posters and what looked like original watercolors. The paintings had an almost Oriental quality to them, as if they had been done very quickly, but with great confidence, using only a few brushstrokes. Despite the economy of line, there was a great precision and realism to the paintings. One was a large portrait of Barbara, nude. In the painting, she was looking out toward me, but not at me. Her attitude was direct, sensual but not provocative. She saw me notice the painting. "Steve did that of me, as a wedding present," Barbara explained, smiling. "So we can both remember what I looked like when I was young and beautiful."

"That's sweet," I said, continuing to look around.

Several smaller watercolors were of a baby, I assumed the baby I had heard crying over the phone. There were a number of cabinets filled with books and records; on the tops of the cabinets were several interesting-looking objects I could not immediately identify. I turned around, in the direction of the front door, and saw a kitchen separated from the rest of the apartment by a half-height dividing wall, over which was a second level, apparently used as an office, accessible by narrow stairs. Opposite the kitchen, across the entrance hall, was a dressing area separated from the main room by a wall that went up to the second level.

It was quite unlike my conception of a New York apartment, which I realized I had imagined would be small and dark and old and depressing, and I felt very comfortable.

"What a beautiful place," I said, putting my suitcase down.

"Thanks," said Barbara with a dismissive smile. "We love it, but we don't know what we're going to do when the baby—"

"Hi. I'm Steve," said the owner of the man's voice I

had heard earlier, coming from the far corner of the room. He walked toward me from what I supposed was a changing table, holding a small infant against one shoulder, and offered his hand. Steve looked a little older than Barbara, perhaps twenty-seven or twenty-eight. He was not quite as tall as me. He had short, straight, light brown hair, delicate, intelligent features, and a friendly, sincere smile. His wife came to stand next to him.

"I'm Nona. I really appreciate—"

"And this is Serena." He turned the baby to face me.

"Although she's not usually very serene," Barbara added with a small laugh. The baby looked at me without focusing very well. I could see both parents in her face.

"She's sweet." I held out my finger to her and waggled it. She looked at it for a moment and then grasped it in her hand and smiled triumphantly, making a small sound. "Hello, Serena," I crooned. "May I hold her?"

"She doesn't usually like strangers," Barbara warned.

Taking my finger back, I put my flute case down on my suitcase and slipped my purse off my shoulder. With the fearfulness of a new father, Steve gingerly handed me the child, and I took her against my chest and put my nose against the top of her head and took a deep smell.

As far back as I could remember, I'd always loved babies, loved their bright, foolish, tiny faces, their fierce little bodies, the smoothness of their skin and the wonderful odor of their hair. As late as junior high school, I was still pestering my mother to have another child, but I had been the only one. I helped the neighbors with their babies whenever I could, and was always ready to baby-sit.

Serena settled against my body and I rocked her gently. Barbara laughed. "That's amazing," she said. "You're very good with her."

As if on cue, the baby began to fuss. We all laughed. "I'll take her," Barbara said, and I gave the baby to her mother.

"Let's sit down," Steve said, gesturing to a grouping of couches at a low, round wooden table to our right.

"Do you want anything to drink?" Barbara asked. "You must be hot after your trip."

"I'd love something, but first I need to pee," I admitted.

Steve gestured back toward the entrance to the apartment. "It's the door to the left of the front door."

When I returned from the bathroom, the Andrews were sitting on one of the couches, and there was a tall glass of lemonade with ice on the table. Barbara was crocheting a small garment, perhaps a baby sweater.

"Do you want to call your folks or anyone?" Barbara asked. "Let people know where you are, that you've arrived safely?"

"No. My mom trusts me to take care of myself," I said, sitting down across from them. "I've really been on my own pretty much since high school. I'll call her when I've got real news—maybe after the audition."

We talked and talked and talked. Or, rather, Barbara and I talked, and Steve mostly listened, smiling and nodding to indicate his interest and his understanding. We exchanged much of our life stories. I told them about my audition later that week, about my hope of being accepted by the music school and becoming a professional musician. I learned that Steve was an art director for a small magazine devoted to new music, and that Barbara was a freelance copy editor. We talked about our mutual friend, Bill Ganz, and how we knew him, and we ran through the names of others we might know in common, but found no one else.

Barbara and Steve seemed like good, decent people; they seemed to be good together, and I liked them very much.

At one point, the baby cried, and Barbara put aside her crocheting and lowered the top of her dress and gave her her breast. In the seventies, you may remember, it had become fashionable for young mothers to nurse their infants in front of others, even in public places, and many women had refined the maneuver to the point that it almost seemed like sleight-of-hand. They lifted the blouse and moved the baby's head in place in one smooth, quick motion, so that their nipple was never uncovered, and their breast barely so. Not so Barbara. She handed the baby to her husband, pulled the top of her dress down off her shoulders and down her arms until chest was bare. Her breasts were almost shockingly large and full, with blue veins seeming to run everywhere underneath the white skin, the nipples darker and larger than I had ever seen. With both hands, she hefted both breasts as if deciding which one to buy, squeezing one and then the other. Apparently making a decision, she reached for her baby and brought it to her right breast. As the baby began to suck, she closed her eyes, leaned her head back, and sighed deeply.

"Some women don't like it," she said in a different voice than I had heard that afternoon, her eyes still closed. "But to me it's usually very sensual." She lowered her head and opened her eyes. "Sometimes it's almost like an orgasm," she said, looking directly at me, smiling easily.

I felt a flush of pleasure in my own breasts and smiled in return. You must understand: It did not seem to me that she was intending to be flirtatious or provocative or seductive. Young women like us were all swept up in the wave of feminism of the time, and we spoke with other women of orgasms and sex as easily as men, I suppose, spoke about cars and baseball.

If I felt at all ill at ease, it was because her husband was sitting right next to her. When I moved my eyes to his, though, he smiled in a friendly, accepting way, and there was no awkwardness between us.

"I can't imagine what that must be like," I said, and immediately felt that that was a stupid thing to say. "I mean, I *do* try to imagine what it must be like, but I'm sure I have no idea."

"I understand, and you're right," she said, and rearranged the baby at her breast, shifting her higher on her chest. "It's nothing like having a man at your breasts. A baby is much greedier." She looked down and caressed her infant's cheek with her finger. "Aren't you, sweetie? Aren't you?"

She looked at her husband. "When a man is doing something you don't like, you can just tell him to stop."

"Does he listen?" I asked.

"He does if he knows what's good for him," she replied. We all laughed.

"Honey," Barbara said, "could you get a cloth? I'm leaking." I saw that milk was dribbling out of her left breast. Steve sprang up. "Out of the house, I wear a nursing bra," she explained, "but I really hate them. I don't really like clothes at all." Barbara put the tip of her forefinger over her nipple, and then put it to her mouth and sucked on it. I watched, and felt another confusing flush —of embarrassment or excitement, I could not tell. But she seemed so casual about it that my feelings, whatever they were, seemed foolish and inappropriate.

"I understand why she likes it so much. It's so sweet. Much sweeter than the milk you buy in the store."

"I wonder why," I said.

"I guess because I eat something other than grass all day," Barbara said, and we laughed. She was continuing to dribble milk from her other breast, and she covered the nipple with her palm. "Want to taste it?" she asked, extending her hand with the wet palm turned up toward me. Our eyes met, and she smiled, and I could not decipher her smile, but I returned it.

"I don't know. I don't—"

"Go ahead," Steve said, suddenly standing next to his wife. "It's really very good."

Laughing, I dipped my forefinger into the palm of her hand, and brought it to my mouth. There was only a little of her milk on my finger, but I could tell that she was right. "Hmmm." I said. "It *is* sweet."

"Here, honey," Steve said, offering what looked like a clean cloth diaper. Thanking him, Barbara took the cloth, wiped herself off, and then moved the baby to the breast that was dribbling.

As Steve cooked dinner, Barbara and I sat at the table on the other side of the low wall. The conversation continued, seemingly inexhaustible. We talked about books we had read that had changed our lives, movies we loved and hated, music and musicians, art and history and politics. I remember being impressed with how well-informed they were, how intelligent, how considered their tastes. Only a few years older than me, they seemed incomparably more worldly and sophisticated, although not in the least patronizing or condescending. I felt so fortunate to have met these people, and they seemed pleased to have me as their guest.

Dinner was chicken, stir-fried vegetables, and brown rice. Barbara put a record of Erik Satie on the stereo system. Steve opened a bottle of red wine, and I had some with him, but Barbara, of course, abstained.

Over dinner, I told them more about my myself: That my father was a jazz flutist, my mother a potter and sculptor, that my parents had never married or even lived together, that I was an only child.

"It must have been wonderful to have such bohemian parents," Barbara said. "I grew up in Brooklyn, and my parents were as conventional as you can imagine."

"Oh, it wasn't so great," I said. "We didn't have a lot of money, and I was jealous of the kids who had a father who lived with them. I didn't even know where he was, half the time. Sometimes he'd disappear for a year or more. I guess for some kids that's pretty normal, but not the ones I went to school with."

"He must have been proud that you took up the flute," she suggested.

"No, not at all. He was completely self-taught, an ear player. He didn't like that I was learning to read music and couldn't improvise. 'It's like a person who never says an original sentence!' he used to say."

"What an awful thing to say," said Barbara.

"Fathers can be real bastards to their children," Steve said thoughtfully, and did not elaborate. It was, it seemed, the first thing he had said for hours.

"My mother's been pretty supportive, though," I said. "She's always been proud of me."

After dinner, I helped clear the table, and then

insisted on doing the dishes as my way of contributing. Barbara sat at the table, nursing Serena again, and Steve dried the dishes and put them away.

Barbara took me to the dressing area. She gave me an unused drawer in an old dresser and cleared a space in the clothes closet and I unpacked the few clothes and personal belongings that I had not already sent back from school to my mother for storage.

While I was unpacking, the phone rang. Steve and Barbara traded knowing looks. "Right on time," she said, rolling her eyes, and went to answer the call.

"Her mother," Steve explained. "Since the baby came, her mother calls just about every day around this time. Before Serena was born, she waited for Barbara to call her."

Barbara stayed on the phone a good ten minutes, answering, it seemed, a series of detailed questions about the baby. Steve and I sat on the couches in silence, listening to Barbara's side of the conversation. Finally she said, "Yeah, he's fine... No, nothing is new...Okay...Okay, speak to you tomorrow... Bye."

"She means well," Barbara said, after she had hung up. "She's really been very helpful. In the first week, I was a nervous wreck. Now I'm a lot calmer."

"You seem completely relaxed with the baby," I said.

Barbara smiled. "Thanks. I'm not."

By nine-thirty, with the summer sky still glowing, we were all yawning.

"We go to sleep pretty early these days," Barbara explained as she gathered things from the linen closet. "Serena doesn't sleep through the night, and she's usually up for the day at six or six-thirty."

"I understand," I said. "I'm pretty tired after my trip. And I've always been a morning person. Getting up at six is no problem."

Steve was at the windows, letting down the five sets of venetian blinds. "It's a problem for *me*," he said good-naturedly. With the blinds down, the loft seemed smaller and more intimate.

Barbara gave me a pillow, pillowcase, sheet, and towels. Steve helped me make the couch up into a bed as Barbara showered. We folded the king-sized sheet in half lengthwise to make a top and bottom sheet. It was warm enough that I didn't need a blanket. When Barbara came out of the bathroom, dressed in a gauzy white nightgown, Steve went in.

"Do you have anything to sleep in?" Barbara asked me, sitting down next to me on the couch-turned-bed.

"I have a nightshirt." I had taken it out of the drawer she had given me, and was holding it with the towels. Now I held it up. It was an overlong cotton T-shirt, decorated with the seal of my university.

"If you want something lighter, I can give you a nightgown," she said, indicating her own gown. "My mother is always giving them to me. She thinks the way to keep your husband happy is with sexy lingerie."

She said it with a smile, and I laughed, but talk of keeping husbands happy—for that matter, of husbands at all—was beyond my experience. Again, although there seemed to be only a few years' age difference between us, I felt much younger than Barbara. "I'll be fine with this," I said. "Thanks."

"I guess you've never had a husband?" she asked.

I shook my head. "Just boyfriends."

Barbara laughed. "Completely different species, husbands and boyfriends."

"Doesn't that depend on the husbands and the boyfriends?"

She patted my knee. "Not in the least." In her crib, Serena started to cry. "You'll see," Barbara said, getting up and walking across the room. "Right on schedule," she said quietly. Then, in the high-pitched voice she used to address her child, "What's the matter, Serena? Hungry again?"

In the bathroom, which was large and modern and full of mirrors, like one in a good-quality hotel, I undressed and showered, thinking about boyfriends and husbands and babies. I knew that I wanted to have babies, but it seemed years away. I knew that, unlike my mother, I wanted to have a husband before I had a child. I was sure that Barbara's joking comments about the difference between boyfriends and husbands were not really jokes at all, but I could not fathom the difference. If her comments were veiled complaints, I did not understand the reason. Her husband seemed like a wonderful, considerate man.

As I dried, I looked at myself in the mirror. In comparison to Barbara's heavy, full breasts, mine looked like a young girl's, round and high. I had always been pleased with how perfectly shaped they were, like ripe peaches, but now they seemed small and immature and somehow silly.

When I came out of the bathroom, wearing my college nightshirt, the lights in the loft were out, and the venetian blinds shredded the light from the street lamps into weird patterns on the ceiling. Not knowing whether my hosts were asleep or awake, I padded as softly as I could to the couch that was to serve as my bed.

"Good night, Nona," Barbara said in a half-whisper.

"Good night, Barbara," I whispered back, slipping into my bed. "Thanks for everything. You've really been wonderful."

"I hope that couch isn't too uncomfortable."

"I'm sure I'll be fine. I'm very adaptable."

"Good night," came Steve's whisper.

"Good night."

In fact, the couch was too short, and I was unused to the noises from the avenue below, and the venetian blinds clattered against the metal windows with the slightest wind, and it was too light in the room. I was so tired I was almost dizzy, but it seemed I lay there for some time, listening to Steve and Barbara whisper unintelligibly on the other side of the room. Although since I had met them I had felt completely comfortable with them, I now felt awkward to be sleeping in the same room as a married couple I barely knew.

I was suddenly awake. For a moment I had no idea where I was, and then I heard a baby's cry, and knew. It was much darker in the room. I could not see a clock, and I had no idea what time it was, but it seemed to be the middle of the night.

Serena's crying had woken me up. I turned on my side, facing the opposite end of the room, and in the darkness I watched Barbara get up, take her baby from the crib, and bring her to bed to nurse.

I closed my eyes, still half-asleep, partly listening to Barbara nurse Serena and partly imagining it. In my dreamy state, I drifted back and forth between the role of mother, feeling a warm ache in my breasts and a sweet, hungry tug on my nipples, and the role of infant, imagining the warm, nurturing breast in my mouth. Barbara crooned softly to her child, and I felt as soothed as if she were my own mother. I began to fall back asleep.

Barbara said something in another tone, and I heard Steve's voice. Though he spoke very softly, I caught the words: "I'll put her back." I listened as Steve took the baby, got out of bed, and returned her to the crib.

He got back into bed and said something I could not make out. She replied. Their tones were intimate and playful, with small laughs.

"What about our house guest?" Barbara asked in a suddenly distinct whisper.

"She must be asleep by now," Steve whispered back, and, without thinking, I closed my eyes like a child whose parents suddenly check on her.

In my imagination I could almost see the two of them, propped up on their elbows, looking across the room at me, holding their breaths, waiting for me to contradict Steve's assertion. I kept my eyes closed and pretended to sleep. Even if I wanted to admit that I was awake, it seemed too embarrassing to do so.

They waited another moment without moving, and then the soft whispering sound of their movements under the sheet resumed. They made small noises that were immediately familiar. I closed my eyes and my dreamy mind filled with images of what they were doing.

Gradually, the sounds of movement grew wetter, and the sounds of pleasure grew louder, and my body filled with my imagination, and ached with pleasure and yearning. Still lying on my back, I opened my eyes and turned my head toward them. My eyes were adapting to the dim light. I could see their bodies, moving under the sheet.

At that time in my life, sex was like a friend I loved but rarely saw, whom I never thought about when we were apart. When I was first with a new boyfriend, the lovemaking was always passionate and frequent, and I would think about it constantly. As the weeks or months would go by, the lovemaking would become more routine and less frequent, but for some reason I would not miss it. By the time we broke up, after a few weeks or a few months or a year, I had almost forgotten the urgent lovemaking at the beginning of the relationship. It was as if, when I stopped eating, I became less hungry rather than more so, and soon had lost the memory of the pleasure of food entirely.

Between boyfriends, I had virtually no interest in sex. Although I had read *Our Bodies, Ourselves* and many of the other books of radical feminism that flooded the campuses and the bookstores at that time, I did not even own a vibrator. I had tried touching myself a few times over the years, after reading an article about it in one of the women's magazines or listening to a solemn feminist discussion group, but, although it felt pleasant, I felt silly doing it, and stopped or simply fell asleep before I got anywhere near orgasm, or even really at all aroused.

It had been over six months since I had broken up with my last boyfriend, and since my last orgasm. With Barbara and Steve making love across the room from me, I was embarrassed and oddly ashamed and as aroused as I could ever remember being. My sex felt full of blood, and the wetness between my lips made them slick and smooth. My mind filled with vivid, detailed pictures of Steve's lips on Barbara's heavy breasts, his delicate hands caressing her soft body, and my body responded as if I were Barbara herself. Without really thinking about it, I put one hand between my legs, stroked my forefinger between my lips until it was wet, and then brought it up to my clitoris. I could not stop watching their shapes in the darkness.

They rolled over. Still under the sheet, Barbara rose up on her hands and knees, and Steve rose onto his knees, behind her. The sheet slipped down from his back and fell away behind him. The room was too dark for me to see well, but I could see the contours of their bodies. I could see the shape of her breasts hanging low and heavy, swaying as she moved. I could see the shape of her upraised buttocks. Although, as I later learned, his penis was of normal size, it seemed huge as he guided it into her.

Hypnotized, I stroked my clitoris in time with his thrusts into her. Although, as I said, I had never had much success touching myself, I suddenly knew just what to do. With the urgent pleasure building so strongly under my finger, I remembered my past attempts with a kind of embarrassed incredulity, as if suddenly getting a joke that everyone else but me had found funny.

As I watched them make love, I felt each stroke of my finger as if Steve were thrusting inside me, and at the same time I ached with a frustrating, inescapable awareness of my emptiness. I lifted my knees and put the soles of my feet down on the bed, and my hips lifted with each stroke.

Barbara's sounds of pleasure were growing louder and more uninhibited. I wanted so much to echo her noises, but I kept my lower lip between my teeth and tried to breathe without moaning.

They moved faster and faster, and my wet finger kept up with them. The slapping sound of his hips against her buttocks was rude and unbearably exciting. Barbara groaned very loudly, and Steve grunted, and they both moved spasmodically, shuddering.

I may have made a small noise as my own orgasm burst from my clitoris and through my entire body. Steve suddenly turned his head in my direction. I closed my eyes and pretended to be asleep, letting my knees fall lazily to the side as I slowly turned my back to them.

Three

Sunday

The room had the strange light of very early morning when the baby's cries woke me up again. My body was bunched awkwardly on the couch, my feet pressing against the armrest and my knees pressing against the back. When I turned, I felt a pain. After a few moments, Steve stirred, got out of bed, took Serena from her crib, and brought her to his wife.

I closed my eyes and listened to intimate, private sounds of the small family slowly beginning its day. They sounded sweet and full of love. I remembered what had happened in the middle of the night and felt a flush of heat in my chest and between my legs.

After feeding Serena, Barbara got out of bed and

went to the bathroom. On her way there, I had the feeling that she stopped and looked at me, but I kept my eyes closed, again pretending that I was asleep. After a while, she left the bathroom. Steve put the baby back in the crib and took his turn in the bathroom. I heard Barbara enter the kitchen and begin to prepare breakfast. Deciding to admit that I was awake, I sat up and looked over at her.

"Good morning," Barbara said, smiling warmly. She was wearing a light robe over her nightgown.

"Good morning."

"How'd you sleep?"

"Okay, I guess."

"I hope this isn't too early for you."

"No, it's fine."

I stood up, and my face must have betrayed the sudden pain I felt in the small of my back.

"I guess that couch isn't very comfortable to sleep on," she said with an apologetic smile.

"I'm just too big for it," I said, shrugging. "I'll get used to it."

"Maybe we can come up with something better for you tonight."

I sat down at the dining table.

"Want some breakfast? Coffee?"

"That would be great."

Steve came out of the bathroom wearing a robe. His hair looked as if he had washed it, and he had shaved.

"Good morning," he said, with a shy, friendly smile as he came to the table.

Watching him walk toward me, I remembered the shadowy shape of his body as he made love with his wife.

"Good morning," I returned as he sat down opposite me.

I glanced over into kitchen and saw that Barbara had been watching me watch her husband. She gave me a small, indecipherable smile as she set a mug of coffee, a spoon, and a creamer in front of me. A sugar bowl was already on the table. "Thanks."

The baby gurgled. "Would you get her and put her in the rocker, hon?" Barbara asked.

Steve made a small face of reluctance. "I'll do it," I volunteered, already getting up.

"The rocker is right next to her crib. Just put her right on the table."

The baby was on her back, smiling drunkenly at the mobile fastened above her. "Hello, cutie," I said, picking her up, watching her bright little eyes try to puzzle me out, and put her into the carrier, which held her in a somewhat upright position, allowing her to see more of her surroundings.

"There's a strap that goes between her legs that meets the one that goes around her waist," Barbara told me as I carried the baby to the table.

"I know. I've done a lot of baby-sitting."

"Great."

When I came back to the table with the baby, Barbara

was just sitting down. Three places were set with cereal, orange juice, toast, and coffee. I put the baby carrier down facing us.

"Hello, sweets," Steve said to his daughter, smiling goofily. She gurgled happily at him. He smiled even more broadly at this reward.

After breakfast, Barbara suggested that I could take a shower, and I took some clothes in. When I came out, dressed, I found Steve and Barbara both dressed, too. We dawdled about the apartment most of the morning, and then around eleven o'clock someone suggested that we all take a walk. Steve put his daughter into a cloth carrier that strapped onto his chest, turning himself into a male marsupial, Barbara put some sandals on her feet, and we all went downstairs. They showed me some of the immediate neighborhood, and then we headed south, into Greenwich Village. The sun was warm and bright. I was amazed at how many trees there were and how green they were. I was fascinated by the crooked, cobblestoned streets and the old brick buildings and the eccentric shops. It was, I knew, long past the prime of New York's famous bohemia, but I fell in love with it nonetheless.

We wound up in Washington Square. I was fascinated by the musicians, the roller skaters, the lunatics, the exhibitionists.

Serena grew hungry, and we sat on the grass under a tree while Barbara nursed her.

It was early afternoon when we returned to the apartment. Serena had fallen asleep on the way back from our walk, and Barbara carefully took her from the carrier and laid her into her crib, which was behind a screen next to their king-sized bed. Barbara and Steve and I ate lunch, which was yogurt and granola and whole grain bread. After lunch, Barbara went up to the loft to do some work, Steve picked up a novel he was reading and sat down on one of the couches, and I took out my journal—which I had not written in since I'd gotten on the bus to New York—and brought it up to date.

Long before dark, Steve went into the kitchen and made dinner. After dinner, we played with Serena. The telephone rang, and it was Barbara's mother. As Barbara and her mother talked, Steve opened a drawing notebook and took out a Rapidograph pen and drew Serena at play.

After a while, Serena began to cry. Barbara tried to feed her, but she would not nurse. "She's tired. It's time to put her down to sleep," Barbara said, rocking her. Her crying grew more desperate.

"I'll put on some music," Steve said, getting up and going to the stereo. "We can dance her." He glanced back at me.

Steve put a Dylan record on the stereo, and then took Serena from her mother. He put the baby against his shoulder and danced with her as if with a woman, watching Barbara and me on the couch, smiling.

"We do this all the time, when she has trouble falling asleep," Barbara explained.

"It's fun to dance with a baby," I replied.

"Want a turn?" Steve asked, smiling.

"Sure." I stood up and took Serena and cradled her against my body as Steve had done, and rocked her gently to the music. Steve continued to dance, although his arms were now empty. Barbara sat and watched us dance. She was smiling.

When it came time to go to bed, I remembered Barbara's remark that perhaps we could find another arrangement for me instead of the couch, but she did not bring it up, and I did not remind her. Instead, I took the bedding I had used the night before out of the closet and made up the couch again.

Again we took turns using the bathroom to change. Barbara was first and came out wearing a saffron night-gown. Steve went next and came out wearing only black pajama bottoms of a satiny material, his chest bare. I went last, and when I came out, again wearing my college nightshirt, Steve and Barbara were already in bed with the lights out. We said our good nights, and I lay down between the sheets on the couch.

Was the sigh I made as I lay down an intentional complaint? Did I anticipate the consequences? And if I had not made that small noise, would it all have unfolded differently? I have my suspicions. Although no one was planning anything, we were all attracted to each other, and the atmosphere was thick with possibility. I didn't plot and plan the small noise of complaint that escaped my lips, but it reflected my vague, unfocused wishes, my longing, my hope, an invitation for an invitation. And I think everything that happened was inevitable, given who we were and what we were and the times we were in.

Barbara spoke as soon as she heard my sigh. "I don't think that couch is too comfortable," she said to Steve, but loud enough for me to hear. "I told Nona we'd find something more comfortable for her tonight."

"Like what?" Steve asked in a neutral tone.

"I think we could make room here."

Steve said nothing for a moment.

"On my side," Barbara added, lightly.

"As long as I don't end up on the floor," Steve said.

Barbara raised the sheet on her side of the bed. "Bring your pillow."

I did so and slipped into bed beside her. "Thank you." The bed was much more comfortable than the couch, and I could stretch out to my full length. "This is great. A big improvement."

We exchanged good nights again.

I lay on my back with my eyes open, as excited as a schoolgirl on her first sleepover. Suddenly my eyes filled with tears. "The two of you have been so wonderful to me. And I'm practically a stranger to you."

Barbara turned on her side to face me, and put her hand on my near shoulder. "You're not a stranger at all. You're a wonderful new friend of ours."

I sniffled back my tears. "Thank you. I feel so silly."

"It's okay," she said tenderly, as you would to comfort a child, and kissed me on the cheek. "Now let's go to sleep," she said.

"Okay. Thank you."

She gave my shoulder a gentle squeeze and then took her hand away, although she still lay on her side, facing me.

I closed my eyes and felt my heart beating very quickly. Lying there next to the two of them so close, the loss of her touch made me feel painfully empty, alone, and incomplete. I wanted nothing so much as to be lying between them, comforted by their bodies against mine, like a baby between her parents.

I was not, at that time in my life, a terribly analytical person. For better or worse, I usually let my impulses have their way. I put one hand lightly on Barbara's waist and moved closer, so that I could almost feel the warmth of her body on mine, but I was ready to withdraw my hand and my body at the slightest suggestion that they were unwanted.

In the shadowy half-light, I met her eyes. I could not read the expression on her face. She lifted her arm toward me.

I took it as an invitation, and I closed the small space

between our bodies, burying my head in her shoulder, feeling her full breasts against my chest, her arms around me. I felt all the comfort and pleasure of a child cradled by her mother.

I had never, as an adult, lain with another woman, much less a woman and a man, and I truly did not know what would happen next. I felt calm and content, excited and nervous; I was drowsy and sleepy, preternaturally conscious and awake; holding her and being held by her seemed natural and simple, revolutionary and dangerous.

My lips were touching the soft skin at the base of her neck, and I kissed her there gently, tentatively. She was stroking the back of my neck slowly and softly.

So much has been made of the question whether women want love or sex or both. Which did I want then? I can't say that my yearning distinguished one from the other. I wanted to be enveloped by Barbara's love, in whatever way she might want to envelope me. Had it worked out that way, I would have been content, I think, to fall asleep in her arms.

But with Steve in the bed, that was not to be. I could feel him nestled against his wife's back. My arm, around her waist, was between them. I could not be sure, but it seemed he was kissing her neck.

He slipped his hand between Barbara's chest and mine, cupping her breast. The back of his hand pressed against my breast. I felt it moving as he gently turned the nipple in his fingers.

If Barbara did not want something to happen, it was the time for her to say so. But she only sighed.

Steve pressed himself against her in a steady rhythm, and I withdrew my arm, which had been between them, and put my hand on her shoulder, lightly, tentatively, ready to withdraw.

I lifted my head to look at her. She met my eyes with a steady gaze, but in the dim light, her expression was undecipherable. My heart was pounding as I had never felt it before. We were, I knew, moving into new territory.

I let my body fall back slightly. The sheet had worked itself down the bed, so we were uncovered to the waist. Steve's hand roamed over Barbara's breasts, stroking them through her nightgown. Her lips parted slightly. He tucked his fingertips into the low neckline of her gown and slipped it down, baring her breasts. When he brought his hand back to her breasts, she sighed deeply. The sight of his hand on her breasts, so close to me, was profoundly arousing. I wanted to touch them as he was touching them, to lower my lips to them. But I lay without moving, watching her become more and more aroused.

After a long time, his hand left her breasts, sweeping down her hip and thigh, pushing the sheet farther down and gathering the fabric of her nightgown's skirt and lifting it up to her waist. He brought his hand to her sex, petting her pubic hair before moving between her thighs. I watched his hand move, incredulous that I was being allowed to witness this, fascinated and terrified and excited.

The aroma of our arousal was almost overpowering. I had the sense that I could distinguish Barbara's odors from my own.

Barbara sighed deeply, and my eyes flew up to her face. I was surprised to see that her eyes were still open. As my eyes met hers, she smiled, and reached out and put her hand lightly on the side of my neck. A shiver ran through me.

I felt a movement, a shift of weight in the bed. Barbara had lifted her upper knee. She sighed again, and I could tell that Steve had entered Barbara from behind. The bed rocked slowly with the unmistakable rhythm of lovemaking.

I did not know what to do, and I looked into Barbara's eyes for a clue. She smiled slightly, and with her hand on my neck drew me toward her. Awkwardly, I slithered forward again, closing the space between our bodies. As I did, Barbara reached for the hem of my nightshirt and pulled it up to my armpits.

I felt our bodies touch in so many spots: our lips and our breasts and our bellies and our thighs and legs. And there, at our centers, keeping our sexes from touching, was Steve's hand where he was caressing her.

But almost as soon as my body touched the back of his hand, he withdrew it, and in the next moment I felt Barbara's sex on mine, pressing and then retreating in the rhythm of Steve's hips. A moment later, I felt Steve's hand on my side.

His hand moved further, to the small of my back, where it met Barbara's hand, and pulled me closer. My upper leg slipped between Barbara's legs, and our sexes touched more fully. I could almost feel Steve's penis as it thrust into her more and more urgently. It seemed he was very close to orgasm. We were all close.

Steve's hand moved down from my waist, at first cautiously, no more than an inch or two. After a moment, his hand moved farther down, cupping one cheek of my bottom.

As soon as he did, he groaned, as if shocked by his own audacity. It was a startled, frightened, almost disappointed sound, and he shook very powerfully, squeezing my bottom as he thrust himself into Barbara. Barbara quivered against me, pulling her mouth from mine as she gasped and moaned. My own orgasm shuddered through me powerfully as I felt them vibrate against me.

Slowly, the arms around me loosened, and we gradually moved apart. Barbara rolled onto her back and, for the first time since we had gotten into bed, Steve and I could look at each other. I saw that he was still wearing his pajama bottoms, and his penis had already disappeared into its folds.

Steve and Barbara kissed each other softly and then, both turning to me, somewhat awkwardly, kissed me.

Drawing apart again, we all looked at each other. It seemed they were as surprised as I was.

I wanted to speak but did not know what to say. My mind was racing with too many thoughts and feelings to catch one. I felt exhausted and exhilarated. I was shocked by what I had done, by what we had done. I felt as if I had committed a revolutionary act, as if I had breached a barrier I had not known existed, as if I passed into another world. I felt fearful and fearless. And I felt, more than anything else, closer to these two people than I had ever felt to anyone in my life. I felt something that seemed to transcend love, that I had somehow merged with them, become a part of them. I was near tears.

"That was beautiful," Barbara said.

"Yes," I said, almost choking.

She spoke hesitantly. "I just want you to know we've never—I didn't—we didn't..."

"No, no—me neither. Nothing ever like this," I said. I felt my tears overflowing my eyes and I sniffled them back. "You've made me feel so wonderful." I put my hand on Barbara's shoulder, and then reached past her and touched Steve on his shoulder. "I love you both," I said.

"We love you, too," Barbara said.

Steve touched me on the shoulder. "We both love you," he said softly.

The three of us shared kisses. I ached with their sweetness.

†††

I awoke to feel movement in the bed and realized that the baby was crying. Steve had gotten up and was bringing the baby to Barbara on her other side. As Barbara made room for Steve and the baby, she slid over closer to me, and I nestled against her soft, sleepy warmth. She took the baby and put her to her breast. The baby began to suckle. Dreamily, I reached out to touch the baby, stroking her small, soft head. Without thought, I found myself kissing Barbara where my lips rested at her shoulder. It was a natural, irresistible progression my lips followed as they moved down her chest to her breast. My hand moved from the baby's head and joined my mouth at Barbara's breast. I guided her nipple to my lips, licking and sucking and drinking the wonderful hot sweet milk.

Barbara's breathing gradually grew labored. "Take her back to the crib," she said in a low, urgent voice, turning toward her husband, handing the baby, now drunk and sleepy with milk, back to him. I slid closer to Barbara, feeling her hip nestle against my groin, my breasts against her arm. I kissed her shoulder. She made a sleepy sound of pleasure. I put one arm under her neck, my other hand on her waist, and squeezed her to me.

Steve returned to bed. As he settled against her, I felt his penis through the silk of his pajama bottoms brush against my hand on Barbara's waist. His penis was hard again. He lay down, pressing himself against her, kissing her. She sighed.

Steve raised himself up on one elbow and lowered

his head to her breast, at the same time putting his hand on her sex. She moaned deeply.

I was consumed with curiosity and desire. I raised myself up to see Steve's hand on her sex. Barbara was caressing his erection through the fabric of his pajama bottoms. She reached up to his waistband and, with his help, pulled the bottoms down. His erection was hard and high. As he slipped his bottoms off, she caressed his naked penis with her hand, pulling him toward her. It was a dizzying sight.

Naked now, he rolled between her legs and entered her. They both were moving very quickly, their pelvises thrusting together almost frantically. Eager, desperate to share their excitement, I pressed myself against them.

Supporting some of his weight on his far elbow, Steve put his arm around me, drawing me against the two of them.

I felt his hand move down my back, stopping at my bottom. I opened my legs and his fingertips slipped into my wetness.

Just as happened the first time, he stiffened and groaned almost the moment he touched me. He shuddered again and again. Beneath him, Barbara moved her hand to her sex and caressed herself with a very rapid circular motion, reaching a loud orgasm only moments later, clutching me against herself with her other hand. As for me, I reached a strangely diffuse climax that left me, nonetheless, content.

Four

Monday

In the morning, I woke to the sound of the baby gurgling, and as I opened my eyes the memory and realization of what we had done the night before flooded my consciousness, filling me with a giddy, drunken excitement. It was lighter in the room than it had been when I had woken the first morning. Barbara was lying next to me, and she saw that I was awake.

"Good morning," she said, with a sleepy, conspiratorial smile. The sight of her beautiful face made me ache with pleasure and longing. I wanted to feel her body against mine again.

"'Morning," I said, smiling back, putting my hand on her cheek. She turned her head and kissed my palm.

"Look who's here," said Steve, holding the baby. He climbed onto the bed on Barbara's other side. Some time during the night, he had put his pajama bottoms on again. "I changed her and now I think she's ready for breakfast."

He handed the baby, who was dressed only in a diaper, to her mother. Barbara had already checked both breasts and had chosen the left, turning on her side toward me and laying Serena on the bed between us.

As the baby took her mother's breast, I slid closer to the two of them until my body touched them everywhere it could. I felt the wonderful rhythm of the baby's suckling in my own breast, which pressed against the back of the baby's head. Her small feet were caught between her mother's belly and mine. Below that, I felt Barbara's groin against my groin, her legs against my legs. It was all deliciously sensual. I put my hand on Barbara's hip and stroked it softly.

Steve had lain down on his side behind Barbara, his head propped on one elbow. "That's so beautiful," he said, reaching across to stroke his daughter's head. His fingertips brushed against my breast, and I trembled. He looked at me and smiled.

In the light of morning, I felt very shy and young, and blushed and looked away.

He leaned over his wife and kissed her on the lips tenderly. "I've got to get ready for work. She slept late. It's already seven."

Barbara yawned enormously. "I'm tired."

He smiled. "I wonder why," he said, slipping out of the bed.

"I'll make you breakfast as soon as she finishes nursing."

"That's okay," he said, crossing the room toward the bathroom. "I'll get it myself." I heard the sound of the bathroom door closing.

I sat up. "I'll make Steve his breakfast this morning," I told Barbara.

She smiled sleepily at me. "That's sweet of you."

Steve and I sat at the dining table. He was freshly washed, neatly dressed in slacks and a short-sleeved white dress shirt, his hair still a little wet from the shower. I was dressed in my nightshirt, my face still unwashed, my hair still uncombed. I watched him as he ate his muffin and drank his coffee.

I tried to make sense of what I was feeling, and could not. I felt enormous tenderness toward him, a kind of love, but it was unlike any feeling I had ever had for a man I had just made love with. The sexual attraction, the memory of past desire and the anticipation of its future, was there, too, of course, but along with all that, I felt a great familiarity, a sweet, warm intimacy, almost as if we were not just lovers, but also sister and brother. It was the strangest situation, I think, I had ever found myself in. We had had orgasms together, but had we actually had sex with each other?

He had been studying the coffee in his cup, and now he looked up and met my eyes. "What are you thinking?" he asked softly, smiling shyly.

I shook my head. It was too much to explain.

He touched my hand softly with his fingertips. I felt it as a jolt of warmth running up my arm to my shoulder and neck. It made me shiver. "You're a beautiful person. Last night was wonderful. I loved the way you shared the love between Barbara and me."

I felt an exultant ache in my chest. I smiled at him, and he smiled back, his fingertips still resting lightly on my hand. I knew that I was crying. I felt the tears well out of my eyes and run down my cheeks. I didn't understand why.

He lifted his hands and brushed my tears away. "It's a whole new way of feeling for us, too," he said softly.

"I think they're both asleep," he whispered, gesturing with a nod of his head toward the bed. We stood facing each other in the entranceway next to the dining area. "Don't wake them up."

"Okay."

He lifted his briefcase and looked at me for a moment. His face was full of boyish shyness and confusion. It was sweet to see. "I'll see you when I get home from work." He smiled awkwardly.

"Have a good day, then," I said, returning his awkward smile.

He leaned forward and give me a small, chaste kiss on the lips, and I was overwhelmed with the need to feel him against me again. I put my arms around him and pulled him against me, my breasts melting against his chest. I opened my mouth, smearing my lips on his.

He dropped his briefcase and put his arms around me and embraced me. I felt his excitement rise, and then he let go of me and stepped back from my arms. "I've got to go," he said gutturally, snatching his briefcase and turning to leave. I caught his wrist and pulled him back for another kiss. "I'll see you all later," he said. I released his wrist and watched him leave the apartment, puzzled and confused and full of desire.

"I'm not asleep," Barbara said from the bed, startling me, as soon as the door had closed. "I'll be up in a minute."

"Okay," I said, wondering what she had heard of my conversation with Steve, what she had imagined had just taken place between us. But when she rose from the bed and greeted me, it was with one of the sunniest smiles I had ever seen. I was even more surprised when, as she joined me at the breakfast table, she leaned over and gave me a sweet, warm kiss on the lips.

"So," Barbara said, as we cleared the breakfast dishes, "what's on your agenda for today?"

"I'd like to practice, if I could. If it wouldn't disturb you or the baby—or the neighbors, for that matter."

"I don't care about the neighbors. As far as me and the baby go, we can try it and see what happens."

"That sounds fair. Other than practicing, there's nothing I really have to do. What is your day like?"

"This and that. I have some editing to do, I have some shopping to do, I have some errands to run, and of course I have Serena to take care of."

"Let me know how I can help. I'll do whatever I can."

"Thanks."

We got dressed at the same time. I found myself once again staring at Barbara's full, heavy, overripe breasts, and she apparently was looking at mine, because she said, "I used to have perfect breasts, like yours."

I put my hands to my chest and laughed. "These? Compared to you, I look like a twelve-year-old. You look like a woman."

"I look like a cow is more like it," she returned. "I worry about what they're going to look like when I stop nursing. Steve is delighted now, but what then?"

Again, I briefly imagined Steve at those breasts, his hands fondling them, his face buried between them, his mouth at those enormous nipples, the milk pouring out, wetting his face. I felt my own nipples grow hard, and my eyes suddenly met Barbara's. She smiled at me indulgently, as if she knew what I was imagining.

I felt my face flush, and I turned away and quickly finished getting dressed.

At breakfast, Barbara took an assortment of vitamin pills and dietary supplements. "And," she said pointedly, taking a pill from its foil-covered cardboard pack, "birth control. My doctor says it's not too soon, even though I'm nursing." She looked at me fixedly. "What do you use?"

"I use an IUD."

Barbara nodded, and the conversation moved to other things.

After we were dressed, Barbara asked me to do the favor of staying in the apartment and waiting for a phone call from one of her editors while she did some food shopping with Serena.

"I could do the shopping for you," I suggested. "Or I could watch Serena and you could go shopping without her."

"I like to get Serena out in the sun first thing in the morning. The experts say that'll help her sleep at night, although I haven't noticed any effect. Anyway, I'm not doing any major shopping, just a few things we ran out of over the weekend. I should be back in half an hour. If the phone rings, just take a message, okay?"

I was disappointed not to be able to go with them, but of course I said yes.

After they left, I sat on the windowsill and tried to

see if I could see them on the Avenue, but I couldn't. I felt inexplicably lonely and sad until I heard them outside the front door again.

"We're back. Any calls?" Barbara asked as she came in.

I went to join them in the entranceway of the loft. "No, not a one. Sorry."

She laughed as she took a small shopping bag out of the mesh carrier at the back of the baby stroller. "It's not your fault."

"Let me take that," I said, taking the bag from her. "You take your baby."

"Thanks."

I took the shopping into the kitchen area and put it away.

"By the way," she said as she unstrapped Serena and took her from the stroller, "while I was out, I had a set of keys made for you." Balancing Serena with one arm, she fished into her purse with her free hand and took out three keys on a metal ring. "That way you can come and go as you please."

"That's awfully nice of you," I said, feeling a wonderful, sad glow in my chest.

She showed me each of the keys and explained its function, and then handed them to me. Our hands touched as I took the keys from her, and I felt a surge of electricity. "Thanks," I said.

"It's nothing," she said, and kissed me softly on the lips.

The phone call Barbara was expecting came as I was holding Serena while Barbara folded up the stroller. After that, we spent the entire day together. Barbara went upstairs to the loft and spent several hours copy editing a manuscript. Serena stayed in the playpen beside her. After a while, I set up my music stand and my metronome and spent that time practicing scales, arpeggios, and trills. Remarkably, Barbara claimed to be undistracted by it, and Serena made no complaint, either.

Barbara fixed lunch for the two of us, and we continued the desultory conversation we had been having, adding more brushstrokes to the already detailed portraits we had been painting of ourselves. I learned more about Barbara's family, and she learned more about mine. We told each other about our boyfriends, the ones we had not slept with and the ones we had. She told me about how she had met Steve when they worked together for a magazine, about their decision to get married, about their wedding. I told her about how I had broken up with my last boyfriend, a young adjunct professor of music, when I discovered him in bed with one of his current students.

We talked about feminism. "I was in a woman's group, a consciousness-raising group, before Steve and I got married. I'm not sure how far we raised anyone's consciousness. We talked about sex all the time". She laughed self-deprecatingly. "Now, I meet on Thursday nights with the other mothers from my Lamaze class. We hardly talk about sex at all anymore."

"I was in a women's group last year in college," I said. "But we never talked about sex. We read books about feminism and then talked about them, tried to relate them to our own lives." I smiled. "I talked about sex with my roommates."

"Steve gets together with some of his old college buddies on Wednesday nights and plays poker. I'm sure they talk about sex."

"Isn't that all guys talk about when they get together?" I asked.

After lunch, Barbara put Serena down on the largest of the Oriental rugs, and we sat down on either side of her and played with her. She liked when Barbara put her face on her belly and shook it back and forth. I tried it, and she liked it from me, too.

"You really love babies, don't you?" Barbara asked, watching me with her infant.

"I do."

"It's a big step to take. A lot of responsibility."

"I know. I'm nowhere near ready."

"You have plenty of time. You're much younger than me, and sometimes I think I should have waited."

"How come?"

"Look at me. I'm only twenty-six and I'm a mother already." She laughed. "My life is over. I spend my life meeting her needs or his needs."

As if to prove Barbara's point, Serena began to fuss. I scooped her up into my arms and tried to comfort her, but I couldn't.

"Give her to me. She's either wet or hungry or both."

I passed the baby to Barbara, who checked the diaper. "Definitely wet."

I followed Barbara to the changing table, which was next to the crib, and watched as Barbara changed the diaper.

"Female genitals are so neat and tidy, don't you think?" Barbara asked as she wiped her daughter. "So much more aesthetic than male."

"I never really thought of it that way," I admitted.

"Male genitals are really ridiculous. As if they really belonged inside the body, with all those other funny-looking things." She put the new diaper on and closed it up. "Male genitals look like something you'd see in an aquarium, like a sea anemone or something."

I laughed. "I suppose so."

She turned to me and grinned. "When you change a baby's diapers twelve million times a day, your mind begins to run in strange directions."

I laughed again. "I can see that."

Barbara finished dressing Serena, who was still crying. "Well, now that we've eliminated one cause for complaint, there's really only one other possibility." She took the baby over to the couch I had slept on, which I had returned to its original condition, and sat down. I took a seat on the other couch, which was at right angles to it, as she lowered the top of her dress. "I don't think I'm going out again today," she said, almost to herself, and took off her nursing bra. The baby, whom she had lain on the couch next to her, grew very excited to see her mother's breasts, the milk already dribbling out of both nipples.

As I had seen her do before, Barbara hefted both breasts experimentally before choosing the one to nurse from first. She took the baby up in her arms and closed her eyes as the baby began to suckle, the milk running down her other breast.

I was fascinated. Barbara let her head loll back against the high back of the couch, and her breathing grew deeper and became sighing. I realized that it was arousing her, and the sight and sound of her so lost in pleasure aroused me, too.

After some time she opened her eyes, smiled at me shyly, and moved the baby to the other breast. This time, although her breathing was still deep, she kept her eyes open. "You have no idea," she said. "You have a baby, and you realize this is what your breasts are *for!* I can't understand women who have a baby and don't breast-feed."

"It looks wonderful," I acknowledged.

Later, Barbara put Serena into her crib and went upstairs to do more work at her desk. I went back to my flute, this time going over one of the pieces I intended to play at my audition.

"Do you ever play it straight through?" Barbara

called down from the loft, having heard me play the same phrase—a technically tricky run—a dozen times in a row.

"Not when I'm practicing it," I said.

"I'd love to hear you really play something. Your audition's tomorrow, right?"

"Yes."

"You nervous?"

"Of course."

"I'm sure you'll do fine. You play beautifully."

"Thank you. Maybe after dinner, I could play something for you and Steve."

"That would be wonderful."

She returned to her work, and I returned to mine.

Later in the day, Barbara was sitting on one couch with Serena on her lap, and I was sitting on the opposite couch. We had been talking for about an hour, our conversation sifting once again through our relationships with our families and friends. We all heard the sound of the front door opening.

"It's your daddy," Barbara said to Serena, who smiled and grew excited. Barbara glanced across at me and smiled. I was still rarely able to interpret her smiles.

I felt a rush of childish fearful excitement, an odd weakness in the backs of my knees, like what I had felt on those infrequent occasions that my father had come to visit my mother and me, overwhelming us, however briefly, with his charm and his love.

"Hello, everybody," Steve said, closing the front door. I heard him put his briefcase down. He walked into the room, looking damp and worn from the heat of the day, but handsome and attractive. He went first to where his wife and daughter were sitting. "Hi, sweets," he said, kissing Barbara, and then took Serena from her mother's lap and swung her into the air. "Hi, little sweets," he said, and kissed her many times all over her face. He seemed genuinely to love his daughter, and I felt a warm pang of pleasure as I watched him.

Holding her in front of his face, he rocked her gently a few more times, and then said, "Back to Mommy," and handed her to Barbara.

He turned to me, smiling, and I felt a great warmth blossoming inside me. I smiled, feeling awkward and very young.

"Hi," he said, softly, almost shyly.

"Hi," I said, barely able to meet his eyes.

He leaned over and kissed me on the lips with great gentleness. I felt a flood of heat in my chest, and my eyes flicked across to the other couch. Barbara was watching us, smiling. She seemed relaxed and comfortable with what she was seeing.

"How was your day?" Barbara asked him.

"Terrible. I couldn't wait to get home," he said. Barbara and I looked at each other. She smiled at me. I was quivering with anticipation.

†††

It was difficult for me to get through dinner. We talked about everything, it seemed, but what was on my mind, and what I'm sure was on theirs as well. Steve briefly told us about his workday, turning what must have been an unpleasant disagreement with an editor into an amusing anecdote. "And what did all you women do today?" he asked when he had finished the story. Barbara told Steve about her day. I added a little about mine. The conversation was lively and full of laughter. I was nervous and excited and I drank more wine than I usually did.

I had done the dinner dishes and we had had our coffee and Barbara had received her nightly call from her mother. Barbara, sitting at the table with Serena dozing in her arms, said, "Nona said she'd play something for us."

Steve looked at me and grinned disarmingly. "I'd love that."

I went to my music stand. When I practice, I sit, but when I perform, I always stand, so I raised the stand higher. Barbara and Steve had followed me and sat down on the couch together. Steve took Serena onto his lap and cradled her in one arm.

I turned the sheet music—it was a piece by Mozart—to the first page, took my flute up, and took a breath.

I'm always a little nervous when I play for someone, no matter who it is. I think most musicians are. But as I focused my concentration to begin, I realized that it was for some reason terribly important that I play well. They were both looking at me, smiling expectantly.

Within eight bars, I knew I was playing well, and I felt a great exultation. It seemed I was playing without effort, as if the flute were playing itself. I skated through the technically difficult passages as if they were the simplest scales. Hearing the music, it was as if I were listening to a virtuoso, and my performance seemed to yield new insights into the phrasings. I was astonished. I played the piece better than I had ever played the piece before. I played beyond myself.

The music ended, and I lowered the flute from my lips, almost surprised to find it there. Shyly, I looked up from the sheet music to my hosts. They were smiling broadly.

"That was beautiful," Barbara said, sounding happy and proud of me.

"It really was," Steve agreed.

"Thank you," I said, looking down, my voice almost breaking, surprised at how affected I was by their praise.

As it grew later, the rhythms changed. As we talked, we touched each other's hands with our fingertips. As we passed each other in the small kitchen, we put our hands on each other's waists or shoulders. As we sat together on the couch, our thighs touched.

By the time the glow of the late evening sky disappeared behind the buildings to the west, and Steve closed the venetian blinds, I was floating in a soft, warm, dreamy sea.

Barbara nursed Serena, got her to sleep, put her into the crib. She returned to the couch where Steve and I were sitting together. She had not bothered to close up her blouse from nursing Serena, and when she yawned, it gaped open, exposing her beautiful breasts, still slick from Serena's saliva and her own milk.

"I'm ready to go to bed," she said to both of us, still yawning. "Would you like a nightgown to wear instead of that cotton thing?" she asked me. "I have some things from before I had the baby that would fit you."

"Sure," I said, my excitement rising another small increment. I stood up and followed Barbara into the dressing area. She gave me a beautiful red satin night-gown with thin straps and a low neckline. "With my breasts the way the are, it just doesn't hang right anymore," she told me. "I'm always popping out of it." I undressed quickly and put it on. "You look great," she said, giving me a quick kiss on the cheek.

She put on a beige gown with a full-cut lace bodice. "After I had the baby, my mother sent me a whole set of these nightgowns for the full-figured woman," she said with a laugh. "C'mon. Let's brush our teeth."

In the bathroom, Barbara headed not for the sink but for the toilet, sitting down and immediately beginning to pee. I was embarrassed at such lack of modesty, but I was also touched and flattered that she was so comfortable in my presence. As if reading my mind, she laughed. "It's like we've always known each other, isn't it? It's almost like we're sisters."

"Yes," I said through my toothbrush. I was near tears, and I tried to hide it. In such a homey situation, it felt absurd to be so moved.

"I'm a little nervous, though," she said as she wiped herself. "I don't know what's going to happen when we all go to bed." She flushed and stood up.

"Nothing has to happen," I said quickly, fearful that she was angry with me, "if you don't want it to."

"That's not what I mean," she said as she joined me at the sink. "I'm not jealous of you. I feel very close to you, like you're a member of the family. I really mean that."

"I feel the same way."

"It's just that it's very powerful what's going on," she said. "I'm feeling things and doing things that've never happened to me before. It's wonderful, but it's a little scary, too."

"I know, I know. I feel exactly like you."

"I'm glad to hear that."

When we came out of the bathroom together, Steve was on the couch, paging distractedly through an art magazine. He glanced up and smiled at us. "The two of you look lovely," he said, sweetly, without being suggestive.

"Thank you," Barbara said for both of us.

"I'll get ready for bed, too," he said, standing up, dropping the magazine on the floor. "I need to shower."

I helped Barbara strip the bedspread from the bed and take the pillows out of their covers. Before we got into bed, Barbara walked around the screen to the crib. She looked in on Serena, and then called to me to come over to her. I went and stood next to her.

Serena was sleeping on her side, as infants do, with her tiny hand curled next to her tiny open mouth.

"Isn't she beautiful?" Barbara asked, putting her arm around my waist.

"She really is."

"I hope you have your own soon," she said, gently tugging me against her side. "When you're ready, of course."

"Thank you," I said, because I didn't know what else to say.

"Let's get into bed," she said, giving my waist a squeeze.

I lay on my back next to Barbara. We were holding hands, and our bodies only touched in a few innocent places. Nothing had happened, but my heart was already thudding with anticipation.

"Would you like Steve to make love with you?" she asked after a moment. "I know he wants to."

I felt a stab of fear in my heart. "Has he said that? Has he told you?"

"No. But I can tell."

"How do you feel about that?"

"I think it would be wonderful. It's not like he would be unfaithful to me. I want to share the love between Steve and me with you."

I felt as I imagined a child bride must feel on her wedding night. "Thank you," I said.

The door to the bathroom opened, and a few moments later Steve came into view wearing a pair of satin pajamas. His face was solemn and intense, as if he were about to participate in the holiest of sacred rites. He met my eyes but said nothing. His eyes shifted to Barbara and they looked at each other for a moment.

"Come to bed, sweetie," Barbara said, reaching across me and patting my side of the bed.

Steve nodded to her, almost imperceptibly. He climbed into bed next to me and lay down on his side where Barbara had indicated, snuggling against me. I felt his penis, already seeming to be fully erect, against my thigh. Barbara reaching across me to her husband, finding his hand and putting it on my chest just below my breasts. I wondered if he could feel how hard my heart was pounding.

Barbara moved her husband's hand up to my breast. I closed my eyes, floating. Between my legs, I was already soaking.

They were both kissing me, first on my mouth and then on my cheeks and then on my neck and shoulders and then on my chest and then they lowered the straps of my gown and kissed my breasts and my nipples. I sighed and sighed, weightless, rocking in a cradle of unfathomable pleasure.

I felt their hands caress my breasts, move down my body, into my wet sex.

With her hand on my shoulder, Barbara turned me on my side, so that I was facing Steve. She pressed herself against me, and I felt her breasts against my back and her pubic mound against my bottom. She kissed my neck as she reached past me to her husband, drawing him to me again. He put his arms around us both, pressing himself against me, kissing me, and I felt his erection nestling against my groin through the silkiness of his pajamas.

Barbara reached down to my sex. She parted my legs and then reached beyond me. I felt her slip Steve's penis out of his pajamas and place it between my thighs.

Steve made a low sound of incredulous pleasure. "You really want me to, sweets?" came his voice, lower than I had heard it before. I opened my eyes and looked at him. It was a strangely solemn moment, as if we were about to perform a sacrament.

"Yes," Barbara said. "I love you."

I began to tremble. "Are you sure?" I whispered. "Are you sure this is all right with you?"

"I want this," she replied, also whispering, kissing my shoulder gently. "For all of us. It'll be beautiful."

Kissing the back of my neck, Barbara guided Steve's penis to the mouth of my sex.

It had been so long since I'd been with a man. I'd almost forgotten what it was like to feel that soft, hard, hot, dull, blind, hungry flesh seeking me. I lifted my upper knee higher, and shifted my pelvis toward him, and I felt the head of his penis begin to enter me. At first, he seemed too big for me, and I felt a wave of fear. Then Barbara brought her hand up to my breast, stroking and caressing my nipple, and I opened like a flower. Steve pressed gently but insistently, filling me wonderfully, putting his lips at the base of my neck and licking and sucking.

With her husband stroking inside me, and her hand still on us, Barbara pressed her body even closer to mine, kissing me just behind the ear. Cradled between Barbara and Steve, feeling their bodies against mine everywhere, I felt loved, beautiful, protected, and safe.

Steve was thrusting inside me ever faster and more urgently. Suddenly he groaned and thrust spasmodically inside me. Barbara thrust her tongue deeply into my ear. Cradled between them, I was coming again, my orgasm flowing endlessly and spreading through my body out to my very skin in a way I had never felt before. It seemed that my consciousness was disintegrating: There was no longer a *me* experiencing the pleasure; there was only the pleasure.

Awkwardly, we all managed to kiss each other. I had

to turn my head sharply to reach Barbara's lips, and Barbara had to raise herself up on one elbow to reach Steve. We were all smiling foolishly, like small children sharing a secret. Then we lay down, still embracing, our bodies still entangled.

The baby was crying. The room was dark. The candle had gone out. I had fallen asleep where I was, still between the two of them. Steve was still nestled against me, but was no longer inside me. I could feel his penis, now soft and wet, against my thigh.

The baby continued to cry. Barbara mumbled, also just waking up. "I'll get her," Steve said, slipping out of bed.

"Change her first," Barbara said in a sleepy voice.

"I know."

I lay with my eyes closed, partly awake and partly asleep, listening to Steve talk softly to his baby as he took her from her crib, changed her diaper, and then brought her to Barbara, getting into bed next to her. Still more asleep than awake, I moved closer to Barbara, nestling against her side, softly stroking her with my hand as she nursed her baby. My hand found the baby's tiny mouth at Barbara's nipple and suddenly I was almost desperately thirsty. I moved my head down and brought my lips to Barbara's other breast. Her milk flowed freely, hot and sweet and delicious.

The baby only took the one breast before falling asleep again. Steve put her back into her crib and returned to bed, again getting in next to Barbara, cuddling up against her, caressing her.

"More?" she asked sleepily.

"Yes. Feel this."

"I want to go back to sleep, honey."

"You don't have to do anything," Steve said, already lifting himself over her.

Making a small, ambiguous sound of protest or incredulity or resignation, Barbara lifted her knees and parted her legs.

Reaching down with one hand, Steve fitted himself to her and entered her. "You're so wet," he said softly as he sank into her.

"It's from before," she said, although her hips were rising slightly to meet his thrusts.

"You feel wonderful," he said, stroking quickly. "I love you."

"I love you, too, honey," she said.

Lying on my side, watching them, I felt painfully separate, and my eyes filled suddenly with tears. I reached over and rested my hand in the small of Steve's back, letting it rise and fall with his thrusts.

He turned his head and met my eyes in the near darkness. Shifting his weight onto his other elbow, he reached his arm out toward me. I slid over on the bed until my body touched them both. Steve put his arm around my waist and squeezed me to them, and then moved his hand down onto my bottom.

He lowered his head toward mine and kissed my mouth, his hand moving lower, finding my wetness, opening me. He had his penis inside Barbara, but he was caressing me with his fingers, and he was kissing me. I was as aroused as I had ever been. I moved my hand from the small of his back onto his bottom, squeezing it. His tongue deep in my mouth, and his fingers as deep in my vagina as he could manage, he groaned. Although he was ejaculating inside Barbara, it seemed he was coming inside me. Pressing my sex against Barbara's hip, I came again.

Five

Tuesday

I awoke to find Barbara nursing Serena next to me. Serena was not even wearing a diaper, and her tiny naked body against her mother's naked chest was heartbreakingly sweet and beautiful. Steve lay behind Barbara, his head propped on his hand, watching her. A feeling of almost delirious contentment suffused me as I watched this beautiful scene, somehow a part of it.

Steve noticed that I was awake, and we all exchanged good mornings, smiling foolishly. We had, in some small way, changed the world.

I wanted to stay in bed with the three of them forever, but we all had things to do. After Barbara finished nursing her, Steve, in his pajama bottoms again, took Serena to the changing table and put a diaper and a T-shirt on her. Barbara slipped on her nightgown and got out of the bed and went into the bathroom.

"Your audition is today, isn't it?" Steve asked as he returned with Serena, now in the infant seat.

I had not put the gown that Barbara had given me back on, and the sheet was at my waist. As we talked, Steve's eyes kept drifting from my face to my chest. It filled me with a strange mixture of pleasure and embarrassment to feel his gaze on my breasts, but I made no effort to cover myself.

"Yes."

"Nervous?"

"I suppose so." Actually, the audition seemed remote and inconsequential. Everything that might possibly happen outside that apartment, or even outside that bed, seemed part of some distant past. "It's just my entire professional future," I said with a laugh. I felt my breasts quiver, and I knew that Steve was watching them move.

"What time is your audition?" he asked, forcing his eyes back to mine.

"Ten o'clock."

"Well, good luck with it." He gave me an encouraging smile. "I'm sure you'll do fine."

"Thanks."

His eyes drifted down to my breasts again, and he seemed to lose himself in thought. Shaking his head suddenly, as if catching himself dozing off, he brought his eyes back to my face and smiled. "Well, I've got to get dressed and get a move on."

After I heard the front door close, I closed my eyes and my mind drifted over what had happened over the last few days. I felt as if I were on a boat on crazy, uncertain waters. But although I was in powerful seas, I had a drunkard's sense of invulnerability. I would not capsize. The currents would not drown me. In fact, the currents were all with me, hurtling me into utterly new, wonderful seas.

I lay there, my hand resting on my sex. The flesh felt tender, almost bruised, but aching as if to be bruised some more. I had remembered what I had forgotten. The appetites that had been dormant had been reawakened, as they always did at the start of a love affair, but this time stronger than I had ever felt them before.

My fingers explored myself, at first simply to assess my condition, but then, remembering their success that first night, I began to look for the places to stroke that had made me feel so good.

I cupped a bare breast with one hand as I stroked my sex with the other under the sheet. I was deeply involved with the sensations I was evoking when I sensed someone beside me, and I stilled my hand and turned my head.

Barbara was standing next to the bed smiling at me. "Good morning," she said.

"Good morning," I said, taking my hand from between my legs.

"It's okay," she said. "You don't have to stop."

I was blushing. "You must think I'm some kind of sex maniac," I said, taking both hands from under the thin cover. "I really don't—"

She sat down on the edge of the bed. "I understand."

"I mean, if you can believe it, the first night I was here was the first time I actually made myself come."

She smiled. "Really?"

I was terribly embarrassed, but what I had done felt like a guilty secret between us. I let the words tumble out before I had a chance to stop myself. "The baby woke me up. I didn't know what to do to let you know that I was awake. It was too embarrassing, so I didn't. Then you went ahead and made love with Steve, and I listened and watched in the shadows. It was incredibly exciting. That's the first time in my life that I made myself come."

"Why'd you wait so long?"

"I don't know. I just didn't get it. I was too embarrassed, I guess, even though I was all by myself. Mostly, when I wasn't with a guy, I just kind of forgot about sex. It's like I went to sleep."

"And now I see you've woken up again," she said with a laugh.

"It's like I'm in a completely new world with you and Steve."

"It's a whole new world for us, too. Since the baby came, we haven't been having very much sex."

"Really? The way you made love the first night I was here, it seemed the two of you were very into it."

"The fact is, I haven't been very interested. With the baby always wanting my breasts, I haven't been in the mood much for Steve. We've only had sex a couple of times since Serena was born. I think it made Steve terribly excited to have you stay with us. His being so excited turned me on."

We held each other's eyes for a moment, and then I glanced away and noticed the clock.

"I've got to get up and get ready for my audition," I said, sitting up and pulling the nightgown on over my head to cover myself.

When I left to go to my audition, I felt overwhelmed by the city streets, like a baby animal leaving its nest too early. Although I had gone out every day since I'd arrived, it was always with Barbara and Serena or with the entire family. Alone, I felt naked and unprotected, as if the light summer dress I was wearing was not there at all.

"So how was it?" Barbara asked excitedly, as soon as I entered the apartment. "Are you accepted?" She had been working in the loft and raced down the stairs to meet me, smiling enthusiastically.

"I don't know yet. They'll send a letter in a couple of weeks. I gave them this address—I hope that's okay. Or I can call and get the results."

Her pale blue eyes darted over my face. "But how did it go? Tell me all about it!"

"Well, it was pretty hard, but I think it went very well," I said, smiling back, her enthusiasm exciting me.

"Oh, that's great, Nona," she said, giving me a sisterly hug. "I'm so happy for you. Tell me all about it." She led me to the dining table, and we sat down.

"The guy giving me the audition is the head of the woodwind department, and he was probably the most intense man I'd ever met. He was in his thirties, and he had a Prince Valiant haircut, and a jaw like a movie star, and these really piercing blue eyes."

"He sounds cute."

"He was too serious to be cute. Even when he smiled, he looked serious, and he didn't smile much. He looked over my transcript and my application and my letters of recommendation and he asked a few questions, and then he had me play my prepared pieces—the one I played for you and Steve last night, and two others."

"How'd they go? The piece you played for us sounded great."

"Well, I don't think I played it as well as I did for you, but it went pretty well. Then he gave me something to sight-read I'd never seen before, something flashy but not too difficult, and then we played a duet."

"And how did that all go?"

"It was all like I was watching and listening to someone else play. I was there, and I wasn't there. It was almost as if I was having an out-of-body experience."

"That's funny," Barbara said quietly. "That's kind of

how I felt when the three of us were in bed together last night."

Barbara and I had lunch, and I spent the afternoon keeping her company and helping her pursue her domestic chores. Normally, I would have spent as much time as I could practicing my flute, but I suddenly had no interest in playing. Instead, I changed the baby and played with her and brought her to Barbara to nurse; I went with Barbara to the laundry room, and helped her sort and fold. Upstairs again, I helped her put the laundry away. Later, we went out to bring Steve's dress shirts to the Chinese laundry, and to pick up those from the week before.

As the day unrolled, the glow of anticipation grew warmer and warmer inside me. I yearned to be once again enveloped in the arms of Barbara and Steve, to be consumed by their love. As it grew closer and closer to the time Steve usually returned from work, I grew as restless as a cat expecting dinner, and, carrying Serena on my shoulder, paced the apartment aimlessly, inspecting the art on the walls, the books on the shelves, the objects and the decorations.

Finally, we heard Steve's key in the lock and I felt myself lurch in surprise, as if I had not been waiting for exactly that sound for hours.

"Hello, everybody!" he called as the door closed. Barbara got up from her desk in the loft and came to the head of the stairs. I walked toward the entrance to the apartment, and saw that he was carrying a bouquet of roses as well as his briefcase.

"Hi," he said, smiling at me boyishly. "How'd your audition go?"

"Fine. It went fine."

Barbara came down the stairs, walking past me toward her husband. "Who're the flowers for?" she asked lightly, reaching for them.

"They're for the three of you," Steve said.

"They're beautiful," she said, taking them from him, and giving him a light kiss. "Thanks."

"I thought we'd celebrate Nona's audition by going out for dinner."

"I don't have a sitter for Serena, and I haven't expressed any milk," Barbara said from the kitchen, where she was unwrapping the flowers.

"We can take her with us. We'll hide her under the table."

With Barbara busy in the kitchen putting the flowers in a vase, Steve closed the distance between us and put his hand at my waist. Our eyes met, and I felt lightheaded. "Hi," he said, softly, almost whispering. The single syllable seemed laden with a thousand meanings.

"Hi," I said, barely able to speak. He kissed me on the lips, and I felt a rush of longing so intense it was painful.

†††

We walked to Greenwich Village, taking turns pushing Serena in her stroller and carrying the empty babyseat. The summer evening was warm and light, and the streets were filled with people. Steve led us to a tiny Japanese restaurant on Thirteenth Street, barely wide enough for three rows of small tables. Steve and Barbara sat opposite each other, and I sat next to Steve so that we could we put Serena's carrier on the chair next to Barbara. The waitresses all came to coo over the baby, and Barbara beamed with pride. I felt strangely jealous, as if the Andrews were mine alone, and no one else had the right to enjoy them.

In the middle of the meal, Serena decided that she was hungry, too, and Barbara had to interrupt her meal to nurse her. I noticed that, when she was in public, Barbara was perfectly adept at the maneuver of bringing a baby to her nipple without exposing her breast to view.

We were having our tea when Serena started fussing again, and Steve hurriedly paid the check and we gathered ourselves up to leave. I was just as glad. I had enjoyed our meal, but I was eager to return to the apartment, which I was thinking of as *our* apartment, *our* home.

Barbara had put Serena in her crib for the night, but it was still too early for us to go to bed. Steve put some music on the stereo system and sat down on the couch with an art magazine. Sitting on the other couch, Barbara took out her crocheting. I stood with my back to the windows, looking at the two of them, feeling oddly unsettled.

"I've always wanted to learn how to do that," I said suddenly, surprising myself. In fact, I had never had interest in any of the traditionally female crafts of knitting, sewing, or crocheting. I had no idea what had made me say it.

Barbara looked up at me and smiled. "Great! Come here and I'll teach you."

"Okay," I said, sitting down next to her, still puzzling over what had made me tell her that pointless lie. She took some yarn and a spare crochet hook from the bag at her feet and began to teach me the craft.

Finally, Steve threw his magazine on the table and stood up. "I'm getting ready for bed," he announced, walking to the windows.

My heart thrummed, and I looked from Steve to Barbara. "Okay," she said. "Let me just finish this row."

Steve was lowering and closing the venetian blinds. "Take your time," he said.

"How do I stop this for now?" I asked her, indicating the baby hat she had started me working on.

"Just leave everything as it is. It'll be fine."

Steve went into the bathroom. I put my crocheting down on the table and stood up. "I guess I'll get the bed ready," I said.

"Why don't you change first, and then I'll help you with the bed?" she suggested, grimacing as she concentrated on her work.

I went to the dressing area and quickly stripped off the few clothes I'd been wearing all day. Naked, I looked over to where Barbara sat working. I felt an uncomprehending gratitude that she had welcomed me into her life and a nearly overpowering desire to feel her body on mine again. I took the nightgown she had lent me—*my* nightgown, now—from the hook on the back of the closet door and slipped it on.

"Okay," she said, as I returned to the living area. She picked up a pencil to mark off her place on the pattern she was following. She looked up and gave me a delighted and delightful smile. "You really look lovely in that."

I felt myself blush, like a little girl in her first party dress. "Thank you."

"Come on," she said brightly, standing up, "let's get the bed ready."

As we had done the night before, we stripped the coverlet from the bed and took the pillows out of their decorative covers, folded everything up, and put it all aside on the trunk at the foot of the bed. I lit the candle on the bureau as Barbara turned off the overhead light. "I'll go change," she said.

I sat down on the edge of the bed and waited.

"I've been thinking about the three of us all day,"

she said softly, when she returned, now wearing her nightgown. Standing before me, she put her hand lightly on the back of my neck. I felt a flush through my chest.

"Me too," I said, looking up at her. "What have you been thinking?"

She shook her head slightly, smiling sadly. "I don't know. It's all been so wonderful. I feel such love for you. I don't understand what's happening to of us. I wonder how we can go on."

I sat in the candlelight and looked at this woman I had known only a few days, and who seemed more important to me than any other woman in the world. In one part of my mind, the notion seemed like a delusion, but in most of my mind it felt inescapably and self-evidently true. I wondered if I was going crazy. I felt my eyes fill with tears.

"You're frightening me, Barbara," I said, choking, and she put her arms around me and hugged me to herself. "I love you so much." I put my head on her belly, still a little round from her pregnancy, and felt her stroke my head. I felt both deliriously happy and painfully sad, and sobbed and laughed at the same time.

She sat down beside me, comforting me with small, meaningless sounds, kissing me softly on the cheeks, as a mother kisses away the tears of a small child. I put my arms around her and nestled against her chest.

Steve came out of the bathroom wearing a satin robe. He knelt before us. "What's the matter?" he asked, quiet and concerned.

I sniffled back my tears, more than a little embarrassed. "Nothing," I said with a dismissive laugh. "I'm just a crybaby."

He came closer, putting an arm around each of us, and kissed me on the cheek as Barbara had done. "Nothing to cry about," he said. "Everything's all right. We love you."

As if choreographed, we smoothly shifted position until the three of us were on our knees in the middle of the bed, embracing and kissing. We moved, at first, in nearly perfect three-fold symmetry. The mood shifted with dizzying speed. Our kisses, which had been sweet and gentle and loving, grew more openly desirous. Our chests pressed together. One of my breasts met one of Barbara's; my other felt Steve's smooth, hard chest. In our embrace, both Barbara and Steve had a hand at the small of my back, as I had a hand at the small of each of theirs. Almost at the same moment, their hands moved down to the rise of my bottom, and then farther down to hold my bottom, pulling me against them. I moved my own hands down as theirs had done. I felt Steve's penis grow hard, awkwardly pressing down against my thigh, and then he moved away slightly and returned, this time with his penis folding up between our bodies.

Once again, I was in a state of almost uncontainable pleasure. But I felt much more than merely sensual pleasure. With their bodies pressing against mine, their hands holding me, and their mouths on mine, I felt a sense of belonging, of acceptance, of love that I had never experienced—that I had never even imagined experiencing.

Our symmetry broke down as we tumbled down onto the bed, throwing off our nightclothes and rubbing ourselves against one another like a primitive, undifferentiated life form. I found myself lying on my back between them. They lay on either side of me, facing each other.

This time they turned me to face Barbara, and we embraced and I felt her wonderful breasts against mine, her sweet mouth on mine, her sex against mine. Behind me, I felt Steve's penis press against my bottom as he reached under me and over me and put his arms around Barbara and me. I lifted my thigh and pressed my bottom toward him, and Barbara reached between my legs and guided his penis into me. We all sighed.

As we moved together, I felt them everywhere against my skin, hands and arms and feet and legs and lips and breasts and bottom and sex. They were giving more stimulation than I could hear. I was almost sick with arousal.

After a length of time that could have been hours or seconds, I felt Steve shudder inside me and ejaculate. At almost the same moment, Barbara, whose sex was pressing against mine, took her mouth from mine and cried out in a deep, wrenching voice. An endless orgasm without climax spilled through my body. My very consciousness was disintegrating with pleasure, and what few thoughts remained were utterly incoherent.

Once again, Serena woke us up with her crying some time in the middle of the night. This time, it was Barbara who put Serena back into her crib after feeding her, and then she came into bed on Steve's other side, so that he was between us. He had been lying on his back, but when Barbara got back into bed, he turned toward her. I sensed that he lay his hand on her breast as he pressed himself against her.

"Oh, come on, honey," Barbara murmured drowsily. "What's gotten into you every night lately?"

"I want to make love," he said.

"Go to sleep," she said, and I could tell that she was pushing him away.

With a groan of protest, he turned onto his back again, and then continued the motion until he was facing me. I felt his penis press against my thigh as he brought a hand up to my breast. Although I was filled with desire for him, I felt a guilt and confusion. Should we make love? What did Barbara want? As he raised himself on one elbow, Steve moved his hand from my breast to between my legs, fondling my clitoris very briefly before reaching lower, I suppose to see how wet I was, whether he could enter me. Uncertain what to do, I reached out and stroked his penis. As I did, I turned to try to see Barbara. She was on her back. Her eyes seemed to be closed, and she was already asleep again or pretending to be.

I didn't want Steve and me to make love without Barbara. As I fondled him, I tried—I hoped subtly—to use my hand on his penis to steer him, gently indicating that he should lie down again. He let himself be persuaded, and I shifted onto my side, snuggling against him as I stroked him. His arm slipped under me and around my shoulders.

After a little while, to my surprise, Barbara shifted herself toward Steve, and her hand joined mine.

"Oh, God," Steve whispered, squeezing me more tightly against him as his pelvis thrust rhythmically, sending his penis back and forth through my fist. Barbara's hand was lower than mine, sometimes bumping into it, sometimes disappearing from contact.

After only a moment or two, Barbara shifted position again, raising herself up and then bringing her face down to Steve's penis. Her mouth engulfed him, her wet lips touching my fingers. "Oh, Jesus, Barbara!" he cried.

I was very surprised—a moment ago she was protesting that she wanted to go to sleep—and deeply aroused.

Her mouth drew him in, and I moved my hand down toward the base of his penis, to let her take him in as deeply as she wanted. Squeezing me even more tightly, Steve turned his head and kissed me hard, his tongue deep in my mouth.

Barbara's hand met mine at the base of his penis. His scrotum was very tight, his testicles seeming almost to be disappearing into his penis.

Steve seemed very close, and Barbara's head bobbed faster. Her hand moved up and down, just above mine. Steve tore his mouth from mine and made a loud, almost frightening groan. Barbara lifted her mouth from his penis. Everything seemed to stop for a moment, and then Barbara moved her hand again. "Oh, Jesus," he moaned, and thrust very hard through our hands, ejaculating, it seemed, all over his chest.

"Now go to sleep, honey," Barbara said softly, and turned her back to us.

Rather than going to sleep immediately, he got up and went to the bathroom. And when he returned to bed, he crawled up from the foot of the bed to put himself between Barbara and me. I had turned away from Barbara to face the edge of the bed. Steve fitted his body against mine. He was hard again—or still—but I pretended to be sleeping, and eventually was.

Six

Wednesday

I never had erotic dreams, but I was dreaming that an old boyfriend was making love with me. The dream was extremely vivid. I was lying on my stomach, my leg bent at the knee, and he was lying behind me and over me, entering me from the rear. His strokes were long and deliberate, each time almost taking himself entirely out of me and then slowly burying himself completely.

Gradually I came awake to realize that I had been dreaming, and that Steve was making love to me as my old boyfriend had been doing in the dream. I was deeply aroused, very wet, but once again I was concerned that we were making love without Barbara. The way I was lying in the bed, I couldn't see her at all. She might have been pressing up against her husband, urging him on, but I doubted it. I suspected that Steve's slow, deliberate movements were to avoid waking her.

From the quality of the light in the room, I sensed that it was early morning, perhaps six o'clock. Serena would stir soon, rousing Barbara. I didn't want her to wake to discover Steve and me making love—not because I thought she'd be upset with me, but because I thought she'd be angry with Steve. I knew I had to make him come quickly, easily, silently.

The way I was lying on the bed, my left hand was up near my head, under Steve, and all but useless, but my right hand was free. I brought it between my legs, and grasped the shaft of Steve's penis where it entered me. I heard him sigh in my ear. He hesitated in his stroke as if waiting to see what I would do next. Improvising, I reached farther down to take his scrotum in my hand. He sighed again. Gently squeezing his testicles, I pulled his scrotum up and down the shaft of his penis. His breath caught, and he sighed. I moved my hand up and down, up and down. His breathing synchronized itself with my hand.

My own orgasm was not my concern, but my wrist was pressing against my vulva, and as I stimulated Steve I was stimulating myself. Gradually, although I was still holding his testicles in my hand, I became more caught up in pursuing my own orgasm than in causing his. I had almost forgotten about Steve entirely when I heard him sigh in my ear and felt his testicles quiver in my hand as he ejaculated inside me. As his tremors subsided, I let go of his scrotum and drew my fingers up to my clitoris and, immediately, came.

He kissed me softly behind the ear and then pulled his penis out of me and retreated back toward the center of the bed. I lay there in the predawn stillness, guiltily feeling the wetness between my legs, trying to sense whether Barbara was awake, not daring to turn to see. I closed my eyes and let myself drift back to sleep.

When I awoke again, the bed was empty. I found my nightgown among the bedcovers, put it on, and got up. Barbara was at the dining table in her nightgown, and Serena was in her rocker on the table.

I looked closely at Barbara, trying to detect any change of attitude.

"Morning," she said, as friendly as always. "How'd you sleep?"

"Just fine," I said, sitting down across from her. "How about you?"

"Fine, once he finally let us." She smiled. "He's been quite the teenager lately."

A few minutes later, Steve came down from the loft with his briefcase, dressed and ready to leave for work. "Good morning," he said to me, smiling a friendly smile that betrayed, it seemed, no hint that we had just had intercourse no more than an hour earlier.

He kissed each of us goodbye in turn, first Barbara, then Serena, and then me. His lips were soft and sweet and melted me like chocolate. When our lips parted and Steve straightened up to leave, I glanced over at Barbara. She was smiling at me, I thought, indulgently.

After we heard the door close behind him, Barbara and I looked at each other. "What do you suppose we're doing, the three of us?" she asked quietly, smiling at me but seeming to be speaking to herself.

"I don't know," I said, a stab of guilt and fear in my chest. "Do you regret it? I don't want to do anything to make you upset with me. You've been wonderful to me. I love you both very much."

She smiled and shook her head. "No, I don't regret it at all." She reached out, covering my hand with her own. "Don't blame yourself for anything. Everything that's happening is happening because we all want it to. We both love you, too. I just think too much, that's all. I just worry about how it's all going to end."

She smiled like a mother reassuring a daughter and patted my hand.

After breakfast, Barbara went upstairs to the loft, and I sat at the kitchen table and wrote in my journal for a while. Around noon, Barbara and I took the baby for a brief walk, and when we came back, we had lunch. Later, we sat on the rug and played with the baby, until we were interrupted by a telephone call, which Barbara took upstairs at her desk.

"I've got to go out again," Barbara said. "I've got some work to pick up, and the editor wants to talk to me. You feel like coming with us?"

"You're going to take the baby with you?"

She grinned. "Do I have a choice?"

"You could leave her with me. I wouldn't mind," I said, smiling at the baby, who was lying on her back and gurgling up at me.

Barbara's eyes searched a far corner of the room as she considered it. "It shouldn't be more than a couple of hours. I guess I could nurse her just before I leave."

"Well, whatever you like," I said. "I'm just saying I don't mind looking after her."

Barbara made up her mind. "That would be great," she said, grinning.

Of course, the baby began to fuss within minutes after her mother left the apartment. I changed her diaper, I put her on my shoulder and danced with her, I sat down on the couch and put her on a pillow on my lap and rocked her up and down and back and forth. Nothing helped.

I toyed with the idea of giving her my breast, even though I had no milk. The thought frightened me, filled me with guilt, and excited me terribly. I did not do it. I rocked her until, finally, she fell asleep.

†††

I was engrossed in reading and I didn't hear Barbara come in. When I suddenly noticed her standing in front of me, I jumped in surprise.

"Oh, I'm sorry. I didn't mean to startle you, Nona."

Smiling, I put the novel aside and stood up. "It's your apartment. I was just in another world."

We faced each other from a distance of about ten feet. I felt awkward. I wanted to approach her, to kiss her, but I did not know how to behave toward her.

She seemed to feel no awkwardness.

"Thanks. How'd your meeting go?"

"Fine," she said, going up to her loft. "I got a nice juicy assignment that'll keep me busy for a few weeks when I finish my current one."

"Great."

She came down the stairs from the loft without her briefcase. "How was Serena?"

Although I had done nothing, I remembered my impulse with guilt. I turned away, as if to look in the direction of the crib. "Fine. No trouble at all. She's sleeping now."

"That baby sure sleeps a lot."

"You should be grateful for that. When she gets older, she'll be a lot more demanding."

"I know, I know. Everybody tells me that," she said, climbing the stairs to the loft again.

†††

"Getting hungry?" she asked as she came downstairs several hours later.

"I suppose."

"I'll start dinner."

"Don't you usually wait for Steve?"

"Wednesday's poker night with the boys," she said, going into the kitchen. "He won't be home till very late tonight."

The fact that we would be alone made me feel giddy and excited. Our eyes met, and she smiled at me. I felt the way I did when a man I found attractive met my eyes. "Oh, yes, you told me. I forgot," I said, looking away.

"I'm usually sound asleep when he comes home."

"Let me help you make dinner," I said, trying to deal with my feelings of awkwardness.

The short time between dinner and bedtime passed with agonizing slowness. What would happen when the two of us got into bed? Without the spark of male desire, would we make love? Barbara's eyes met mine again and again and again, and she smiled at me as a lover might, but perhaps I was reading too much into her smiles. I knew one thing: I would let her take the lead.

When it was finally time for bed, Barbara turned off the lamp. The only light in the room came from the street and a small light she had left on near the door, for Steve when he came home. We got into bed on opposite sides and lay on our backs under the sheet without touching. Neither of us spoke for a moment.

Suddenly Barbara laughed. "Now I'm feeling kind of nervous again," she said to the ceiling.

"Me, too," I confessed, also looking up rather than at her.

I sensed her hand moving toward mine, and I moved mine toward hers, and we held hands without speaking. My heart was lurching in my chest.

"We can just go to sleep," I suggested. "If that's what you want to do."

"Once," she said, "in my women's group we each got up on the kitchen table one at a time and looked at each other and ourselves with a mirror, but no one touched anyone." She had not acknowledged what I'd just said, but it was clear that she didn't want to go to sleep.

"Wow. My women's group never did anything like that," I said.

"I've always wanted to know what it was like to touch another woman," Barbara said. "Haven't you?"

Although she and Steve and I had by then made love several times, she and I had never actually touched each other's sex. And, in fact, I had never actually been curious about touching another woman. But it seemed it would be hurtful not to agree. "Yes," I said.

She drew back from me so that she could look at me in the shadowy light. Her eyes danced over my face, and she raised her knee. The hem of her nightgown slipped down her leg, exposing her to the hip. I wanted so much to please her, but I met her eyes and hesitated.

"Go ahead," she said softly.

Our eyes stayed on each other's, and my hand trembled as I reached for her. At first, I let my hand rest on her inner thigh.

"Go on," she murmured.

I moved my hand up her leg until it reached the very beginning of her labia. She sighed. I brought my fingertips up into her bush, inexplicably afraid to touch her sex. My fingers ran through her soft, curly hair, and tentatively pressed the soft pad of flesh over the bone beneath.

Although I was touching her more intimately than I had ever done with any woman, I felt unconnected with her, and I needed to establish another link between us, so I began to talk. "It's so strange to be touching you. It's like it feels completely familiar, and completely different." Talking was helping me relax. I took my fingers from inside her and slipped them up between her labia. "It's like I'm not sure exactly what I'm touching, because I can't feel it from the inside. Does this feel good?" I asked, stroking the side of her clitoris.

"Yes. It's wonderful."

"What feels best to you?" I asked, running my forefinger around her clitoris in a circle.

"Just pretend you're touching yourself."

"I don't know what I'm doing," I said with a nervous laugh, and ran my fingers up and down her cleft. "I told you, I just learned how to play with myself the other night."

"You're doing fine," she said, and her hips rose up to press her sex against my hand, and she closed her eyes. All her attention, it seemed, was on what I was doing to her.

Gradually, her breathing grew more labored, and her face more tortured. Uncertainly, I tried to move my fingers the way her hips signaled me. Soon, she opened her mouth, and she made small mewing sounds. I touched her more rapidly, and her mews turned into deep moans, and her entire body quivered, and she came.

She opened her eyes, smiling. "That was wonderful," she said. I felt proud and pleased.

I squeezed her hand. "I'd like you to touch me, too," I said, barely able to speak.

"Lie down," she said, turning on her side. She put her other hand on my vulva. Hungry for her touch, I opened my legs and moved my hips forward, pressing my sex against the palm of her hand. I sighed deeply as her fingers slipped into my wetness. I had never felt anything so soft and tender.

"This is what I usually like best," she said, putting three fingers together, flat, over my clitoris and labia and pressing in a quick, light circular motion.

Perhaps because she was a woman, and knew what

she herself liked, or perhaps simply because of the situation, I was almost immediately ready to come. I turned my head and met her sweet, sparkling eyes. She smiled, and my orgasm burst out from under her hand.

She planted small kisses on my cheek as I let my hips fall back to the bed and caught my breath. "You were beautiful to watch," she said softly.

We reached out for each other and embraced, breast to breast and mouth to mouth and groin to groin, our legs interlacing. She kissed me tenderly, and I returned the kiss.

"I love you," I blurted out, surprising myself.

"I love you, too," she said, smiling, and we kissed again and again, no longer shy with each other at all. Barbara slowly stroked my back through the smooth, thin fabric of the nightgown she had given me, her hand gradually moving down past the small of my back to my bottom, and I copied her motions with my own hand on her body.

"I want to kiss your breasts," Barbara said softly.

"I want you to," I told her.

She lowered one of the straps of my gown and bared my breast, whose nipple had swollen past the point of hardness, and then brought her lips and tongue to me. Her kisses were softer and sweeter and more tender than I had, in those brief moments of anticipation, imagined. The pleasure of her mouth on my breast was so great it was almost beyond comprehension. I wanted her to stop; I wanted her to go on forever. I closed my eyes and turned onto my back, and I felt Barbara move over me, her breasts grazing my belly. She lowered the other strap of my gown and kissed my other breast, still holding the first in her soft, small hand. Shifting her body again, she moved herself between my legs, which opened without thought as she lay her body on mine. I felt her breasts melt against me, and I lifted my knees to welcome her.

She kissed her way slowly down my chest, skipping over where my nightgown had bunched itself just under my breasts. I felt hypnotized with pleasure. A sort of delirium came over me as I felt her lips on the soft skin of my belly just above my navel.

We both knew with certainty where her lips were heading, and I still do not know which of us was more excited, more full of anticipation.

She lowered her head and kissed me just above my bush.

When her mouth first reached my sex, I groaned. Her hands reached under me and took hold of my bottom, one hemisphere in each hand. Her tongue licked my clitoris, at first cautiously, tentatively. I knew that she had never done this before. The touch of her tongue was so light as to be almost imperceptible.

Some of my boyfriends had used their mouths on me, some perfunctorily, some enthusiastically, some awkwardly, some expertly, but none the way she was using hers. It was intensely pleasurable, but frustratingly elusive, indistinct, diffuse. I was close to orgasm, and far away. As when she had licked my breasts, I wanted it to go on forever, and I was impatient for my climax.

Gradually, Barbara became less cautious and more enthusiastic, covering my sex with her mouth, pressing her tongue firmly against me. I closed my eyes and heard myself sighing deeply again and again. It seemed I was floating in space, or rocking on a gentle sea. My body seemed infinitely large, my pleasure filling the entire world. I sighed and sighed.

She pressed her face even more deeply into me, and now her lips caught my clitoris, hot and swollen and wet and aching, and sucked it in a slow, persistent rhythm. It was as if she had reached the conclusion that I tasted good, and now she wanted to consume me. I felt her move one hand from my bottom and stroke me between my lips until she found my opening and gently entered me with her finger, moving it in time with her mouth. I was dizzy with arousal, and I was moaning with every breath. The sensations of pleasure rose within me and filled me, making my skin feel too hot and tight for my body, making me lift my hips off the bed to press myself against her face.

Suddenly, confusingly, she lifted her head from me before I reached my climax. Straightening up on her knees, she pulled her nightgown over her head and tossed it aside, and then, turning her back to me, threw one leg over my chest and lowered herself onto me.

I was abruptly confronted with her sex only inches from my face. I was shocked and, in truth, repelled. As much as I wanted to give her the enormous pleasure she was giving me, I was not sure that I was really ready to put my mouth on her sex. The odor of her arousal was strong, and although it was exciting, I did not really want to taste it. I was more familiar with the male sex and would sooner have taken Steve's penis into my mouth, had he been with us.

But there was something touching about her sex, resting there, anonymous, mute, like a closed mouth, waiting for me. With the forefinger of one hand, I parted her inner lips experimentally. An incongruous thought passed through my mind: *The baby came out of here.* It seemed impossible. I moved my finger up and down in the small, wet slit. I heard a low, imploring moan.

Hesitantly, my heart beating more in fear than in arousal, I put my hands at her hips and lifted my head slightly and brought my mouth to her sex.

The flavor and odor were much stronger than I had anticipated, and at first I actually gagged a little, and shuddered. I had a feeling of awful panic, as if I was going to drown, or suffocate. For the briefest moment, I had no idea where I was, or with whom.

But Barbara moaned deeply as my tongue touched her sex and gave me a long, hard lick with her tongue.

I felt connected with her again, and I knew that I wanted to give her all the pleasure that I possibly could, all the pleasure she was giving me. I pressed my tongue against her, licking in hard, long strokes, as she was doing to me, and took her bottom in my hands. She brought her sex more fully onto my mouth, and I licked and licked, letting the saliva pour from my mouth, diluting her flavors.

I was as overwhelmed by the intimacy of our acts as by the intensity of sensation on my sex as she licked and sucked urgently, her hands squeezing my bottom. It seemed for some reason much more intimate than oral sex with a man. I licked her the way I wanted to be licked, and the way she seemed to want. It was impossible to tell which of us was leading and which was following. Soon I felt her entire body quivering beneath me, and she pressed herself harder against my mouth. I sucked as much of her sex into my mouth as I could and flicked my tongue against it as rapidly as I could, and she copied me. It was unbearably stimulating. Suddenly we were both shuddering. I felt my orgasm begin in the tips of my ears and my toes, rushing through me like two tidal waves that met at Barbara's all-consuming mouth. I cried out, but my groan was suffocated by Barbara's own sex. The next moment, she pulled her mouth from me and groaned hugely as she crushed herself against me.

Carefully, we disentangled ourselves from each

other. Barbara turned around and lay down next to me, smiling triumphantly. Her hair was wet and tangled. She looked beautiful. We embraced, kissing, tasting our own fluids on each other's faces. I can't say that I actually liked the flavor of my fluids, but it was deeply exciting to taste them everywhere on her face.

We fell asleep in each other's embrace.

I was lying with my eyes closed, half asleep, as Barbara nursed Serena when I heard the front door open and Steve come into the apartment. The door closed and locked as quietly as I had ever heard it, and then I heard the sound of Steve's stockinged feet as he padded into the room.

"D'you win or lose?" asked Barbara in a whisper.

"Lost. I couldn't keep my mind on the cards tonight," he whispered in reply.

"Why not?"

He made a whispered laughing sound. "Why do you think?"

"I think she's done nursing," she said. "She's asleep. Could you put her back in her crib?"

"Sure."

He walked around to Barbara's side of the bed and took Serena. "C'mon, honey," he whispered to his daughter.

I listened to the sounds he made as he returned the baby to her crib, and then I heard him undress. He slipped into bed next to Barbara. "I couldn't wait to get home," he whispered.

Barbara gasped.

"I've had that all night," he whispered, and I knew he had to be referring to an erection.

A regular movement began in the bed, not of intercourse, but as if she was caressing him, or perhaps he was rubbing himself against her. As I lay there with my eyes closed, I imagined the one possibility and then the other.

"Is Nona awake?" he whispered as the regular rhythm continued.

"I don't know."

"Nona?"

I felt a stab of fear as I heard my name. I still don't know why I didn't answer.

"I guess not," Barbara whispered.

"Did you make love with her?"

I could hear Barbara's hesitation before she answered. "Yes."

"How? How did you make love with her?"

"First with our hands, and then with our mouths."

"Oh, Jesus," he said, and the bed trembled, and, whatever they had been doing, I knew he had come.

Seven

Thursday

In the morning, I awoke once again to discover Barbara lying next to me nursing Serena. Steve lay behind Barbara, watching. They noticed that my eyes were open, and we said good morning to each other.

I felt wonderfully listless, a pleasant, lightheaded exhaustion. My body felt tender, almost sore, as it did after strenuous exercise. I stretched, and felt the muscles in my inner thighs ache.

Eventually we began our day, getting out of bed one at a time, visiting the bathroom. Steve got dressed and joined Barbara and me at the dining table, where we had already set breakfast for the three of us.

We all spoke softly, almost in whispers, although

Serena was awake and sitting in her carrier right there on the table. It was as if we were sharing something so delicate even a loud voice would destroy it.

"What's happening today?" Barbara asked Steve.

"I'm having lunch with Mike." He turned to me. "He's a friend from college." I nodded.

"I'm dropping off the manuscript I finished yesterday," Barbara said.

"Why don't you just send a messenger?"

"It's better if the editors see you. It reminds them you're a real human being who needs more work. Besides, I need to get out into the real world occasionally."

Steve nodded at Barbara and then turned to me. "What about you?"

I shrugged. "I have no plans. I'll just help Barbara with Serena and whatever." Steve nodded. I suddenly felt the need to explain. "Once I find out that I got in to the school, I'll start looking for a job. But right now my life's kind of in limbo. If I don't get in—"

Steve nodded. "It's okay. We understand."

"And I have the mothers' group tonight after dinner," Barbara said. "So don't be late coming home."

Steve smiled as he got up from the table. "I wouldn't dream of it."

As he had done the morning before, Steve kissed each of the three of us in turn on his way out. For the briefest moment, it seemed completely normal.

As Barbara and I cleaned up the breakfast dishes,

she told me about the mothers' group she attended on Thursday nights. "It's mostly the women I attended Lamaze classes with, plus a few others. We all just liked each other so much, we felt it would be a good idea to keep meeting afterwards. The Lamaze instructor lets us use the space she gave the classes in. It's really great. We talk about problems we have, with nursing or with getting the babies to sleep or whatever. It's very reassuring to hear that other women are having the same difficulties you're having."

"I'll bet."

"It's only a few hours that one night a week, but it makes me feel like I'm not completely alone in this."

"But you're not alone. You have Steve."

"And he's great, but he's not a mother. He just doesn't know what I'm going through. He can't."

The fact that Steve and I would be alone together that evening hung over the day, casting a strange shadow on the time Barbara and I spent together. They both knew what had occurred between Barbara and me when we were alone together. What were they each expecting to happen when Steve and I were alone?

In preparation for going out that night, Barbara used a breast pump periodically during the day to fill a bottle with her own milk. I watched, fascinated, as Barbara evacuated whatever milk Serena didn't drink each time she nursed.

Just after lunch, Barbara left to deliver the work she had completed. I walked aimlessly around the apartment. I played briefly with Serena in her playpen. I tried to continue the crocheting I'd begun the other night and became immediately confused. I looked at my flute case but did not open it. I sat on the broad windowsill and worked on my journal and stared at the traffic on the avenue below and thought about my life.

The telephone interrupted my meditations. I debated whether or not to let it ring, and then hurried over to answer it. "Hello? Andrews residence," I said, sitting down on the edge of the bed.

Over the telephone, I heard a man laughed. "Nona? It's Steve," he said, still amused.

"Oh. Hi," I said, feeling flustered, like a young teenager. "I didn't know how—"

"It's okay, it's okay. Is Barbara there?"

"No, she's delivering the manuscript she finished working on. She said she'd be back in about forty-five minutes. I'll tell her you called."

"It's nothing important." He paused.

"Okay."

"Nona?"

"Yes?"

"I was thinking I want to do a watercolor of you."

I turned and looked at the nude he had painted of Barbara.

"Nona?"

"Yes?"

"What do you think of that? Do you think you might like to pose for me?"

I stared at the portrait of Barbara and felt an ache inside me. "Yes."

"Maybe we could work on it tonight, while Barbara's at her mothers' group."

"Yes," I said, full of a sudden excitement. "Yes."

"Okay. Tell Barbara it's nothing important. Tell her I love her. I'll see you later."

We hung up. I lay back on the bed and closed my eyes and thought about Steve and Barbara and put my hand under my skirt and made myself come.

"Hi. Anything doing?" Barbara asked when she returned.

"Steve called but he said it wasn't anything important," I said. "He asked me to tell you he loves you."

She smiled, and I felt a strange guilt. Although I felt extremely close toward her, I knew that I was not going to tell her about my conversation with Steve, or his suggestion. "How's Serena doing?" she asked.

"She's been fine."

On cue, Serena started to whimper, and Barbara went to the playpen and scooped her up.

Steve came home at his usual time, and as usual he kissed the three of us in turn. This time, it seemed he gave me a conspiratorial smile.

Dinner was hurried—Barbara was getting a ride to her meeting, and she wanted to be ready for it. I kept waiting for Steve to bring up his idea, or Barbara to ask us how we were planning to spend our evening together, but neither did. Instead, Steve talked about his workday, and Barbara talked about her meeting with her editor. I said very little.

After dinner, Steve cleared the table and I washed the dishes as Barbara nursed Serena, put her in her crib, and then expressed a little more milk into the bottle she had been filling all day. She had just put on a nursing bra when the buzzer sounded and she jumped up.

"You don't have to wait up for me," she said to Steve and me. We were standing side by side in the kitchen, finishing up the dishes. I turned off the water and dried my hands on a dishtowel. "You have fun," she said, smiling and giving me a quick kiss on the lips.

I smiled back at her, but did not know what to say. I could not tell whether her remark was meant to be especially meaningful.

She turned to her husband and gave him a longer, more intimate kiss. "Hmm," he said. "We're going to miss you."

"I'll bet," she said with a small laugh.

"Are you going to be all right?" he asked.

"Don't worry about me," she said. "You two have fun. I'll be home my usual time. There's milk for Serena in the fridge if she's hungry." The downstairs buzzer rang again. "Gotta go."

She hurried to the intercom. "I'll be right down," she said into the metal grille. A metallic voice replied something unintelligible.

Barbara picked up her purse and was gone.

As soon as I heard the door to the apartment close and latch, I felt a dull ache in my belly and my chest. Our work in the kitchen was done, but Steve and I still stood there, not quite looking at each other.

"Have you thought about my suggestion?" he asked quietly.

"You mean, to paint me?"

"Yes."

"All day," I admitted.

"What do you think?"

"It's very flattering," I said, and laughed suddenly. "It makes me nervous, for some reason."

"Why?"

"I don't know." I still was unable to look at him except obliquely, like a child caught in a lie. "Everything makes me nervous."

"Do you want to give it a try?" he suggested.

I laughed again. "Sure. Why not?"

"Great. I'll go get set up," he said, walking past me out of the kitchen area.

"If I'm going to have to hold still for any length of time, I better go pee first," I said, and went into the bathroom.

When I came out, the blinds had been lowered and Steve had set up an easel at the windows, facing into the room. He seemed to be absorbed in thought and apparently did not hear me.

"Where do you want me to go?" I asked.

He looked up, unstartled. "Why don't you just sit on the couch there?" he suggested, pointing to the couch on which I had slept the first night, which was at an angle to his easel. "Sit with your back against the side, with your arm along the backrest and your legs up on the seat."

I crossed the room and sat down as he had told me. "Like this?" I asked, feeling terribly self-conscious.

He smiled a sweet, indulgent smile. "Like that, but without your clothes on," he said.

I laughed giddily. "I wasn't sure what you meant."

"Is that okay?"

My heart was pounding very hard. I felt foolish and naive. After all, he had seen me naked. We had made love. "Of course," I said, with a resoluteness I did not feel, and stood up and very quickly took off the clothing I was wearing, painfully uncomfortable, with the awareness of his calm eyes on me.

"You're very beautiful," he said softly, once I was naked.

"Thank you," I said, barely able to speak, as I assumed the position I had taken earlier. "Like this?" I asked.

"Bring your left knee up. Put the left foot flat on the cushion," he said. I did what he told me. "Let your right hand rest on your right thigh." I moved my hand onto my thigh. It felt stiff and unnatural. "No, just relax. Let your shoulder drop. Loosen your elbow. Turn your hand over. Just let it fall there."

I tried to follow his directions, but they seemed to make no sense. I laughed nervously. "I'm sorry. What did you say?"

He stepped from behind the easel and walked over to me, kneeling next to the couch. "You look like you're waiting to see the dentist. Just relax," he said, putting one hand on my shoulder and the other on my hand. I felt a flush of warmth where he touched me. "It's okay," he said, gently squeezing my hand.

I turned toward him. "I've never posed for anyone before," I said.

Our eyes locked on each other's, and I felt a wonderful warmth flood through me. I knew what I had not allowed myself to know all day: That we were going to make love. I was so excited my scalp felt tight.

He rose a little higher on his knees and kissed me on the lips. His kiss was slow and gentle and sensual, and my mouth opened to his. His hand left mine and rose to my breast. He kissed me for a long time. My sex felt so swollen and wet, it was as if he was kissing me between my legs.

I knew it was inevitable that we would make love, but there was still a point of resistance. I took my lips from his. "What about Barbara?" I asked.

"Didn't you hear what she said?" he said urgently, almost whispering, and kissed me again. "'You two have fun. Don't worry about me.' She was giving us permission. She *wants* us to make love tonight."

I felt lightheaded, dizzy again. I took an enormous breath and let it out in a long sigh. Of course I had heard what she had said, and could not interpret it in any other way.

"Why?" I asked.

He gave me another small kiss on the lips. "Because she's not afraid. She loves us, and she knows that we love her."

A quiet voice in my mind told me that no matter what Barbara had said, I was courting disaster, but a much louder and persuasive voice in my chest and between my legs told me that I wanted this man at that moment more than anything else in the world. I put my hands on his shoulders and closed my eyes and drew him to me.

We made love hurriedly, without finesse, like a couple of furtive teenagers, right there on the couch, with all the lights still on. Neither of us had the patience for Steve to undress completely. I lay on my back on the narrow couch, and he pumped into me frantically, as if he had not had a woman in a long time. The very impatience of his lovemaking was extremely exciting, and I raced toward my climax with him, lifting myself off the couch to thrust my pelvis against his. He clutched my bottom in both hands, squeezing so hard it almost hurt, and I dug my fingers into his shoulders as I fought to keep up with him. We were no longer kissing, needing our mouths open to get enough air to power our efforts and for the animal noises we were making. I came before he did, my orgasm feeling like a seam of heat and pleasure ripping me apart from my groin to my throat. His orgasm came a moment later, loud and almost frighteningly violent. After his spasms subsided, he collapsed upon me, and I relaxed the grip I had on his shoulders and let my legs down from his waist. My heart was beating crazily. We were both out of breath and covered with sweat.

After a few minutes, he gave me a small kiss on the edge of my mouth and sat up. "Do you still want to pose for me?" he asked with a playful smile.

"Okay. Let me wash my face first."

"No," he said, standing and pulling up his pants, but not bothering to button his shirt or even tuck it in. "Don't wash. Just sit up."

We looked at each other a moment. Finally, I nodded. "Okay," I said, sitting up and assuming the pose he had arranged me in earlier. "Like this?" I asked. I felt entirely at ease with my nudity now.

"Yes. Perfect," he said, looking at me from behind his easel, his pencil already moving quickly over the surface of the paper. After perhaps half an hour, he put down the pencil and began to work with brush and paint.

It was strange and exciting to sit there naked, as still as I could, with his fluids slowly seeping out between my labia, his eyes intently on me, on my nakedness, the memory of our lovemaking still fresh in my body. I wanted to feel his arms around me again, to nestle against his chest, to feel him grow hungry and hard for me again.

"Okay!" he announced, just as I was about to tell him that I had to go to the bathroom. "You can move now."

"May I see?" I asked.

"Sure."

I stood up, acutely aware of the sticky fluids at the mouth of my sex, and walked barefoot to the front of the easel.

"What do you think?" he asked, putting an arm around my shoulder, squeezing me to him. "I might add a little detail, after it's dry, but it's basically finished."

It was shocking and surprising to see myself so deftly captured in the painting. It was unmistakably me. I had a slight smile, playful and confident. I looked proud of my body, sure of my desirability. I had not intended to pose suggestively, but I looked lascivious.

I laughed, covering my face with both of my hands, no longer so comfortable or confident. "It's wonderful," I said, "but I'm not sure I want anyone to see it."

"I'm glad you like it. It's yours. That way, you can decide who sees it and who doesn't."

I showered and put on the nightgown Barbara had given me. While Steve was in the bathroom, I returned to the easel and stared at his portrait of me as if at a tantalizing puzzle. While I was in the bathroom, I saw, he had cleaned up his work. The paints were all closed, and the brushes were all washed, standing up in a glass jar.

Just as Steve came out of the bathroom in a fresh pair of the black silk pajamas he favored, Serena started crying. "I'll go warm up the bottle Barbara left."

"I'll go get her," I said. "What time will Barbara be back?"

"She's usually not back until about eleven-thirty," he said.

On my way to Serena's crib, I looked at the clock behind their bed. It was only a little after nine-thirty. I was surprised. It seemed deep into the night.

By now Serena was crying enthusiastically, and I picked her up as gently as I could, cradling her against my chest and cooing to her, promising her milk, promising her her mother, telling her that everything was all right. She did not believe me.

After a few minutes, Steve pronounced the bottle he had placed in the pot of water on the stove warm enough, and I handed him his daughter. He sat on a kitchen chair and smiled down at her with enormous love. I had never seen him give Serena the bottle before, and I was touched at how sweetly and tenderly he cradled her. She blinked up at him as he whispered to her, her small, sweet face sleepy and confused.

"I'll go turn off the lights," I said. "They seem to hurt her eyes."

When I came back to the kitchen, the apartment in darkness except for the light coming from the street, Serena was asleep again. I put the bottle back in the refrigerator as Steve put the baby into her crib.

"I guess we might as well go to bed, too," Steve said, as we met in the dark living room.

"I guess so," I said.

We met in the middle of the bed, under the single sheet. I snuggled up against him, feeling secure against his chest, his arm around me.

He sighed deeply and turned on his side toward me. "I want to make love with you again," he said, drawing me against himself powerfully. Through our nightclothes, I felt his penis against my groin. He was already hard.

This time, we made love more slowly, as if to make up for our previous haste. We kissed a long time. He caressed my breasts tenderly, squeezing them, licking my nipples, sucking on them, nibbling them. He reached between my legs and stroked me with an exquisite tenderness, until I longed to feel him inside me again. When he finally entered me, it felt as if he were made especially for me, and I for him, so perfectly did he seem to fill me. He reached beneath me and held my bottom in both hands, guiding me to him with every stroke.

My arousal rose imperceptibly but inevitably higher and higher. The silk of his pajamas against my bare skin was delicious. The silk of his penis inside me was indescribable.

He rose up on his knees, withdrawing from me. It was, momentarily, a puzzling shock. Then, with his hands on my hips, he indicated that he wanted me to turn over.

I rarely made love in that position, but I followed the suggestions of his hands unresistingly, arranging myself on my knees and elbows. It was the position he and Barbara had assumed that first night, when I had watched them make love. I felt atavistic, bestial, like nothing more than a female animal in heat, offering herself to the dominant male. I had never felt more exposed, more vulnerable, more yielding.

Immediately, I felt his penis enter me again. It seemed it was deeper than I had ever felt a man inside me before, deeper than I knew was possible. Leaning over me, he caressed one of my breasts with one hand and my sex with the other. He was moving quickly now, and with every stroke I felt his hips rock against my bottom. I remembered watching him make love with Barbara, remembered imagining myself in Barbara's place. Now, imagining myself lying on the couch and watching myself, with Steve's penis filling me to the womb and his hands everywhere on me, I overflowed with pleasure.

I woke up with a start to the sound of the apartment door opening. How would Barbara feel to see me in bed with her husband? She had all but told us it was all right with her, but I still felt a glow of guilt and apprehension in my stomach.

The door closed quietly, and I heard what sounded like Barbara putting down her keys and her purse and taking off her shoes. I was nestled against Steve, who was lying on his stomach at the side of the bed. Although he was facing away from me, I could tell that he was asleep. I moved apart from him, to the opposite side, rolled onto my belly, and closed my eyes.

My eyes still closed, I listened to Barbara padding about the apartment on bare feet. It sounded as if she walked over to the bed to look at us, and then over to the crib to check on Serena. After a few moments, she walked back past the bed and into the bathroom.

When she came out and approached the bed again, I wanted to open my eyes and end the pretense that I was asleep, but I could not. I kept my head half-buried in the pillow and my eyes closed, breathing as evenly as I could.

I felt a shift of weight at the foot of the bed. She crawled up the center of the bed, between Steve and me, and lay down with a sigh. She lay without moving for perhaps a minute, and then she rolled on her side, away from me, toward Steve.

She was not still. I sensed that she was trying to rouse him, gently kissing and caressing him. After a little while, I heard him make a sound of protest, and felt him roll over.

"Hi, sweetie," he whispered sleepily. "How was your group tonight?"

"Awful," she whispered back. "I kept thinking about the two of you here together. What did you do while I was gone?"

"I painted her portrait."

"Nude, I'll bet."

"Yes. It really turned out well."

"Did you make love with her?"

He did not answer. My heart and my loins were pounding.

"Did you?"

"Yes. You said..."

She sighed deeply. "It's okay. I knew you would. How many times?"

"Twice."

She sighed again. "Make love to me now," she whispered. "I want you very badly."

"I don't know if..."

I felt another shift of weight. "It feels like you'll be able to manage."

I felt them moving together on the bed as they fitted themselves into each other's limbs and heard them kissing.

"We're going to wake her up," he whispered.

"I don't care," she said.

The movements on the bed had assumed a slow, regular rhythm, and I knew that he was inside her. My heart was pounding and my body was aching everywhere, but especially in my breasts and in my sex, which felt warm and thick and full and heavy. I didn't know what to do. I lay there, unable to move, as I felt the rhythm grow faster and heard Barbara's sighs grow deeper. It was just like that first night, when I lay on the couch across the room pretending to be asleep as they made love.

I wanted to join them, but I was afraid to. She needed him all to herself then, to reclaim him, to reaffirm their connection. But their lovemaking was even more arousing than it had been that first night. Surreptitiously, I brought my nearer hand under myself, under my nightgown, to my sex. With one finger, I stroked myself rapidly.

Steve was moving very quickly now, and Barbara was sighing loudly and deeply. It was absurd to pretend that I was still sleeping, but I continued the pretense, not moving except for my one finger, around which my body, the bed, the room, the entire universe, seemed to be spinning.

Barbara made a loud, wrenching sound, and the bed seemed to quiver and shake. In the next moment, Steve made a startled, guttural sound. I could almost feel him inside me, filling me, emptying himself into me. I stroked my clitoris another time and, keeping as still and as silent as I could, felt my orgasm flood through me.

Beside me, Steve and Barbara were still. Unable to keep apart from them any longer, I rolled over to face them. Steve was lying between her legs. They both turned toward me. We all looked at one another in the shadowy darkness. I could not read their expressions at all.

Eight

Friday

When I woke up the next day, I was alone in the bed. Arching my head back to look at the clock, I saw that it was already after eight. I was surprised that I had slept through so much of the morning routine. I yawned and stretched and got out of bed.

It looked as if Steve had already gone to work. Barbara was in her bathrobe, sitting alone at the dining table. She held her head propped against her fist, her other hand holding a cup of coffee. She looked like she had been crying.

"What's the matter?" I asked, approaching her.

Her eyes flicked up at me and then back down to the table. "Sit down," she said.

"What's wrong?" I asked, sitting down across the table from her.

"I don't know how to say this to you," she said, not looking at me.

"What?"

Her eyes darted up to me and then away again. "I don't want you to stay here anymore."

I felt a thick hot shard of pain in my chest, and my eyes filled with tears. "Oh," I said, feeling small and cold and empty. "Oh."

Her voice rose, plaintive and indignant. "I really like you, Nona. I think you're a sweet person, a wonderful person, but you can't just come into our lives the way you did and just stir everything up." Fresh tears were streaming down her face, and I felt my own tears overflow my eyes.

"I didn't mean for any of this to happen," I said, through my sobs. I felt scalded by her anger and her pain.

"You show up at the door like a kitten out of the rain, homeless and hungry and adorable. How could we not open our home and our hearts to you?"

"You've been wonderful. I—"

"He's in love with you!" she cried, rising from the table and dashing into the living room.

"He loves *you*, Barbara," I called back. "And I love both of you."

She was at the easel. "Look at this!" she shouted, turning it around so that the portrait of me he had painted the night before faced me. "He loves you! He painted this after you made love, didn't he?" She was shouting.

"You all but told us it was all right with you!" I shouted back.

"I was wrong!" she shrieked, tearing at the portrait with both hands. The easel fell, and the pad of watercolor paper slipped off. The weight of the pad tore the page with my portrait, and she let it drop. In her crib, Serena started crying.

Barbara and I looked at each other for a moment without moving. Then Barbara ran over to the crib, stepping on the painting on her way.

When she returned, her baby in her arms, she was calmer. "Let's sit down," she said very quietly, walking toward the couches.

We sat down on the couches, facing each other. She opened her robe and, this time without showing her breast, lowered the strap of her nightgown and brought Serena to her nipple. She closed her eyes for a moment, and then opened them and looked directly at me. "I was wrong. I thought I was beyond the sort of possessiveness and jealousy of my parents' generation. I thought I was liberated. I thought I could let Steve satisfy his fantasies and his desires in a safe way. I thought it would make up for the fact that we haven't had much sex lately. I thought it would be fun. I thought I might like making love with a woman. I don't know what I thought."

She shook her head. "Maybe if we were Mormons, I'd have no problem sharing my husband with another woman. But I think even the Mormon men didn't go to bed with more than one wife at a time, and the wives didn't go to bed together by themselves. And we're not Mormons. And none of us can handle this situation, not really."

She paused and looked at me, giving me a chance to speak, but I was silent. "And what about you? What did you imagine you were doing with us? Did you think you were going to become a member of our family? Did you think you'd become Steve's second wife? My sister? Our daughter? What?"

She stared at me until I felt compelled to speak. "I don't know," I said. "It just happened. One thing led to another. I didn't know where it would go."

She spoke very softly. "It wouldn't go anywhere. It *couldn't* go anywhere. You can't be a part of our life, and we can't be a part of yours. And I'm really sorry, because I think you're a sweet person, and I really liked you, and we might have become very close friends."

The pain in my chest had grown heavy again, and I was weeping: For the pain I had caused her, and for the loss of her love, and for myself. "I thought we *were* very close friends."

"No," she said, shaking her head slowly. "We were lovers. But we didn't know each other well enough to be very close friends, not really." Deftly, she shifted

Serena from one breast to another without exposing herself to me at all. "We've only known each other seven days. *Seven days!*"

"It seems like I've known you and Steve all my life."

She looked at me thoughtfully. "This must be a difficult time for you, waiting to find out what you're doing with your life."

"That's not why it happened," I said, wounded by her psychologizing.

She seemed fully self-possessed now. "This is what I want you to do, Nona. I want you to find somewhere else to stay. And then I want you to pack your things and leave."

"Right now?"

She nodded her head slightly. "I know this sounds cruel, but yes. We need to make a clean break. It'll be for the best."

I couldn't say anything for what seemed like a long time, and then I felt something pass through me. I knew that it had all been inevitable. I must have been crazy—we all must have been crazy—to think otherwise. "All right."

I wiped my tears on my arm and stared at her for a moment. She didn't look angry anymore, but remote and inaccessible. "May I go to the bathroom first?"

"Of course."

†††

She stayed on the couch with Serena while I used the bathroom and while I got dressed and while I dug out my address list with my list of names in New York and sat down next to the telephone.

The last name on my list was Uncle George, my father's older brother, a large, gruff man who lived in Brooklyn. I had not seen him in more than six years, and he had always frightened me a little. His name was on my list not because I had considered asking him for a place to stay, but because my father, who knew a lot about emergencies, had always assured me that Uncle George was good in them. With Barbara sitting across the room, I felt reluctant to call any of the other friends of friends on my list. I imagined her imagining me coming into another couple's lives and wreaking the havoc I had wrought on the Andrews.

My father had given me two phone numbers for Uncle George, his home and the bar he owned. Not knowing the hours a bar owner worked, I called him at home and woke him up. But once I had established who I was, he insisted that I come to Brooklyn and stay with him.

"Okay," I said, looking across at Barbara as I hung up the phone. "I've found a place to stay."

"Good," Barbara said, evenly. "I'm glad for you."

She continued to sit on the couch as I got up and emptied the drawer she had lent me into my small suitcase, as I dug through their hamper for the clothing I had put in it, and as I gathered my music stand and my flute and my music from where I had left them next to the window, not too far from where my ruined portrait lay on the floor, and as I put the keys she had given me on her dining table.

Everything I had come with was finally assembled in the entranceway, next to the dressing area. I walked back into the main room and looked down at Barbara, who was cradling her sleeping baby in her arms.

"I'm ready," I said quietly.

She looked up. "All right."

"I'm sorry," I said. "I'm truly sorry."

She nodded. "I am, too."

"What are you going to tell Steve?" I asked.

"That's no concern of yours, Nona," she said softly.

"Would you tell him I said I'm sorry?"

"I'll tell him that."

"Please don't think badly of me, Barbara," I said. "I didn't mean to cause you any pain."

"Good luck, Nona. I hope you have a good life."

"Thank you," I said, and turned and gathered up my things and left, quickly, before I broke down again.

Nine

There was one conversation I had with Barbara that I've saved to describe out of chronological order. It took place on Monday morning. After we'd finished with breakfast and got dressed, Barbara headed upstairs to work, and I took out my journal and sat down on the couch. At the head of the stairs, she looked back down at me. "What are you writing?"

"I keep a journal."

"Are you writing about us?"

"I write about everything that happens in my life."

"You're not going to make it public, are you?"

"I'm not planning to. It's just for me."

She nodded. "I used to keep a diary, when I was a

teenager. I wonder what happened to it. I think my mother probably threw it out."

"That's terrible."

"It wasn't important. I didn't write much in it. It didn't seem there was much going on in my life."

"I try to write every day, if I can. Otherwise I seem to forget too much."

She didn't say anything for a moment. "If you change your mind and publish any of it, promise that you'll disguise us, that you'll change our names and everything."

"I promise," I said, and of course I have.

After the disastrous beginning I've described, my life in New York worked out well. Uncle George was a widower with two grown children, and he had an entire house to himself. I stayed with him all through music school, working as a waitress in his bar. I never saw Barbara or Steve again and, despite occasional temptation, did not go to bed with more than one person at a time for a long, long while.

THE AUDITION

Sam Rosenberg, Certified Public Accountant, husband and father, was sitting in the tiny, windowless, overcrowded office of Jimmy Conti, in the basement of Heaven, the all-nude nightclub that Jimmy managed. Sam and Jimmy were going over last month's books. Sam was embarrassed to have Heaven as a client—it was the one client he lied to his wife about. But Sam was the junior partner of Rosenberg and Rosenberg, and when Rosenberg the father gave Rosenberg the son an assignment, Rosenberg the son took it. "A client's a client," his father had said. "They pay their bills just like everybody else."

Sam wished he could get out of there, but it was

taking longer than he had hoped because they had been interrupted by phone calls that Jimmy apparently had no choice but to take.

Shortly after Sam had begun doing Heaven's books, he had started to notice other such clubs everywhere. Telling himself that it was just to satisfy his curiosity about them—so that he would not have to lie awake nights beside his sleeping wife, wondering about what went on at Heaven—he went to a joint in Queens, which was where he lived—but in a neighborhood distant from his own. He sat and watched, burning with shame and discomfort, nursing a ridiculously overpriced non-alcoholic fruit punch. After twenty minutes or so, he left, telling himself that he had learned what he had set out to learn, and that he would never have to go to such a place again.

Less than a month later, on his way to a client, he noticed another such place on a commercial strip in New Jersey. After meeting with his client, instead of driving straight back to the office, he found himself inside the club, wondering what the hell he was doing.

After two years of visiting nearly every such establishment in the greater metropolitan New York area (except Heaven and the ones too near his home), he still had no idea what the hell he was doing. He was no less fascinated than he had been that first time, and no less uncomfortable. His greatest fear was of meeting someone who knew him—although, he realized, whoever he met would be as likely to want to keep his presence at such places as secret as Sam. Nonetheless, when he imagined running into a client or a relative at a club, the feeling he got was as if that person had walked in on him while he was masturbating.

There was a knock on the door. Startled, Sam looked up and saw Hector Rosario, one of the employees, stick his head in.

"We're busy," Jimmy said, automatically, without looking up.

"There's a girl here. Says she's here for an audition."

Jimmy looked at his watch. He looked at the calendar. "Yeah," he said. "Tell her she's early. Tell her to cool her heels."

Hector nodded, removed his head from the doorway, and closed the door.

"I'll tell you what," Jimmy said. "After we finish up here, you can audition this new girl with me. I've seen so much pussy, I can't tell one from another. I could use a new opinion."

"I've got an appointment in New Jersey, Jimmy," Sam said nervously. Sam made it a point always to come to Heaven well before it was open for business. It was the only sensible time to come, but even if it had been possible to work when the club was open, he would not have been able to bring himself to do so.

Jimmy turned to look at Sam. "When's the appointment?" he asked.

Sam grinned with embarrassment. He was, he knew, not a skillful liar—something of a liability in his profession. "Three this afternoon," he admitted.

"Then what do you say?" asked Jimmy, grinning back.

"What do I know about this kind of stuff?" Sam asked.

"Isn't an accountant supposed to know figures?" Jimmy asked with a laugh, pleased with his own joke.

"Very funny."

"Every man likes to look at pussy, don't they? That's all the qualifications you need."

"I don't know, Jimmy," he said, blushing.

Finally, ten minutes later, they had actually finished, and Sam followed Jimmy up the steep, narrow stairs. Hector was mopping the floor. None of the other employees was there yet. The club was not due to open for another hour. All the chairs were upside down, resting on the tables or the edge of the stage.

"Where's the girl?" Jimmy asked Hector. Hector gestured with his mop toward the front of the club, where a doorway led to the entrance vestibule.

Sam stood as Jimmy walked up the narrow aisle to the entranceway. He could hear the conversation, although he could not see Jimmy or the girl.

"I'm Jimmy. You here for the audition?" came Jimmy's voice.

"Yeah. I'm Bettina," came the girl's voice. She sounded young, about the age of Sam's daughter. Involuntarily,

Sam imagined his own Jenny coming to such a place to audition. He often tortured himself with such thoughts as he sat in these places. "I spoke to you the other day."

"Yeah, yeah. I remember. You worked in Jersey. Topless."

"Yeah. I've been doing topless for about a year."

"You understand this ain't just topless? This is all-nude. You show everything here."

"I understand. It's no big deal."

"How old are you?"

"Twenty."

Jennifer, Sam's daughter, was just eighteen.

Sam had recently read in a magazine that most men his age did what he had thought was his own private idiosyncrasy—when he read the obituaries, he immediately figured the difference between the age of the men who had died and his own age. Sam wondered whether most men also compared their own age to the age of the girls in the magazines and the clubs, as Sam did. When he had first started looking at men's magazines, they had been much older than he, but gradually he overtook them, as he aged and they did not. For the past eight years or so—since his daughter's breasts had begun to bud—he had also figured the difference in age between the women in the magazines—and, lately, in the clubs—and his own daughter. Now that she had turned eighteen, she was finally as old as some of the models in the magazines and, he supposed, in the clubs.

"You got ID?"

"Yeah. Just a second."

"Okay," he said after a moment. "You're twenty years old. Now I need to get a look at you."

"You just want to see my body, or you want to see me dance? I got my outfit on under my street clothes."

"I wanna see you dance. Follow me."

Sam watched Jimmy reemerge from the vestibule into the main room of the club. Behind him came the girl. She was a brunette, like Jenny, but not nearly as pretty as Jenny. She looked younger than the twenty-years-old she was claiming to be.

Sam couldn't tell what kind of body she had, because she was wearing a long leather raincoat. If he had seen her on the street, Sam wouldn't have looked at her for more than a moment, but now he was unable to stop staring. He couldn't wait to see her naked.

He had not really seen his daughter naked since she was a child, although of course he saw her all the time in bathing suits and nightgowns and things like that. Occasionally he caught glimpses of her as she ran naked between her bedroom and the bathroom, which he always yelled at her not to do. It was impossible not to be aware that she had become an attractive young woman—as attractive as the girls in the magazines and the clubs—but that awareness was abstract, compartmentalized. Only when a girl in a magazine actually resembled Jenny did it become a problem. Then he was careful to avoid looking at pictures of that girl when he masturbated. Once in a while, though, when he used a magazine that he hadn't paged through in advance—which was always more exciting, even though he couldn't usually restrain himself from previewing the magazine as soon as he could—he'd find himself with his hard cock in his hand, suddenly staring at a girl who reminded him of Jenny. Depending on how far along he was, he'd either lose his erection or come—sometimes both at once. Either way, it was always upsetting.

"Take two chairs down at the stage," Jimmy told Sam as he passed by. "And sit down."

Sam unbuttoned his suit jacket and sat down. Jimmy led the girl back to the room the girls used for a changing room.

Sam sat and stared at himself in the mirror on the wall behind the stage. At the other clubs, Sam never sat at the stage. He was one of the ones who sat in the back, never said hello to anyone, never smiled, trying to avoid the eyes of everyone there—men and women, staff and guest, alike. He never tipped anyone—not the bartenders, not the waitresses, and not the dancers. He never paid for anything extra—table dancing, lap dancing, slow dancing, private rooms, girl-girl shows, limousine rides. And he never bought more than the minimum, usually one drink, which he nursed for as long as he had time to stay and then left. Although he'd been to some of the clubs several times, he avoided going to any one place regularly—if he thought someone at one of the clubs recognized him, he would stop going there for a while.

"You can leave your stuff here," Sam heard Jimmy say to the girl. "When you're ready, the stage is just through that curtain. I'll be sitting out front with that other guy. You can make like we're customers."

"How about some music?"

"I'll see what I can do."

Jimmy returned to the main room. Hector had finished mopping and was beginning to set the chairs back down on the floor. "Put on a tape," Jimmy told him.

"Sure thing, man," Hector said.

"And turn on the stagelights, too," Jimmy added as he sat down next to Sam.

Hector went to the control booth, which was at the very front of the room, in the corner next to the stage.

Sam met Jimmy's eyes in the mirror and then looked away. He felt exposed, his guilty secret discovered.

The spotlights went on, illuminating the stage in bright pink light. After another moment, loud music abruptly came through the speakers, startling Sam. A bright light began to flash in synchronization with the music.

He watched the curtain for the girl's entrance. After a moment, she pranced out. She was dressed in black leather—high-heeled shoes, what used to be called hot pants, a bikini top, and a choker.

She looked much prettier than she had seemed when he had first seen her. Her face was animated. She wore a confident smile. But she still looked so young. Sam wondered if she was really as old as she'd claimed, or whether she'd shown Jimmy fake ID. He was sure some of the girls had fake ID.

She definitely didn't look twenty-years-old. She looked like a young girl playing dress-up. Sam remembered his daughter's fourteenth birthday, when his wife had hired some women who made up Jenny and her guests and did their hair. It had seemed like an innocent idea, and the girls all enjoyed it, but when the women were finished, Jenny and her friends looked like whores. Sam was still disturbed whenever he saw the pictures they'd taken at the party.

The dancer seemed to know the routine well enough, though. She covered the entire stage—as if the club was filled with patrons—running her hands over her body, leaning over with her arms together to exaggerate her cleavage, doing high kicks, turning her back to the audience and bending over to emphasize her buttocks, making provocative faces at herself in the mirror, crouching down on her heels in front of her customers—Sam and Jimmy—and thrusting her pelvis forward in rhythm with the music.

She made eye contact with Jimmy, who nodded encouragingly, and with Sam, who blushed and looked away.

"You're making her feel bad," Jimmy told him. "She wants you to look at her. She wants to make you happy. That's why she's here."

Sam coughed and said nothing. She didn't want to make him happy. At the moment, all she wanted was to get the job. Later, when she was actually working, all she would want would be the money—the money and the feeling of power she'd have over the men, making them stare like fools. The men, for the most part, would try to act casual, indifferent, as if they were used to having naked young women flaunting themselves in front of them. They reminded Sam of small boys, daring each other to do frightening things and then trying to pretend that they weren't scared.

But for all the smiles that passed between the dancers and the patrons, it seemed to Sam to be a relationship built largely on mutual need and mutual contempt, to which Sam himself added a strong measure of self-contempt and shame. He wondered whether he was unique in this respect. Most of the other men at the clubs didn't seem to be in the least ambivalent or embarrassed about being there, or maybe they were just better than Sam at masquerading their discomfort.

Sam had never been able to sort out his feelings about the girls who danced or posed for the magazines. He certainly felt men had a right to see such things, which had to mean that the women had a right to perform for them. And he'd believed—or tried to believe

—that sex was natural and good: He and his wife had given both their children sex education books that emphasized that. But Sam couldn't convince himself that dancing or posing naked was an acceptable profession. If Jenny were a dancer at such a club, Sam knew he would feel not just shame and embarrassment, but also a deep sadness, a conviction that he and his wife had failed terribly in raising her.

No, these girls had crossed some kind of line—whether out of greed or need or neurosis or something even darker and more disturbing—into a life where there could be no dignity or self-respect, only degradation and shame. As his kids' sex education books said, sex was something private and intimate, a physical expression of love between two people.

Except, Sam acknowledged, when it was jerking off, or mentally recording images of a naked dancing woman for jerking off to later, as he knew he was doing right then.

The woman reached with both hands behind her back and unfastened the black leather bikini top. She turned her back to Sam and Jimmy. When she turned around again to face them, she held the cups of the top in her hands. It looked as if she were going to have nice breasts, Sam noticed, as she worked the cups down ever so slowly.

He was impatient to see them, and he was, as usual, angry with himself. He was staring like a cat following a bird on the lawn. What did he think he was going to see? How could this girl's breasts be so much more wonderful than those of any other? He forced himself to look away for a moment.

But only for a moment. He could no more ignore the girl than the cat could ignore the bird. When he looked back, she had dropped onto her heels directly in front of him, still holding her top to her breasts. "Would you give me a little help, honey?" she asked him, just as if he were a customer, and shrugged her shoulders suggestively.

Sam glanced at Jimmy. "Go ahead," Jimmy told him.

Hesitantly, Sam took the free ends of the top and pulled. As he did so, the dancer loosened her grasp of the cups, keeping her hands where they were, and stood up. The leather slipped from between her hands and her breasts. Sam looked at the empty leather bra he held in his hands, and then back up at the girl. She was still hiding her breasts. He tossed the top onto the stage at her feet, and she kicked it to one side.

Just then, Sam heard the telephone ring three times and then stop. After a moment, Hector approached Jimmy and whispered in his ear.

"Shit," Jimmy said. "Okay." He stood up. "I gotta take this call," he said to Sam. "I'll be back as soon as I can." To the girl, who had not stopped dancing, he said, "You keep dancing, honey," and then walked away.

The girl danced with her hands covering her breasts. Gradually, almost imperceptibly, she spread her fingers apart, until the pink of her nipples and the surrounding rosettes peeked out from between them.

Sam was unable to keep himself from staring. He sensed that the girl was watching his eyes, and when he glanced up, he saw that he'd been right. She smiled then, and her pleasure seemed genuine and innocent. For the briefest moment, her smile reminded him of the smile Jenny used to give him when she noticed that he was watching her play in her room by herself. Then the dancer winked at him lasciviously and the resemblance disappeared.

With her fingers spread wide, the girl danced from one end of the stage to the other, and now she began to move her hands further apart, drawing her fingers across her breasts, the middle fingers running directly across the nipples, which were standing fully erect.

Sam sighed heavily. He realized that he had grown hard, something that rarely happened to him in the other clubs. Fortunately, his erection was pointing in the right direction, running inside his underpants just behind the fly of his suit, so it was not terribly noticeable or uncomfortable.

The dancer's breasts were lovely, not too big and not too small, with a soft curve to them. The nipples and rosettes were round and sat just above the center of the breasts, pointing slightly up. They were definitely real—not that he had anything against the implants—half the girls in the clubs had them—but real breasts were softer and more appealing, he thought.

Sam found himself remembering the last time he'd glimpsed Jenny's breasts—he'd accidentally walked in on her in the bathroom when she was getting out of the shower—and he realized that the dancer's breasts looked a lot like his daughter's.

It was as if he was looking at a doubly exposed film. One image was what he was actually seeing—the girl dancing. The other image was what he was imagining—his own daughter Jenny, dancing in exactly the same way. The one image fascinated and aroused him. The second image sickened and frightened him, but he couldn't dismiss it from his mind. He brought his eyes up to the girl's face, to reassure himself, but it didn't help—he saw his own daughter as clearly in his mind's eye as he saw the girl before him.

As the girl danced, she started to call more attention to the leather shorts she was wearing. She ran her hands over her crotch and her buttocks. She rocked her pelvis forward and back rhythmically. She turned her back and bent over, keeping her legs straight, running her hands up the inside of her thighs. The shorts were so brief Sam could see the beginning of her buttocks.

When the girl turned around and straightened up, the zipper on her shorts was open, and suddenly—almost before Sam realized what was happening—she had stepped out of them, hooking them on one of her heels and kicking them aside.

She still was not completely naked. Now she wore a brief pair of panties—what they called a thong—consisting of little more than a triangle of thin, opaque black fabric covering her pubis. The girl turned around. From the rear, she was, for all practical purposes, naked. The thinnest band of black elastic rested high on her hips, meeting another band that disappeared between her buttocks.

From the rear, she could have been any young woman. Sam's double vision seemed to merge. He was watching both the girl and his own daughter dancing naked. He felt dizzy, and he tried to find the dancer's face in the mirror, but his view of her face was blocked by her body. He felt the urge to get up and run away, but he was paralyzed.

The dancer turned around again, and he looked up at her face again, eager to confirm that she was a stranger. Misinterpreting his expression, she gave him a broad smile. In his mind, Sam saw his daughter smile.

Just as if he were watching two different women dancing at the same time, Sam felt as if he were two different men. One was the father who wanted to rush up to the stage to cover his daughter's nakedness. The other was the man impatient to see the girl remove that last article of clothing, to expose herself completely.

Sam looked up and down from her face to the thin triangle of black fabric. He was sweating with fear and anticipation.

More and more, the girl emphasized her pubic

mound and the narrow space between her legs still hidden by the thin strip of fabric. She dropped to her heels and rubbed herself. She put her hands on the floor behind herself and rocked forward, spreading her knees, thrusting her pubic mound forward, stretching the fabric so taut that the contours of her labia were unmistakable. She rolled onto the floor, facing away from him, spreading her legs wide, raising and lowering her pelvis in an obvious allusion to intercourse.

Her bare buttocks looked delicious and inviting. Sam sighed and wiped the perspiration from his upper lip.

She stood up again, strutting to the very edge of the stage, directly in front of him, so that he had to look almost straight up to see her. She shifted her weight from one leg to the other, and Sam stared as if he'd never seen a girl dance before.

She ran her hands up her body to her breasts and back down to her hips. Abruptly, with a quick move of her hands, she unfastened clasps at her hips and made the panties disappear. Suddenly he was staring up at her pubic mound, at her triangle of light brown curls.

The girl danced away, covering the entire stage, pretending that the entire room was filled, doing high kicks so that the men would have quick glimpses of her vulva, flashes of labia. After a tour of the stage, she returned to the center, where she turned and leaned over, making her labia peek out from between her legs.

When Sam had first started sneaking looks at his

older brother's girlie magazines, they didn't even show pubic hair, much less labia. The first time he saw a woman posing the way the dancer was now posing, he didn't know what he was looking at—the woman's labia looked like a deformity, like a strange small second pair of buttocks. He was shocked, almost revolted. Now he found it terribly arousing.

She put her hands on her ankles and ran them up her legs. When she reached her upper thighs, she pulled them apart, spreading her labia, showing the pink.

It was a standard part of every girl's act, but until then Sam had never liked it. A girl's mouth might be pretty, he told himself, but that didn't mean you wanted to see what was inside. But now he found himself staring as hard as any other man.

The girl raised her hands a little further, to her buttocks, and did something else Sam knew was coming but had never had an appetite for: She spread her cheeks and exposed her anus. For the first time, Sam found himself excited rather than repulsed by this. It was newly exciting to see this part of her anatomy, to receive this demonstration that she would withhold nothing whatsoever from him.

She took her hands away and went down onto the floor of the stage. She rolled onto her stomach and then rose up on her hands and knees, rocking back and forth and rotating her pelvis, her buttocks only a few inches from Sam's face.

He had never been that close before, at least not under such good lighting. He could see the creases and folds, the ridges and furrows and openings, the wet and the pink. He remembered seeing Jenny, of course, when she was just a baby and he had to change her diaper and clean her up, but that was different—it had never aroused him, although he had to admit he found it interesting. He didn't understand why it was so fascinating and arousing now, but it was. It really wasn't very pretty at all, not the way a woman's face and breasts and shoulders and neck and back and legs and ankles and feet were—it just looked wet and raw, like a mollusk without a shell, like something meant to stay inside the body.

He had never liked this part of the dancers' routine before. But inside his pants he was hard and aching. And what if he saw Jenny like this, now that she was a woman? Would he find her as exciting as he found this dancer? As soon as he asked himself the question, he saw her there before him, doing what this dancer was doing, and yes—he was sickened to admit—he was finding it as exciting.

She rolled onto her side, onto one hip, raising her upper leg into the air, using her fingers to spread her inner labia and apparently even pressing down inside herself to open her anus slightly. Sam could not believe how aroused he was. He felt lightheaded, almost dizzy. With both hands, he gripped his thighs just above the knee, and he was appalled suddenly to realize that he was shifting his own pelvis in his seat in the same rhythm as the girl.

She met his eyes, and he looked down, burning with shame. It was as if Jenny were seeing his arousal. He could not let her see it.

She shifted position again, now sitting up and putting her legs over the edge of the stage. She spread her legs and actually began to stroke her clitoris with her middle finger up and down. Although the dancers often ran their hands over themselves, he had never seen a dancer in a club go this far. He'd seen it often enough in hard-core movies, but to have a real woman actually masturbating right in front of him was incomparably more arousing. Did Jenny actually do this? It was a question he had never before been able to bring himself to ask. And would she ever do such a thing in front of a stranger in this way? The very question appalled him.

But was he really a stranger, after all? Sam found himself confused and stupid with excitement. Staring at her finger moving up and down on her clitoris, he barely knew where he was. His hips followed her rhythm, pressing his erection against the soft cloth of his underwear again and again.

She moved her leg, lifting her foot and putting it directly against his fly. As soon as she pressed her foot against him, he erupted in orgasm and, at the same time, tears. He lifted her eyes to her face. "Oh, Jenny," he sobbed, horrified.

FANTASIES

"Do you have any fantasies?" he asked as they lay naked together in bed. They had just had sex.

"You mean sexual fantasies?" she asked in reply.

"Yeah."

"Sure. Doesn't everyone?"

"I guess so," he said. "Did you ever tell anyone yours?"

"No. Did you?"

"Not really."

There was a long silence.

"Is that what you want to do?" she asked. "Tell each other our fantasies?"

"Do you want to?"

"What if we don't like each other's fantasies? What if you're freaked out or something?"

"I promise," he said. "I won't be freaked out. They're just fantasies. I understand."

"Well," she said, deliberately. "I'm willing if you're willing."

"Great."

"Who should go first?"

"Ladies first," he said.

"Okay." She took a long breath and closed her eyes. "One morning I wake up to discover that I've been abducted. Instead of being in my bed, I'm in a large steel cage in an enormous room with concrete walls, and I'm completely naked. The cage is on a circular platform about three or four feet high, and it's about thirty feet across, but the roof of the cage is so low I can't even sit up, much less stand up. The floor of the cage is some kind of tough rubber padding, so it's not uncomfortable, and it's pretty warm, so it's not a problem that I'm naked.

"Of course I realize that I'm being kept like an animal. For some reason I'm not afraid or angry or even surprised, just curious as to what's going to happen next.

"At first, I'm all alone, but after a while some people come into the room and come near the cage. They don't look like any people I've ever seen before. They have very pink-white skin and pink eyes. It's like they're a race of albinos, but instead of having white hair, their hair is black. They're dressed in clothes that look like a cross between what they wear on *Star Trek* and something medieval. There are men, women, and children. Even though I don't understand their language—in fact, it's completely unlike any language I've ever heard before —I can tell that these people are families visiting a zoo, and I'm on exhibit. There are benches around my cage, and some people sit and watch me for a while, even though I'm not really doing anything.

"When the people first come in, I have the impulse to cover myself, but I realize that there's really no point, so I just lie there and let them see me. I listen to what they're saying and I try to figure out their language, but I can't even tell when one word ends and another begins. From their tones of voice, though, I can tell that they're admiring me, that they think I'm pretty.

"After a while I realize that I'm hungry. Just inside the cage at one side, where there's a pass-through, there are two stainless steel tubs, one with water, the other with food—raw meat and vegetables of some kind, all chopped up and mixed together. To get around the cage, the best I can do is to walk on all fours. When I do, I become very conscious of how exposed I am. I can hear the people outside my cage talking about me, and I feel my entire body blushing. I walk on all fours over to the food, and try to figure out how to eat. Eventually I find that I just have to stick my face in the bowl, on all fours, like an animal. I drink from the water bowl the same way.

"A little while after I finish eating and drinking, I have to go to the bathroom. Of course, there's no bathroom in my cage, not even a hole in the floor. I walk on all fours across to the other side of the cage. The ceiling of the cage is so low I can't even crouch, so I just have to spread my knees and let it go. Some of the urine splashes on my calves, but it's not too bad. Fortunately, the floor of the cage is banked a little bit so that it's highest in the center and lowest all around the edge, so that the urine runs into the trough. Right outside the cage, a number of teenage boys and girls are sitting and watching, and I can hear them laughing and commenting. For the first time I become really embarrassed. I have to make a bowel movement, too, and it's incredibly awkward in that position. I'm afraid I'm going to soil myself. But I have to go, so I just spread my knees a little wider and I force myself. It's really pretty gross, because I know the people can hear everything, and they're laughing and joking, and I can smell my own bowel movement. As soon as I'm done, I crawl as far away as I can get. I can feel that I'm not too clean, and I wish that there was something I could use to wipe myself, but there isn't.

"I get off my hands and knees and onto my side, with my back to the bars of the cage. I sort of snuggle down and get as comfortable as I can, and I put my hands between my thighs. When I do, I realize that I'm kind of excited in a funny kind of way, and I play with myself a little bit the way I sometimes do when I'm falling asleep, with one hand covering the other, but I don't actually make myself come. Pretty soon I'm asleep. I doze on and off the entire day. After a while the visitors leave, and the lights in the room are dimmed a little, and I fall asleep for the night.

"I wake up because the lights are on again and a man is hosing down my cage. He looks like the others, with the weird skin and eyes and the dark hair, but I can tell he works for the zoo, because he's wearing a uniform, and there are no visitors yet. He talks to me in their language, the way you talk to an animal, and I don't bother to say anything back because what would be the point. As soon as he finishes washing away my bowel movement, I put my hand out toward the hose and ask him with my eyes to give it to me. He seems confused, and I pantomime hosing myself off. He's a little hesitant, but he lets me take the end of the hose. I use the water to try to clean myself from my bowel movement, but I don't have any soap so I just have to use my fingers. Even though my back is to him, I can tell that he's watching me. As I clean myself, I find that I'm getting very excited, and I just bring the hose and my fingers up a little, from back to front, and pretty soon I'm having an incredible orgasm.

"The man seems very upset, and he turns the water off and pulls the hose out of my hand and puts it away on the side of the platform where I can't see. He uses the pass-through to change my food and water bowls with fresh ones and hurries out. A little while after that, the doors open and the day's zoo visitors come to look at me.

"Life goes on like that. At first, I use my fingernail to make a mark in the pad where I sleep for each day, but after a while I stop doing that. I almost forget my own name, and I find that I'm no longer even thinking with words. I'm barely more than the animal they're treating me like. I sleep, eat, go to the bathroom, and stare at my visitors. I get my period, and there's nothing I can do about it. It just runs down my legs.

The zoo worker who cleans my cage and feeds me only lets me have the hose about once a week or so, so I get pretty dirty and smelly between times. If I use it on my entire body, I'm too cold afterwards, since there's nothing to dry myself with, so I just use the hose to wash my privates, and then I use it to give myself an orgasm if he'll let me, which he doesn't always do. If he doesn't, I just do it with my fingers. After I've been living in the cage a few months, I play with myself as often as I feel like it, whether there's anybody watching or not. In fact, it's pretty much my only entertainment, so I do it all the time.

"It makes me laugh to see the peoples' reactions. The parents hustle their children away, the teenage girls blush, and the men and boys just stare. Most of the time I pretend that I'm oblivious to them, but sometimes I push myself up to the bars and invite the men or the teenage boys to have sex with me. They don't understand the words, but they get the point. They joke with each other, slapping each other on the shoulders and laughing, but I can tell from the bulges in their clothing that they're excited. Of course, there's a low fence around the cage about four feet away, so that the zoo visitors can't get close enough to even touch me, much less actually have sex with me.

"I think that's going to be my whole life, but after a few more months, I wake up to see that a group of zoo workers are wheeling a small cage toward mine. When it's close enough, I see that there's a man inside. He's naked like me, and he doesn't have the weird skin and eyes the other people do. He looks like a normal person. The zoo workers wheel the cage up to mine and raise it up so that its door aligns with the door to my cage, and they open both doors. At first, he refuses to come out, but the workers prod him with some dull sticks until he gets out of the portable cage. As soon he's out, they close both doors again, and they go off and leave us alone.

"The man is huddling against the cage door. He's a little younger than I am, maybe twenty-two or twenty-three, and he's very muscular and handsome, but I can see that he's very frightened.

"'Do you speak English?' I ask, but I get no response. '*Habla Español? Sprechen Sie Deutch? Parlez-vous Français?*' I try all the languages I know, even the littlest bit, but he says something in a language I don't recognize. Even though he doesn't understand me, I try to reassure him. I tell him my name, and I tell him that he's not going to be hurt. I try to approach him, but I can see that I'm frightening him, so I back off.

"The zoo opens, and the visitors come in. Everyone is very interested in the man. For the first few hours, he doesn't move from his spot near the cage door, but he watches everything I do. After he watches me eat and drink and I've moved away from the food, he goes to it, on all fours, like me. I notice that he has a large penis, and it hangs down between his legs. He eats the way I do, on all fours, like an animal. Of course, eventually he has to go to the bathroom. He raises one leg, like a dog. It gets me excited to watch the thick stream of urine pouring out of his penis. He watches me when I go to the bathroom, too, and that gets me even more excited. When I have a bowel movement, I try to hide, but I know that he can tell what I'm doing. When I'm finished and I move away from it, I can see that he's looking at it on the floor of the cage. It gets me very embarrassed, but it's also very exciting. When the visitors are all gone and they lower the lights in the room so that we can sleep, I wait until he falls asleep and I masturbate again and again.

"The next morning, when the zoo worker comes to hose down the cage, I grab the hose from him and make pleading sounds until he lets me keep it. The man in the cage with me watches me very carefully as I use it to clean myself off, but I don't use it to masturbate. Instead, I offer it to him. He doesn't seem to understand, so I raise the stream up toward him. He's lying on his side, and I play the water over his feet. He seems to like it, so I bring it higher. Gradually, I bring it up to his penis, which becomes erect very quickly. I run the stream back and forth over his penis, and almost immediately, he ejaculates, grunting like an animal. I come without even touching myself. I wash his semen away, and the zoo worker pulls the hose back from me.

"Pretty soon, we're eating at the bowls together, and one night as I'm going to sleep he comes up to me looking kind of lonely and forlorn and I let him cuddle with me. I feel his penis against my back. At first it's soft, but it quickly gets hard, and I get terribly wet, and the next moment, without any preliminaries at all, we're on our hands and knees having intercourse, just like a couple of animals. Even though he comes very quickly, I have a wonderful orgasm. After that, he wants to have sex with me all the time, whether there's people watching or not. And I still use the hose on myself, and on him, too, whenever I get the chance.

"And that's my fantasy," she said. "What's yours?"

"Wow," he said. "I just meant, like, you know, my fantasy is that I'm in bed with two girls at once, and one sucks my cock while the other has my balls in her mouth."

There was a long silence.

OH, BROTHER

After more than a month of living together, my girlfriend Jean and I were becoming more and more casual about our bodily functions. "I had an older brother," she explained early in our relationship. "Until he was about eight and I was about six, my parents used to bathe us together."

At night, before going to bed, Jean and I usually showered together, and it wasn't unusual for me to take a leak while she was adjusting the water.

One night, we'd been out to dinner, and I had had a few more beers than usual. We'd both gone into the bathroom and taken off our clothes, as usual. But rather than waiting for her to start the shower, I began to use the toilet while she was still standing at the sink taking off her makeup.

She looked over as I aimed the thick yellow stream into the water.

"When I was a little girl," she said, "I was jealous of my brother. I wished I could do that."

"What? Pee standing up?"

"Yeah. It always looked like fun."

With some effort, I cut off the flow. "Want to try it?" I asked, half-joking.

She looked down at my hand and my penis and then raised her eyes to meet mine. "Sure."

"Come here, then."

She came over to me and stood at my side, close enough that our bodies touched. One of her breasts flattened against my arm, and her pubic mound touched the side of my thigh. I let go of my penis and she took it, holding it with her thumb on top and the other fingers on the bottom, just as I had been holding it.

"Go ahead," she said.

I looked down at her small hand on my penis and tried to start the flow again. Of course, her hand had been on my penis before, but never under circumstances quite like those. Despite the fact that I really had to go, nothing happened at first.

"What's the matter?" she asked with a small laugh. "Feeling shy?"

"A little," I admitted.

"Maybe this will help," she said, giving the underside of my penis a tickle with her middle finger. I shuddered and the urine began to flow. She laughed triumphantly.

"It *is* fun," she said with a giggle.

I felt the strangest sort of arousal, because although my penis felt as if it was growing larger and thicker, it stayed completely soft.

"I used to watch my brother do this," she said, aiming the flow to various spots in the bowl. "Target practice, he called it."

It seemed that I urinated for minutes, but eventually my bladder felt empty. I squeezed the muscles inside a few times to finish emptying myself.

She stood there, still holding my penis, as if uncertain what to do next.

"Now you shake it off," I explained.

She gave it a shake, but not a very effective one. At least, not effective for its intended purpose, although very effective in another respect. Now that my bladder was empty, my penis was beginning to lift.

"More like you're shaking down a thermometer," I suggested.

She gave it a more vigorous shake, and a drop or two flew off from the tip into the bowl. "This is fun, too," she said, and gave it another shake, and another, and another, and I was completely hard. Staring down at her hand on my erection, where my own had been so often, was terribly exciting.

"Once I watched my brother do this," she said, in a husky voice, her hand moving steadily. I stared, fascinated.

"Did he know you were watching?" I asked, sensing or knowing that she, too, was staring at her moving hand.

"No—that is, I don't think so. I'm pretty sure he thought he was alone in the house. He had the habit of not closing the bathroom door completely. I don't know. Maybe he wanted to be caught. I just stood in the doorway—I wasn't going to walk in or anything, but I couldn't bring myself to walk away. I think I held my breath the whole time. He was standing facing the toilet, just like you are, and I couldn't hear sound of peeing, and I could see his arm moving up and down."

I was hypnotized by the sight of her hand on my penis, and by her story.

"Is this the way you do it?" she asked. "I couldn't really see how he was doing it."

In answer, I put my own hand around hers, forming it into a fist, and showed her the rhythm I preferred.

"Okay," she said huskily. "I get it."

I took my hand from hers and watched as she continued on her own, the sensations and the experience at once so familiar and so novel. As she stroked me, she pressed herself against my side. I snaked my arm around her waist and gripped her bottom. With her free hand, she reached out and held my buttock.

"Finish your story," I told her. The first clear drop of liquid had formed at the tip of my penis.

"There isn't that much to tell. Gradually, his arm began to move faster and faster."

"Show me."

"Like this," she said. Her hand moved faster, a little rougher and harder than I did it. "And then at the very end, his arm moved very, very fast."

"How?"

"Like this," she said, shaking her fist up and down my penis as quickly as she could. I tensed my body as the intensity reached its crest, steadying myself with my free hand against the wall. "I remember the sound he made as he came," she said.

I groaned as the pleasure overflowed. My muscles squeezed spasmodically as her hand continued to move.

We both watched the semen fly out of my penis and splash into the yellow water.

I heard Jean make a throaty sound I'd heard her make before, and her hand stopped moving. I turned my head to meet her eyes. Blushing, she smiled and nodded. The knowledge that she'd come, too, excited me powerfully. I put both hands on her buttocks and lifted her onto my still-hard penis. She was deliciously wet and open. "Oh, brother," she sighed, as I buried myself in her. "Oh, brother!"

BILLIE

I was going to one of those parties that you go to on the chance of meeting a woman. I didn't expect to know anybody except the guy I was going there with, someone I knew from work who knew somebody who knew somebody. It was in a photographer's studio down on West Fourteenth Street, in the meat-packing district. On a hot summer Saturday night, the street was dark and deserted.

Somewhere above us, rock music was thundering through open windows. Kenny, the guy from my office, found an intercom next to a large gray metal door. He pressed a button and we heard a buzzer sound.

We went up three long, steep flights of stairs, passing doors with names like LUCKY RENDERING and BUCCI PORKS and WEISS PRODUCE ENTERPRISES.

The door on the fourth floor said TOMPKINS PHOTOGRAPHY. You could hear the party through it. The door was open. We went in.

Down a short hallway, we turned a corner and came into an enormous room, maybe thirty by eighty, with the ceiling at least fourteen feet high.

The music was deafeningly loud, and most of the room was crowded with people dancing. They looked like artistic types, or artistic wannabes. Some of the women looked good—in fact, some looked very good—but they didn't look like my type, and I was sure I didn't look like theirs.

Kenny said he was going to look for the guy he knew, and disappeared into the party as if the jungle had swallowed him up.

I noticed that some of the guests who weren't dancing had drinks in their hands, so I decided I might as well find the bar.

It wasn't that hard to find. To my left, behind a partition, was a kitchen and dining area. The space wasn't nearly as crowded or as noisy as the other room. On a counter were a couple of gallon jugs of wine and stacks of clear plastic cups. A large garbage pail held a plastic bag filled with ice water and bottles of beer. I helped myself to a bottle, twisted off the cap, and took a long swig.

A wall next to a dining table was covered with

framed photographs. I went over to inspect. They were mostly advertisements and magazine covers of women modeling one thing or another—shoes or hats or other clothing. The guy was good. The women, of course, were tall and beautiful.

"Are you interested in photography?" said a soft, husky voice just behind me.

I glanced over my shoulder. The voice had come from a tall woman with very dark eyes, very white skin, and long, straight, dark hair. She was smiling one of those smiles. She was gorgeous, as beautiful as any of the women in the photographs, tall and on the thin side, small-breasted, the way those kinds of models are. "Not really," I said, turning toward her. "Just in women."

She laughed, and I realized that she *was* one of the women in the photographs. She must have seen the recognition on my face, because she nodded and said, "And how do *you* come to be at a Carl Tompkins party?"

"You mean, I don't look the type?"

"Well, you're tall and handsome enough," she said, "But you *do* look a little too uptown."

"Thanks," I said. "A friend from work knows somebody."

She nodded. "And work is?"

I shrugged the question off. "You guessed right. Something uptown. In an office. Boring stuff. This is the weekend."

She laughed. "I can't remember the last time I met a

guy who didn't love to talk about work. Or professional sports."

"I hate pro sports. Who cares what team wins, when they're just a bunch of hired hands?"

She laughed again. I couldn't believe I was making such easy conversation with a woman as beautiful as she was, the kind of women that, up until then, I'd only seen in magazines and movies.

"That's just the way I always felt," she said.

"I guess we must be kindred spirits," I said, only half-joking.

"I guess so."

"I'm Bill," I said.

"Isn't that funny? I'm Billie."

I smiled. "Further proof we're meant for each other."

"You must be right," she said, smiling a heart-stopping smile. "Let's get out of here, then."

I stared at her for a moment. I could hardly believe that a woman that beautiful—who could have left with any man she wanted—was choosing me. And she was moving so quickly she was stealing my lines.

"You mean that?"

"Sure," she said, putting her hand out toward mine. "C'mon."

"You have to let anyone know you're going?"

She laughed. "I should hope not. Do you?"

"No."

We put our drinks down on the counter and left. I still could hardly believe what was happening.

Even though that block of Fourteenth Street was deserted, there were plenty of cabs cruising down Tenth Avenue, and we got one immediately. Since I lived on East Eighty-fourth Street and she lived on Prince Street, we decided to go to her place. During the ride, we didn't talk much, but it was a comfortable sort of silence.

Her place turned out to be a large studio on the second floor of a walk-up, over an antiques store. "Welcome to my humble abode," she said with a laugh, putting her purse down on a side table by the door and turning on a light.

"Thanks. It's very nice."

There wasn't much furniture. Against the far wall was a king-size bed.

"Thanks. Want a drink or something like that?"

"No thanks," I said, stepping further into the room.

"Excuse me a moment," she said, and went into what I assumed was the bathroom.

There were a lot of pictures of Billie on the wall, some framed, some just tacked or taped. Some of them were nudes, not the kind you see in men's magazines but the black-and-white kind you see in galleries and books. I walked over to look at one more closely.

She was standing just behind me, and I heard her

husky voice intimate in my ear, giving me hot chills. "You like what you see?"

"I suppose you hear this all the time, but you're very beautiful."

"I never get tired of hearing it," she said.

I turned to her, and before I knew it we were kissing, not the tentative kind of kissing you usually start with, but the hot, deep, thorough, no-limits, take-your-breath-away kind of kissing, all tongues and open mouths and arms around each other everywhere. She wasn't wearing a bra under her simple silk shift, and her breasts were small and firm and wonderful under my hands. Her nipples were stiff and I imagined how good they would be in my mouth.

As we kissed, she squirmed her hands between our bodies and unbuttoned my shirt, pulling the tails out of my pants, and then put her hands on my bare chest, squeezing the nipples with her thumbs and forefingers. I must have made a sound, because she broke the kiss and lowered her head to my chest and took one of my nipples between her teeth and bit, just a little more than gently. The sensation shot through me, right into my penis. Then she licked the nipple, ever so gently, and I know I moaned.

I reached behind her and found the zipper of her dress and worked it down to her tailbone. I slipped my hand into her dress and put it around one buttock and pulled her even closer to me, grinding my erection against her groin.

She straightened up, almost reaching my height, and met my eyes. There was no question where we were headed. We walked to the bed, our arms around each other's waist. She pulled off the coverlet and exposed the sheet and the pillows. Still wearing her dress, she turned toward me and reached for my belt. I stepped out of my shoes as she opened my pants and pulled them down, dropping to her knees as she did so.

Through my underpants, she cupped my penis with both hands, squeezing. She worked her fingertips into the waistband and pulled them down smoothly, managing to avoid snagging my erection.

She made one hand into a loose fist around my penis, stroking it up and down. With the other hand, she cupped my scrotum, squeezing firmly but not hard enough to hurt. She seemed to know exactly what to do, just what it all felt like.

I thought that she was going to use her mouth on me, but she didn't. Instead, she put one hand on my hip and turned me toward the bed. "Lie down," she said, her voice even huskier than before. I stepped out of my underpants and pulled off my socks as I did as she'd told me.

I had never been with a woman like this. There I was, lying completely naked on the bed, my erection standing as proud as it had ever done, and Billie was only out of her shoes.

She fixed that now, shrugging out of her dress and letting it drop at her feet.

"You look even more beautiful than in your photos," I said.

"Thanks," she said, with a promising smile, and used both hands to tug her panties down. The dark tuft of hair was even more promising than her smile.

She climbed onto the bed, walking on her knees, and covered my body with hers, straddling me, rubbing her pubic cleft against my penis as she kissed me deeply on the mouth. There was hardly anything for me to do but respond to her. I put my hands on her back and ran them down to her buttocks, and then into the cleft between them.

I could hardly believe how wet she was. Most women I'd been with—and I'd been with a decent number—needed some time to get warmed up. Most women expected at least some foreplay, some caresses and stroking. But I'd barely done more than kiss Billie, and she seemed as ready as I was—maybe even readier.

Without getting off me, she reached over to the bedside table. When she straightened up again, I saw that she had a condom packet in her hand. She tore the foil open and took out the condom. When she smoothed it down over my penis, she made it feel more like another caress than a practicality.

Tossing the empty packet aside, she raised herself up and, guiding my penis with both hands, enveloped me. As always, the pleasure of the sensation was even keener than the anticipation,

As soon as I was inside her, she lay her chest against mine, snaking both hands under my armpits and up to my shoulders. With her pelvis, she started a steady rhythm, up and down, almost completely unsheathing me and then plunging down and enveloping me again. It felt great, and, once again, there was almost nothing for me to do but lie back and enjoy it.

After a few moments, she straightened her legs and squeezed them between mine. Automatically, I had to lift my knees somewhat to accommodate her. She could no longer raise her pelvis as completely as she had before, but she still could thrust against me in a strong rhythm.

I've been with a few women who prefer to be on top, and it's a position I enjoy, especially with a few pillows behind me so that I can easily reach the woman's breasts. But I'd never tried it like this before.

It felt terrific, but it was odd to be so passive. It seemed that she was making love to me more than I was making love to her.

She took her arms from under my shoulders and brought them down to my legs, spreading my thighs further apart and lifting them up toward my chest. This let her sink more deeply between them. She brought her hands down and cupped both my buttocks, as I was doing to her.

It was the strangest thing. With her thrusting so powerfully between my upraised thighs, my pleasure was extremely intense, but I couldn't quite tell where I was feeling it. Of course I knew that I was the one with the penis and that I was the one inside her, but it was almost as if my penis was a part of her body, and that she was thrusting it inside me.

It hardly mattered. Her mouth was planted at the base of my neck, sucking and licking, and her small hot breasts were crushed against my chest. With our hands on each other's buttocks, we pulled ourselves against each other again and again.

She came just before I did, groaning deeply against my neck, grinding her pubic bone against mine. Somewhere—deep inside my own body, deep inside hers, I could no longer tell—I felt a flash of the most intense sexual pleasure I'd ever felt. The lightning struck twice more in the same spot, and then we were both calm.

We lay still a moment, and then she rolled off me and lay down heavily next to me.

"Wow. That was great," she said huskily, reaching over and toying with my penis, soft now but still in the condom.

"Yeah," I agreed. I hesitated, and then spoke again. "I don't know how to say this, but...you make love like a man."

She continued to play with my penis. "Maybe that's because," she said, with a husky laugh, "I used to be one."

GOING NATURAL

The third time our Brooklyn garden apartment was robbed, my wife Claudia and I decided to move to the suburbs, even though we didn't have any children yet. Unsure of whether we'd actually survive the transplantation, we chose to rent for a while rather than immediately buy. We found a small house in Rockland County, New York, not too long a commute to our jobs in the city.

Just behind the house, at the edge of our backyard and those of our neighbors, was an old stone wall. On one side were mostly well-tended lawns. On the other side was what looked like completely wild forest. The woman who lived with her husband and three children in the next house up the street had told us that it was a nature preserve of over a hundred acres, a former estate. On the first nice spring day after we'd moved in, we decided to explore it.

Of course, once we climbed over the wall, we saw that it wasn't completely wild. There was a well-defined dirt path leading deeper into the woods. Some of the trees along the path had a spray of paint to mark the trails. Inevitably, there was some litter of beer cans and candy wrappers and empty cigarette packs and butts.

I followed Claudia along the narrow path, enjoying, as always, the sight of her bottom as it moved in her shorts. Claudia didn't especially roll her hips when she walked, and her shorts weren't particularly tight or revealing, but I found myself more than vaguely aware of my own body. A walk in the fresh air—even in the city—always seemed to heighten my libido.

It wasn't long before we were completely enfolded by the woods. Within only a minute or two, we were out of sight of any other houses, and the litter and other evidence of past visitors had thinned out. And, although it was a beautiful day, if there were any other people in our part of the preserve, we had no evidence of them.

"It's hard to believe we're just a few minutes from our house and the town," Claudia said as we walked along, echoing my thoughts, as she so often did.

"An escape from civilization," I said.

"I don't want to escape from it," she said. "But I like a brief vacation from it."

The day was unseasonably warm, and we were walking briskly, so we worked up a decent sweat. After about half an hour, up one hill and down another, we came to a small lake—little more than a pond—completely surrounded by dense trees. We walked up to the edge, which had a narrow grassy bank on one side. The water looked as clean and pure as a mountain stream. Claudia slipped one sandal off and tested it. "It feels great."

"It must be freezing."

"It's warmer than you'd think. See for yourself," she said, slipping off her other sandal and stepping into the water up to her ankles. "It's really nice. Come wading with me. C'mon."

"I don't want to get my clothes wet."

"C'mon," she said sweetly, and turned back to me with the smile that I'd first fallen in love with. At moments like those, I want to do whatever she wants me to. I sat down on the grass and slipped off my running shoes and my socks.

She'd waded out as far as her calves, and I stepped into the water. It chilled me, but I walked out to join her. She took my hand and we walked out a little farther.

"Have you ever gone skinny-dipping?" she asked me. Of course, she knew that I'd never gone skinny-dipping with her.

"Never," I said. "Have you?"

"Only as a child, a few times in the summer, with my cousins in Pennsylvania."

"I'm sorry I missed that."

"You didn't miss anything. It was completely innocent. We were children."

"It doesn't matter. I'm still sorry I missed it."

"Let's do it now," she said, already turning and walking back to the water's edge.

"We have no towels," I said, following her.

"We'll dry off on the grass."

"What if someone sees us?"

"There's no one here but us. And if they do, so what?"

"Well, what if someone comes and steals our clothes?"

"We can sneak back into our house. I left the back door unlocked."

My heart was pounding. Claudia is sometimes more impulsive than me, but sometimes she just says things to try out what they sound like. "You really want to do this?" I asked her.

"Yes," she said, and, as if to demonstrate, reached down and pulled off her T-shirt and let it drop to the grass. She was wearing a simple beige bra with a front clasp, and she unfastened it and shrugged it off. Her nipples were hard, and my penis felt suddenly hard enough to rip through my shorts.

Of course, I'd seen Claudia naked virtually every

day for the six years we'd been married and the two years we'd been together before that. And though her breasts still looked to me as beautiful as the first time I'd seen them, it was a very long time since the mere sight could give me an erection. I reached out and put my palm against one of them, but she stepped away. "C'mon," she said, "we're going swimming now." She reached to the elastic waist of her shorts and, hooking her thumbs into it, stripped them and her underpants off in one motion.

The sight of her completely naked against the backdrop of the forest was uncannily beautiful, reminding me of those voluptuously sensual nineteenth century paintings that have gone out of fashion. I was unable to move for a moment. Looking over her shoulder, she gave me her playful smile and stepped quickly into the lake. I watched the water rise up her legs to her lovely bottom as she waded out deeper. Then she walked out ever farther, and when the water was halfway up her back she began to swim. "C'mon," she said, turning back to me and treading water. "It's wonderful."

I felt adventurous and foolishly excited, like a child doing something daring and naughty. I stripped, my underwear snagging awkwardly on my erection, making Claudia laugh. I stepped to the water and waded out into the chilling water quickly. My erection wilted as soon as the water reached my thighs, although I still felt full of desire.

We swam out to the center of the small lake unhurriedly. Claudia turned onto her back to float, and the sight of her bare breasts, pillowing on her chest, the nipples dark and erect, rekindled my arousal. I turned onto my back, too, and my penis, not completely hard and not completely soft, emerged from the water as if it were a strange kind of fish.

"My cousins' penises didn't look at all like that," she said with a laugh.

"What were you doing looking?" I asked. "I thought it was completely innocent."

"Well, it was innocent. Innocent curiosity." She turned and began to swim back toward where we'd left our clothes. I followed.

When she got close enough to shore to stand, she stopped swimming and waded onto the bank. I followed, hypnotized, watching the water run off her skin.

Not too far from where we'd left our clothes, the sun found a patch of grass through the trees, and we lay down to warm up and dry off.

"Now we've really escaped from civilization," Claudia said, turning on her stomach, her face toward me. "We've gone completely natural."

Just being naked as we were, with the possibility of strangers coming upon us, was almost unbearably arousing. As soon as the chill of the lake began to leave me, I was completely hard again. The sight of her naked on the grass was irresistible. I ran my hand down her spine. I was afraid I was going to come just from the excitement of touching her,

Usually, I'm silent as we begin to make love, but now my nervousness seemed to make me keep talking. "Not really. I shave my face, and you shave your armpits and your legs and God knows where else." I moved my hand down the small of her back and cupped her nearer buttock.

"I wouldn't mind giving that up," she admitted. "I especially wouldn't mind giving up the bikini waxes every summer. They hurt like hell."

"So stop doing it," I said, putting my fingertips where her thighs met. "I don't mind seeing your pubic hair creeping out of your bathing suit." She let her legs fall gently apart. My fingers slipped between them. "No shaving. No makeup. No haircuts. No shampoos. No permanents." With every item on my litany, I stroked between her labia.

She closed her eyes and made a little wordless sound, a sound from before civilization. I'd heard that sound before, and although it seemed like it had been in another life, another time, I knew exactly what it meant.

In the eight years we'd been together, we'd always made love facing each other: me on top, her on top, lying down, standing up, sitting down, on a bed, on the floor, in a chair, in the bedroom, in the living room, in the shower, but always facing each other.

Claudia began to roll over, but this time I used my hand to stop her, to signal that she was to stay on her belly. I lifted myself over her, putting myself between her legs, and fitted my penis between her thighs.

"What are you doing?" she asked, not alarmed but surprised, giving her behind a little shake that had an effect exactly the opposite of what she may have intended. The head of my penis found the cleft of her labia.

"This is the way people did it before civilization."

"How do you know?"

"I read a lot of books," I said. *Too much, in fact,* I said to myself. Even during the height of passion, I could never quite completely throw off that gift of civilization: The educated, self-conscious inner voice that narrated and commented on everything, even what should have been our most natural and spontaneous act.

Still very nervous and pretending to be feeling more uncivilized than I really was feeling, I pressed my open mouth to her shoulder and bit her, none too softly. Claudia made a guttural sound and lifted her hips. At first I thought she was protesting, but then I felt myself slipping inside her more deeply. She was as wet as she had been the first time we'd ever had sex, all those years ago. As I entered her, she made another deep wordless sound.

Claudia was on her knees and her shoulders, and the image came into my mind of a cat in heat. I slipped my hands up her rib cage to her breasts. They were hanging down in an unfamiliar way. My hands did not recognize them, but they felt hot and full under my fingers. I kneaded them roughly, pulling at her hard nipples.

"Like savages," she said, in a voice I'd never heard before.

"No, not even savages—animals," I said, straightening up at the waist, gripping her hips.

"Like animals," she said. She thrust her buttocks up and back toward me, offering herself even more completely.

"Animals don't talk," I said. My hands at her buttocks, I withdrew almost completely.

Claudia made a noise in her throat I'd never heard before, turning her head to look back at me. I barely recognized her. Her eyes were half-closed, her mouth was open. I buried myself in a long, hard thrust. My thighs slapped against her buttocks, making an unlovely sound.

She made a wild cry that seemed to fly up into the trees, inviting an answer from the other animals.

Immediately, I withdrew and thrust, again and again, uncontrolled, unwilled.

Her body was rocking hard each time I buried myself, and each time she made a sound that started low in her chest. The small part of my mind that was still watching and observing realized that I was making such a sound, too.

In my mind's eye I saw two early humans, no more than animals, long before any trace of civilization, copulating on the forest floor. My body seemed to remember it all, moving with more urgency and feeling than it had ever moved before. Claudia's buttocks rose up to slap against my thighs with every thrust, and her noises were louder and stranger than I had ever heard. For the first time in my life, all volition was originating entirely in my groin rather than my mind. I felt myself gather in my testicles like a storm.

Suddenly the storm broke and my animal body shuddered against hers with a series of movements that were in no way under my control. I heard a series of inhuman grunts that I realized were coming from my mouth. I felt a release that was far more powerful than mere pleasure, a primal, instinctive release.

She was shuddering and writhing, too, and making noises I had not heard except from animals.

After a moment more, we were both still, and then we collapsed onto the grass together. We were both covered with sweat and breathing heavily, blinking up at the sky, the bright sunlight. As she fitted herself against me, I could feel her heart beating hard, like mine. The odors of sex were everywhere.

"You okay?" I asked after a while. My words felt choked, as if I had not spoken in a long time, or ever.

"Yeah. You?"

"Yeah."

We were silent for several seconds. "Back to nature," she said.

"Back to nature," I echoed.

I'm growing a beard. It's a start.

WAKING

In her dream, she was alone, naked in a strange old house she did not know. It was night, and the room was lit only by candles. She was not frightened, but she was cold. It was winter in the dream, and all the windows were open. She tried to close one, but they were stuck. Outside, she saw bare trees and formal grounds covered in snow.

Shivering, she walked down a long hall with marble floors and came upon a bedroom, dark except for the light from a single candle. The windows were open there, too, but there was an old-fashioned wooden four-poster piled high with thick comforters. She slipped into the bed, gasping at how cold the sheets were. The bedcovers started to slip away. She clutched at them, but she was too late to catch them.

Suddenly she realized there was a naked man sleeping next to her in the bed. He was a stranger, but she needed his warmth. She moved against him. It was wonderful how warm his body was. She pressed herself against him everywhere, fitting her body into his, working herself into his arms, and she stopped shivering.

Still sleeping, the man put his hand on her breast, stroking her nipple with the palm of his hand. Against her thigh, she felt his penis quickly grow hard. He rocked his pelvis rhythmically, blindly stroking his erection on her smooth, soft skin.

She was frightened and excited to be caressed by the sleeping stranger. Her nipple grew hard under the palm of his hand, blooming with pleasure. In her chest, her heart was beating rapidly. Between her legs, she felt herself becoming dangerously aroused. She should not be in bed with a strange man, letting him touch her like this, making her so hot.

He swept his hand down from her breast to her pubis, pressing the soft flesh against the hard bone beneath. Her thighs parted involuntarily, and his fingertips slipped down into her folds and creases. She was wetter than she had ever remembered being. Her clitoris felt like a hot, swollen finger. He caressed it confidently, as if he knew exactly what she was feeling.

She sighed and sighed, rapidly climbing toward orgasm.

She came to wakefulness gradually, realizing she had been dreaming, and had not only been dreaming. She was actually in bed—not with a stranger, but with her husband. They had come home from their friends' party just after midnight, hot and tired, turned the air conditioner on to its maximum, slipped out of their clothes and into bed without bothering to shower, gave each other a quick kiss good night, and moved apart to fall asleep.

The room was too cold, and their thin blanket had slipped off the bed in reality just as in her dream. In her sleep, she must have pressed herself against her husband, just as she had done to the stranger in her dream, and, sleeping or not, he must have responded as the stranger in her dream had done.

She was awake, but not yet fully awake, and she closed her eyes as her husband caressed her. He was probably awake, too, she decided, as he moved his lips to the base of her neck. She realized who the stranger in the dream had been: A young man at the party—a man she had found obnoxious but almost rivetingly handsome, with dark hair, dark eyes, and a lean, muscular body. Although she was no longer dreaming, she realized that she was still imagining she was with him. She felt a little guilty at first, but she had seen how her husband had looked at the other women, too, especially the pretty one with the slim hips and the large, shapely breasts.

Was he imagining her now, as he moved his mouth down from her shoulder? He licked her breast everywhere, rubbing his face against her like a hungry infant. Was he pretending she was the woman all the men had been staring at? She was surprised to realize that the thought aroused her rather than angered her. Perhaps if he was the handsome young man, she was a pretty young woman.

No matter who they were, she loved the way he was making love to her, boldly, demandingly, self-assuredly, so unlike his usual diffident and overly considerate approach. She wanted him—husband or stranger—inside her, and she put her hand on his hip and pulled him toward her. Her eyes still closed, she felt him lift himself up and position himself between her upraised thighs, and then gracefully lower himself against her.

She felt his hard penis caught between their bodies. She was as ready as she had ever been, but still she gasped as he entered her. His penis seemed larger than usual, seemed to fill her more deeply, more completely.

And when he began to move inside her, he moved with more assurance, more authority, more passion. She rocked her hips up toward him, raising her knees toward her chest, to feel him even more deeply. Now she could feel the tip of his penis at the mouth of her cervix with every stroke. Her husband had never penetrated her so deeply. She remembered the stranger's arrogant smile, imagined him the one above her, inside her.

It was easy to believe that she was still dreaming. With her eyes closed, it was almost as if she were back in her dream, in the old four-poster in the old house with the stranger from the party.

But who was he with? Her husband seemed more filled with desire for her than he had shown for her in a long time. Was he with the pretty young woman with the beautiful breasts? She brought her hands to her chest and found that her breasts seemed to overflow her hands. They felt as large as the young woman's had appeared, and suddenly it was easy to imagine that she *was* that woman. Her breasts ached as she remembered the men's eyes on them. She squeezed them, feeling their wonderful heaviness, lifting them up to offer them to him now.

He must have had his eyes open, for she felt his mouth on her breasts again almost immediately, one and then the other. Still holding them in her hands, she rubbed them against his face, urging the nipples into his mouth. It drove him to a new intensity, making the old four-poster rock and creak with every thrust. She lifted her body up to meet every thrust with her own. Each time their bodies met, her clitoris was caught between their pelvic bones, and she rotated her hips to squeeze yet more stimulation from the contact. It made him sigh as she had never heard before.

She opened her eyes, and she lifted her head to look down at the man who was still kissing and sucking her wonderfully large breasts so passionately. Perhaps sensing her movement, he lifted his head to meet her eyes.

In the darkness of the bedroom, she saw for a moment the man from the party, and in that moment she did not know whether or not she was dreaming. He brought his mouth to hers and forced it open with his tongue, kissing her with an urgency that was entirely unfamiliar to her, at the same time thrusting his penis into her with a frightening and exhilarating energy, as if attaining his orgasm was a matter of life or death, and she came as hard as she had ever done, making sounds she had never heard herself make before. The pleasure seemed to burst from her clitoris and radiate in dizzying waves into her fingertips and her toes and the tips of her ears and especially into her breasts. In the midst of her pleasure, she felt him tremor and come violently, heard him make the sounds of a stranger.

They were still. He lay with his head between her breasts. She felt her own heart's labored beating and heard her own heavy breathing. Perspiration beaded on her face and her chest. After a few moments, he rose up and looked at her. She saw that he was, of course, only her husband. He kissed her softly, almost chastely, and disentangled himself from her, his waning penis easily slipping out of her. She got up to turn down the air conditioner and pick the blanket off the floor. When she returned to bed, he seemed to be already asleep again.

In the morning, the alarm went off and, automatically, she turned it off. She felt a movement in the bed and turned to see that he had rolled onto his side to face her. He was smiling at her with a shy, playful smile she had not seen in a long time.

"I had a wonderful time last night," he said in a soft voice.

"Me, too," she said, feeling the pleasure of his eyes as he looked at her.

"That's never happened before," he said, puzzled and pleased. "I woke up and you were coming on to me."

She realized that he didn't understand what had happened. "No," she replied. "I woke up and you were coming on to me."

He laughed. "You started it."

"No, you."

Laughing like the newest of lovers, they rolled into each other's arms. This time as they made love, there was no doubt as to who was who.

PLAYTHING

The gallery was crowded with guests, and the conversation was so loud it was hard to hear. No one seemed to be paying any attention to the paintings I'd spent so long hanging and lighting.

"Janice," said Paul Watkins, the host and my employer, directly into my ear, "my wife and I would like you to stay after the party's over." It was Paul's gallery, and I had been working for him for six weeks. The party, which was taking place in both the gallery itself and in Paul's living loft on the floor above, was in celebration of the successful completion of my first assignment—the installation of a new show. At least, that was the way I chose to look it. Others—especially the artist himself—probably thought that it was to celebrate the opening of the show.

I'm twenty-five years old, and I don't consider myself at all unsophisticated or unworldly, but I looked at Paul guardedly. I had always understood that it was a bad idea to mix business with pleasure, but that rule was all but ignored by Paul, who conducted his business as often from his loft upstairs as from the gallery, and who not infrequently had me running personal errands for himself or his wife during my normal working hours.

"What for?" I asked, and laughed—something I do a lot when I'm nervous.

"We'd like to have an after-party party," Paul said, with a conspiratorial smile.

I wasn't absolutely sure that he meant what I suspected, but I didn't ask him to be more explicit. I told myself that I didn't want to risk endangering my job by refusing, although that wasn't what I really believed. I was fairly sure that if I'd declined the invitation, he wouldn't take it personally, and I wouldn't lose my job. The fact was, I was intrigued and curious and flattered and excited. "Sure," I said casually, with a shrug, hoping to convey that I wasn't reading too much into his smile.

"Mara will be so pleased," he said, smiling but already turning away to tread his way among his guests.

†††

Paul was somewhere in his forties, but he looked at least ten years younger. He seemed to be the intellectual type, with a high forehead and intelligent brown eyes, although he was tall and had an expensive exercise machine in his loft that he seemed to use regularly. He wore his brown hair long, in a ponytail, and he had a diamond stud in one earlobe. Mara, his wife, was about five years younger, and still very attractive. She had a round face with mischievous brown eyes and full lips. She was said to be a writer, although I had never heard of her and had never been shown anything she'd published. Occasionally when an errand required me to go upstairs, I'd find Mara at her computer, but just as often she'd be in a nightgown with the newspaper and a cup of coffee, no matter the time of day. "You're very pretty," she said the first time we meant.

"Well, that's done," he said, locking the last of the many locks on the front doors of the gallery as the last of the guests finally left. "Now it's up to the reviewers and the collectors. It's a good show. You did a good show, Janice."

"Thanks, Paul."

He walked across the gallery, toward the cast-iron spiral staircase that led to his living space, and I followed him. "Go ahead," he said, motioning to the metal stairway. "I have to turn on the alarm."

I climbed the narrow helical steps. I heard the series

of beeps that told me that the alarm was set, and then I heard and felt his steps below me on the stairs.

On the floor above, the metal stairs opened onto the living area of the loft. Mara, still dressed in the single-shoulder black dress she'd been wearing to the party, was sitting on one of the overstuffed white linen couches. She had a glass of something red in her hand—a real glass, not one of those disposable plastic tumblers we'd had at the reception—and there was a wine bottle on the table along with two glasses already filled.

"Those are for you," she said, as Paul and I approached.

"Thank you," I said. I'd had a glass or two at the party, but I'd been too excited to notice any effect. I put my purse down on the table and picked up my glass, and Paul picked up his.

"To a terrific installation," Paul said, raising his glass. "You're very talented."

"Thanks," I said, and laughed. We all put our glasses to our lips. I know very little about wine, and I drank mine quickly.

"You look so pretty tonight," Mara said. "I love the way you look in that dress."

"This?" I asked with a laugh. It was a chemise in a dark green crushed silk, and it was about all I owned that I could wear to such an occasion. "I've had this since my junior year in college."

"But we've never seen you in it before, so it's new to

us," said Paul, standing very close. "*You're* still so new to us," he added meaningfully.

"Why don't you come sit down?" Mara asked, patting a place on the couch next to her. "I'll pour you some more wine."

I did as she suggested, leaving a little space between us, and Paul immediately sat down on my other side, leaving no space at all. Mara leaned forward to reach the bottle of wine, and as she straightened back up and refilled my glass and Paul's, she somehow managed to close the gap between us, so that her thigh now pressed against mine.

"Drink up," she said cheerily, and put the bottle down again.

This time I only sipped.

"Tell us about yourself," Mara said.

I shrugged. "Nothing much to tell. Paul must have told you what I've told him."

"Oh, Paul never tells me anything. Besides, I'd like to hear it from you. Where are you from? How do you come to be working at the Watkins Gallery?"

"I'm from Eau Claire, Wisconsin. When I was in sixth grade, my parents took me to New York for Easter vacation. We visited the Metropolitan Museum of Art, and I fell in love with it. I decided I wanted to work in a museum when I grew up. I went to the University of Wisconsin, and I majored in fine arts, and then I went to graduate school in museum studies at Columbia. I got my degree, but my assistantship at the museum ran out. I probably could have gotten a job at a museum somewhere out of the city, but there were no openings anywhere in New York. A friend of a friend of a friend mentioned that the Watkins Gallery was looking for someone, and here I am." I finished my second glass of wine, and put it on the table.

"How come you didn't want to leave the city?" Mara asked "Boyfriend?"

"No, I just like it here. This is where everything is happening."

"But you do have a boyfriend?"

"No, not at the moment," I said with a dismissive laugh. The fact was, I'd broken up with my last boyfriend —a Ph.D. candidate who'd expected me to do his research for him while he was screwing one of his undergraduate students—almost nine months earlier.

"A girlfriend, then?"

"No, not at the moment," I said, intentionally repeating myself.

I think I surprised her. "You *have* had girlfriends, then?" she asked.

I don't know why I was willing to tell her. "I experimented a little in college."

"What do you mean?"

I think she knew, but she wanted me to speak less obliquely. "I've been to bed with a few women a few times," I said, and felt a small hot flush of excitement in my belly, just above my groin.

"How many women? How many times?"

"Three or four. Once or twice each."

"And how'd you like it?"

"It was interesting," I said noncommittally.

Actually, it wasn't all that interesting, even though we'd made sure we each had an orgasm or two. We'd gone to bed with each other because it had seemed like a good idea, and we hoped that we could manufacture a genuine desire for each other. We couldn't. We told each other how beautiful our bodies were because that was the right thing to say, and we'd put our fingers and our mouths places we knew our parents wouldn't approve of because that was going to liberate us from our narrow, sexist, middle-class upbringings. It didn't.

Mara had turned slightly toward me, and she put her fingertips ever so slightly on my knee. "Have you ever been to bed with a man and a woman at the same time?" she asked, stroking softly.

What was I thinking then? Of course I had known what Paul had in mind all along, but Mara's question removed all traces of ambiguity. Did I really want to go to bed with the two of them?

It was difficult for me to imagine getting up and leaving at that point and then coming to work the next Tuesday morning. It was equally difficult for me to imagine going to bed with them that night and then continuing to be an employee. But it seemed I had reached a point of no return, and events would unfold as they would.

"Not yet," I said, turning toward her, meeting her eyes.

Her hand swept up my leg, met my own hand in my lap, and traced a path up my bare arm to my shoulder. She drew me closer, and she kissed me on the mouth, letting her lips go soft and wet. Turning her head slightly, she opened her lips, penetrating my mouth with her tongue, and I felt myself falling backward, my body pressing against Paul.

The women I'd been to bed with in college were as inexperienced and tentative as me. We hadn't spent much time kissing, and our kisses were more of tenderness and affection rather than need and desire.

But Mara was kissing me the way a man kisses, the way I kissed men, with passion and urgency, and I was responding the way I did when a man I desired kissed me that way: I was becoming aroused. Her hands stroked my bare shoulders, and then skipped over the thin straps of my dress to stroke the broad expanse of bare skin above the low neckline. Behind me, Paul shifted slightly, and I felt his lips on the back of my neck, and a hot shiver ran through me.

Still kissing me, Mara moved her hands up to the straps of my dress, and then pulled them down my shoulders. A moment later, I felt Paul's hands at my back, unzipping my dress. I have small breasts, and I was not wearing a bra, and my nipples burned as Mara drew the top of the dress down below them. I felt Paul's hands reach around me and cup my breasts from beneath, letting the nipples peek out between his fingers. Mara took her mouth from mine and lowered her head. Paul lifted my breasts toward Mara's lips, and she kissed one nipple and then the other. My rosettes are large and very sensitive, and I know I sighed audibly.

I wondered whether this was a familiar routine for the two of them, whether Paul had murmured in many a young woman's ear, whether many had preceded him up the spiral staircase, whether he had offered other girls' breasts to his wife's mouth. The suspicion that I was not the first made it all even more arousing.

Mara spent a long time mouthing and licking and tonguing and biting my nipples and my breasts, and all the time Paul's hands were on them, squeezing rhythmically, as he used his own mouth on my shoulders and the back of my neck. His fingers pinched my hard nipples, and Mara took his fingers and my nipple into her mouth, and I was close to coming.

"You have wonderful breasts," Mara murmured, lifting her head and looking past my shoulder. "Bring her to the bed," she told her husband, and stood up.

Paul slipped an arm under my legs and the other

under my shoulder and effortlessly lifted me up. Following his wife, he carried me past the partition that separated the living area from their sleeping area, bearing me like a wonderful present he was bringing her. I didn't mind—in fact, I felt honored and flattered to be so prized a gift.

They had the largest bed I'd ever seen, in a hyper-modern black frame with a high, flat canopy. As Paul lay me down on my back I saw that there was a mirror on the underside. I looked into my own half-drunk eyes as I let Paul finish undressing me. When I raised my hips to let him slip my panties down, the thick aroma of my own arousal filled the air. Paul stood on one side of the bed, Mara the other. They both looked down at me with tender smiles.

"You look lovely," Mara said, as she began to undress.

I looked up in the mirror at my own naked body. My nipples seemed distended, the rosettes even larger than usual. I was wetter than I had ever remembered being. I looked from the mirror to either side of the bed, where Paul and Mara were looking at me as they undressed. The sight was so arousing that I almost came without even touching myself.

Paul and Mara finished undressing. They were no longer young, but both of them looked youthful and fit. Mara's breasts were full and rested on her chest in twin graceful curves. Her stomach had a slight roundness to it, but her thighs looked firm and strong. Paul's chest and stomach were muscular and well developed. His penis stood at a lower angle than those of the younger men I had known, but it looked just as hard as theirs. The head was large and deep purple.

Just before they got onto the bed, Paul turned a knob on the wall that dimmed the lights. Then they were on the bed on either side of me, their bodies pressing against mine, each with a hand on my pubic mound. Automatically, my knees lifted and my thighs parted. I closed my eyes.

It's difficult for me to describe the sensation of their two hands between my legs. It was almost as if they were two small animals scampering and playing, teasing and chasing each other. Where they were seemed almost incidental to them, but it was making me more and more aroused. I had the impulse to reach up and caress Paul and Mara as they were caressing me, but it died before it reached my hands. I felt completely passive, almost paralyzed with pleasure. If they were disappointed with my passivity, if they wanted me to reciprocate, they gave no indication. Soon they each had their forefinger inside me and their thumb on my clitoris, and I was floating into a long, effortless orgasm.

As I came, I sensed a shift of weight in the bed. I opened my eyes to see that the two of them had raised themselves up and, with their hands still sharing me, were kissing. I had the sense—not for the last time that night—that I was no more than an element in a ritual they were enacting.

They lowered their heads to my chest, each finding a nipple. Still stroking my clitoris, they kissed and sucked and licked for a few moments, and then turned to each other and, their heads on my breasts, kissed.

They worked their way slowly down my body, licking and kissing me and then turning their heads and kissing each other. Just before they reached my pubic mound, Paul got up from the bed for a moment. When he returned, he was carrying something light and filmy—I suppose it was a sheet of plastic. I lifted my hips and let him arrange it on me like a diaper. He spent a moment taping the corners together at my hips, and then he turned me on my side and he and Mara put their heads between my upraised thighs. The plastic felt a little strange and awkward at first, but it was so thin and pliable—and I was so wet—that I all but forgot about it. It felt as if their tongues were directly on me, even in me. When Mara sucked my clitoris into her mouth as Paul licked me between my buttocks, I came as I had never come before.

I'm not usually multiple orgasmic. It's not that I'm incapable of it, it's just that I rarely pursue the goal. Often, as I'm on my way to a first orgasm—alone or with another person—I tell myself that I'm going to continue directly to a second, but I'm almost always satisfied with the first, and end up changing my mind.

But Paul and Mara weren't pausing after each of my orgasms to find out if I were yet satisfied. *They* obviously were not, and that was what mattered.

Even as I was still sighing and shuddering from the orgasm they'd just given me, they shifted their heads slightly and kissed each other, once again, this time between my legs.

After a moment, they broke their kiss and rearranged themselves.

Mara rolled herself on top of me, using her arms to support her upper weight, and her full breasts hung down and grazed my chest. She shifted her lower body, putting one leg between mine, and gently lowered herself until her pubic mound was pressing against my hip and my mound was pressing against hers. She rotated her pelvis against me and I gasped. It was somehow as if she were penetrating me. I lifted my hands to her buttocks and pulled her against me as I shifted my pelvis up to press myself against her. The intensity of pleasure seemed to double. She smiled and lowered her lips to kiss me. Her breasts flattened themselves against mine. My fingertips slipping into the wetness between the cheeks, we thrust against each other in a gradually quickening rhythm.

I was very close to another orgasm when I felt a shift of weight on the bed and, a moment later, felt Paul position himself between our legs. I moved my hands farther down between Mara's buttocks and felt Paul's bare penis brush against my fingers as he entered her. Mara tore her mouth from mine, groaning deeply, and shuddered against me with his very first thrust. Her orgasm seemed enormous, and it transmitted itself to me as if telepathically. I rubbed and rocked against her, almost feeling his penis inside me, the pleasure almost too intense.

Somehow they managed to keep their weight from crushing me. I wasn't at all uncomfortable as Paul thrust in and out of his wife in a slow, deliberate rhythm. Each thrust pressed Mara and me against each other. Paul slipped his hands between our chests, turning one to palm one of my breasts, one to hold one of his wife's. I took one hand from between them and reached up to hold Paul. The contrast between Mara's soft round buttocks and Paul's hard flat buttocks was wonderful and exciting.

Paul's rhythm changed. He seemed to hesitate, withdrawing from Mara almost totally, and then he made a low, guttural sound and thrust forward spasmodically. As he came, Mara rotated her pelvis against my hip, groaning again, and it was almost as if he were ejaculating inside me. I rocked my pubic mound against Mara and came harder than ever, and I lost all touch with reality.

When I became aware of myself again, Paul and Mara were lying in each other's arms next to me, murmuring softly to each other. I got up and went to the bathroom, where I discarded the plastic diaper Paul had put on me. I looked at myself in the mirror. I looked tired.

When I walked back to the sleeping area, Paul and Mara seemed to be asleep in each other's arms. I had intended, I suppose, just to slip back into the bed with them, but I felt completely superfluous to the two of them lying there. It was clear that they were finished with me. I realized I wanted to go to sleep in my own bed. As I leaned over to pick up my clothes, I sensed a stirring on the bed, and I raised my head to meet Paul's eyes.

"I think I'm going home," I told him, straightening up. Mara shifted position in her sleep.

"If you like," Paul replied.

"Good night," I said, turning toward the living area.

"We had a wonderful time," he said to my back.

"Me, too," I said, but as I walked away I realized that I didn't know whether I meant it. I'd had more orgasms in a shorter period than I could ever remember having, and they were some of the most intense I'd ever had, but I wasn't sure that I liked being anyone's plaything. What had seemed daring and exciting now seemed demeaning.

"See you Tuesday." he said. (I didn't work on Sundays, and the gallery was closed on Mondays.)

"Sure," I said automatically. I went to the living area to put on my clothes. I sat down on the couch and dressed quickly. I picked up my purse and went out the front door of the loft and down the stairs to the street as quietly as I could. I wondered if I'd come back to work on Tuesday, if I'd ever see Paul and Mara again.

TOES

Sheila and I were lying naked side by side on the bed in the tiny attic bedroom of the old beach house. We had just come in from the beach, showered, and made love.

We were still at the stage where everything is tentative and new. She worked in the same office as one of the women who lived in the house three houses down. I had met her two weekends previously, when I'd visited one of the guys renting the house we were now in. We'd gone out drinking and dancing along with several others from the two houses, and we'd had one date in the city. We'd slept together for the first time the weekend before. It had been wonderful. I had

had to go out of town that week, but I made sure we'd both be back at the beach the next weekend. This was only the fourth time we'd made love.

We were lying naked side by side. Our bodies touched in a few inconsequential places, shoulders and hips and knees. I was thinking that I was falling in love, and I had the feeling that she was thinking the same thing. It was scary and exciting, as it always was.

"Do you like my body?" she asked, playful but serious.

"I'm crazy about your body. Didn't I just demonstrate that adequately?"

"I think I'm too skinny." In fact, she was very skinny. Her hip bones stuck out, and she had almost no breasts and no bottom. I didn't care.

"I thought you can never be too rich or too skinny."

"And my feet are really funny-looking," she said, turning them this way and that, as if looking at something she was thinking about buying. "I hate them."

"Let me see," I said, and impulsively turned around and lay down with my head at her feet.

Until that moment, I'd never given her feet—or any woman's feet—much thought at all. But I took both feet in my hands and pronounced, in my worst French accent, "Zees are *beautiful* feet! I *adore* zees feet!" and planted exaggerated, theatrical kisses on them, on the instep, just below the ankle.

She giggled, which I enjoyed and took as encouragement, and I continued to plant small, noisy kisses on them, moving down from instep to toes, still playing and teasing.

When I reached her toes, I gave a lick, darting my tongue gently into the small space between the big toe and the next. Her giggle turned into a small, speculative noise, as if she was considering a suggestion I'd just made.

The sound she made opened a world of possibility to me. I could give her feet a few more playful kisses, and then return to lying beside her in my original, conventional position. Or I could take that sound as an invitation to continue more seriously.

We didn't know each other at all, really. A single upsetting sexual experience would be enough to douse the flame. It would be safer, much safer, to take her sound as nothing more than a playful response to my own joking.

And yet...and yet, I'd suddenly glimpsed a plane of intimacy I'd never explored with anyone. I was sure that she hadn't either. The thought of exploring it together with her was powerfully inviting.

But did I dare? If my attentions to her feet became more serious, would she be repulsed? Would she think me perverted?

But the sound she made was of pleasure, of invitation. Would she make such a sound if she didn't want me to continue?

All these considerations passed through my mind in the space of a moment. I had all but decided not to dare it, not to risk the new relationship for a pleasure I had not even imagined more than a few seconds before, but my penis was already stirring, and despite my caution, I licked that small space between her toes a little more deeply.

She made another small sound, still a little tentative, but leaning more in the direction of pleasure. I took this as further encouragement, and I pushed my tongue even further between her toes.

She made a surprisingly low, throaty, sigh, and I knew we were over the border. We were going to explore this entirely new terrain. My penis was suddenly hard again, twitching in the air between our bodies.

Holding her left foot in my left hand and her right foot in my right hand, I licked the space between each toe and the next, one after the other. They tasted a little salty and sandy from the beach, and the slightest bit soapy from the shower, but I didn't mind. When I reached the last space on her left foot, she spread her toes wide to let my tongue slide between them, and I was astonished how exciting I found this.

With her toes still spread widely, she moved her foot toward me slightly, and I realized she wanted me to take her toes into her mouth. I started with her smallest toe, sucking and nibbling on it as if it were her nipple, or her clitoris.

From the sigh she made, it might have been. As I

took her next toe into my mouth, I moved my hand up the outside of her leg, and then, awkwardly, onto her vulva. She bent her knee slightly, just enough for me to put my hand between her legs. She seemed wetter than she'd been when we'd make love.

I had never caressed a woman in the position I was in, and it took me a moment to find a comfortable way to caress her, half-twisting my arm and using my thumb, with my other fingers resting between her labia and against her upper thigh.

But my thumb on her clitoris was almost beside the point. Most our attention seemed to be on her toes. I had gradually and deliberately kissed and licked and nibbled and sucked each toe in turn, and now, inevitably, reached her big toe.

I surrounded it with my lips, and she curled her other toes to make it easier for me to suck it into my mouth. Gently, she moved it in and out, and I sucked it in and then pushed it out with my tongue in the rhythm she established. Almost automatically, my thumb fell into the same rhythm on her clitoris.

Sheila was sighing deeply, and I knew that she was very aroused. I was too, but I was still shy about this and kept my penis from touching her, still afraid that having an erection from mouthing her foot would seem perverse, even if she was enjoying and encouraging it.

As if in reassurance, I felt her hand groping blindly along my body until she found my erection and gently pulled me toward her. I shifted forward on the bed until, still in her grasp, I felt the head of my penis against some smooth part of her skin—thigh or hips or waist, it didn't matter. She squeezed my penis in the same rhythm that her toe was entering my mouth, in the same rhythm that I was stroking her clitoris, and lightly rubbed the head back and forth on her skin.

Her right foot—the one not in my mouth—twisted around in a slow circle. I caught it in my hand and stopped it. I slid my hand up her foot to the toes, and then pressed my fingers between them, intertwining them. She made a new, deeper sound of pleasure.

Still sucking the big toe of her left foot, I worked my four fingers in and out between the toes of her right foot.

Her hand holding my penis began to quiver, making the head and the sensitive spot on the underside move rapidly against her skin. I adjusted all of my rhythms—my thumb on her clitoris, my mouth and tongue on her big toe, my fingers between the toes of her other foot—to copy hers.

Her orgasm seemed to erupt everywhere at once, with a loud, guttural sound from deep in her belly, and for a moment I had the illusion that her toe was actually ejaculating into my mouth, as my penis was in fact ejaculating on her body and on mine. I would not have believed I could have so powerful an orgasm outside a woman's body.

We lay for a moment in that odd position, and then I slowly and carefully extricated my fingers from between her toes.

"That tickles," she said, with a small laugh.

I let her toe slip out of my mouth. "You thought that was tickling?" I asked.

She laughed again. "You know what I mean."

I rearranged myself, bringing my face to hers. My penis slipped from her hand. We smiled at each other, as new lovers do.

"That was wonderful," she said. I kissed her on the lips, and she kissed back.

"Yes, it was," I said.

I turned and let myself down once again beside her on my back, as we'd been. I groped with my hand at the bedside table, looking for the box of tissues.

"You know," she said in a playful voice, "I'm not too crazy about my knees, either.

NO MAN'S LAND

The first time I grasped that there must be male human beings as well as females, I was ten years old. I was at the New York Wildlife Preserve with both my mothers and one of my greatmothers, in the Hall of Darkness. The exhibits were illuminated with red light, to which the animals were not sensitive, so they behaved as they did during the night.

I was looking through the window at a colony of small monkeys when I noticed one of the monkeys near the glass raise its hindquarters. Another monkey abruptly approached the first monkey from the rear, its small, hairless penis erect like a pointing finger, and mounted the first.

"Do you know what they're doing, Ellie?" whispered my birth mother in my ear.

"Not exactly, mama."

"Well, this is called sex. The male is raping the female, so that the female will have a baby. It's very painful for her."

"Why doesn't she try to stop it?"

"She can't, hon. It's holding her down, forcing her. Besides," my mother continued, stroking the back of my neck, "she wants to have a baby. She'd do anything to have one."

It was all over in less than a minute. At the end, the male moved a few times even faster and made a grotesque face.

"See right then?" my mother asked. "At the climax, the male passes its seed. That part is very painful for it, too."

"Then why does it do it?"

"It has to. The pressure builds up inside and it has to release it. Otherwise it gets very sick."

The male let go of the female and withdrew. Although the red light made it impossible to tell what color anything really was, in my mind the penis was a startlingly bright, wet pink.

"What happens when the female makes her seed? Does that hurt, too?"

"No, that's different. Females never go through the terrible pain the male does when it climaxes and discharges its seed. We're very lucky to be female."

†††

Later, when I was in bed, my birth mother came in to my room and sat down on the side of the bed.

"Do you understand what you saw at the zoo today, honey? What the monkeys were doing?"

I hesitated. "I understand that he raped her so that she'd have a baby. The part I don't understand is... how come *people* aren't male and female, like all the animals?"

"Well, a hundred years ago there used to be male humans, just like there are male animals. But males were mean and cruel and just couldn't be civilized. They raped and killed everybody all the time."

"And they used to live right along with women and girls?" I asked incredulously.

"Before the Great Cleansing. Now we don't have any males at all. Except for the ones we keep as semen donors. And they're kept in special places, so they can't hurt anyone anymore."

My mind was filled yet again with a picture of the monkeys copulating. "Do people have sex, like those monkeys...?"

She laughed indulgently. "Don't worry, honey. Not anymore. At least not in the civilized world. We're very lucky to be living now."

I was awake. It was very dark and our house seemed completely still. Not knowing why, I got on my knees and pressed my cheek against the pillow. I raised my nightgown, reached behind, and put my pinkie in the little hole I knew was there. It hurt a little, at first, and then, as I cautiously moved it in and out, it felt strange and inexplicably comforting. I closed my eyes and pretended to be a little monkey getting raped. Although it began to feel nice in a way, nothing much happened, and I took my finger out and rolled over and went to sleep.

After that, whenever I couldn't fall asleep, and sometimes before I'd even tried, I'd play monkey. As time went on, I graduated from pinkie to middle finger.

One night when I was twelve years old, I tried using two fingers. As I pressed them in and out, I felt a peculiar tugging toward the front, just where the fine, downy hair was beginning to darken and thicken. I snaked my other hand under my body and touched myself at the front of my slit and discovered the hard, tender kernel of sensitivity.

I thought of the monkey's long thin naked penis. The sensations inside my body climaxed, erupting through me. I remembered the monkey contorting its face in apparent pain, and realized that I must be experiencing what it had been feeling.

Either my birth mother was wrong, or I was a freak. Females *did* feel what males felt when they passed their seed...or at least this female did.

†††

Somewhere along the way, I had stopped pretending that I was a monkey and started trying to imagine what a male human was like. The only pictures I had to guide me were from the fairy tales I'd watched on the eyephones. In my mind, I was happily raped by trolls and ogres and giants and monsters.

By the age of sixteen, I was no longer content with my fantasies. I wanted to find out what male human beings really looked like. As an upper school student, my access authority in the virtual library was quite limited. There was no trace of male human beings anywhere I looked.

In college, things changed. As a history major, I was finally allowed to view materials that predated the Great Cleansing. As soon as I had been granted the authority, I put on my eyephones and asked to view a news report from the year 2043. Immediately, in the virtual space before me, I saw a newscast from one hundred years ago. Standing behind a wooden lectern were a woman and, next to her, a man.

I gasped. The fairy tales I'd viewed as a child had parodied the aspects in which males were different from females: the greater size and bulk, the coarser features, the facial hair, the deeper voice. The person who stood and spoke before me in the virtual space looked more like an ugly woman than a fairy-tale monster.

The virtual scene before me dissolved as the first story was presented. I saw a meeting of the political leaders of the time, most of whom were men. Some of them, particularly the younger ones, were not at all repulsive.

That night in my dormitory room, I waited for my roommates to fall asleep. I got up on my knees and shoulders, my chest heaving and my vagina already wet and aching. I imagined the news reporter on his knees behind me, between my legs, but I was more revolted than excited. Then I remembered one of the younger men in the first news story. He was blond, with delicate features, and he wore no hair on his face. As I rubbed my clitoris, I pushed three fingers into myself and imagined that they were the blond man's penis. I reached my climax almost immediately.

In the days and weeks after this, I immersed myself in the times before the Great Cleansing.

Nearly everything I saw surprised me. Not all the men acted like fairy-tale monsters: Some were gentle and kind, and they didn't all rape or kill anyone. A great many of the audiovisuals were stories about the attraction males and females felt for one another. Men and women often touched and kissed each other tenderly, as mothers do.

The greatest surprise was that the woman was commonly shown experiencing a climax, just like the man, just as I did. My mother was wrong. I was not a freak.

In the scenes of love between a man and a woman, the woman was usually bare-breasted and often totally nude, but in the dozens or perhaps hundreds of visuals I watched, I never saw the man's penis. It was obviously a taboo. I was almost tearful with frustrated curiosity.

I neglected my studies entirely. Pretending to be doing research, I spent hours at the library watching story after story, lost in the era when the pursuit of love between man and woman seemed to be the major preoccupation.

I don't know how many weeks it took, but one morning I woke up to realize that the biology and medicine of the era would have to account for the male. Elated, I got dressed and raced to my carrel without stopping for breakfast. I put on my 'phones and quickly navigated through the library, out of the room I had inhabited for so long and back to the main foyer.

It took me a number of tries before I found the room that had the ancient anatomy texts, but I was finally successful. The books contained detailed illustrations of the male anatomy, and some had actual photographs. Disappointingly, none of the illustrations I found showed the penis erect.

At end of the first term of my junior year in college, having spent the last several months doing nothing but watching visuals, I failed all my examinations and was requested to take an indefinite leave of absence. At first, I lived at home, but soon I found a job in New York City, and I moved out. I took a small, cheap single room in an apartment house in a run-down neighborhood of Manhattan near the Central Park homeless encampment.

At first, I was ashamed of what I had made of my life, and I hurried from place to place without meeting people's eyes and speaking as little as possible. But gradually, I began to relax. Now, when a woman on the transitstrip or the sidestrip met my eye, I didn't immediately look away.

One midday, I was eating lunch as usual at the mealshop near my workplace. I heard a woman ask, "Mind if I sit at your table?" I looked up from my plate. I had seen the tall, heavyset woman in the shop before, although we had never spoken. She was a little older than me, about twenty-five years old, I guessed. She had short, straight, unnaturally black hair. Her clothing was very plain and dark. She seemed rougher than the women I had grown up with.

"It's kind of crowded here at lunch hour," she said with an apologetic smile, glancing around the small restaurant. Her voice was low-pitched but not unpleasant.

I followed her glance and saw that it was true: There were no empty tables and few empty seats. "Sure, go ahead," I said.

"Thanks." She slipped into the chair opposite mine and put her tray down on the small table.

"My name is Stephanie," she said. "Stephanie Helenchild." She offered her hand.

"Ellie," I said. "Ellie Susanchild." Over our two trays of food, we shook. Her hand was large, with long fingers, and strong.

She picked up her utensil and looked at her food. "Nutritious and appetizing," she said sarcastically.

"Cheap and edible," I replied.

We talked all through lunch. I learned that she lived in another run-down neighborhood bordering Central Park. Like me, she performed maintenance on the virtual space.

As we were leaving the restaurant, she turned to look at me. "Doing anything after work?"

"Not really," I said.

"I feel like going out after work. Want to join me?"

"Where are you going?"

"I don't know exactly. I thought we'd get something to eat, and then maybe go to a Madison Avenue music club."

I hesitated.

"Come on, Ellie. I'll look out for you. It'll be okay."

†††

Stephanie took my hand and led me from one deceleration strip to the next until we reached the sidestrip. "Here we are. World-famous Madison Avenue," she said, sweeping her arm grandly along the rows of seedy storefronts. Women went in and out of the shops, loitered on the sidestrip talking with each other, or simply leaned against the walls and watched the passersby.

Stephanie led me several blocks north. A garish sign projected over the avenue announced *The Classics Club*. "This is it," she said. Inside, the club was dark and crowded. I recognized the style of music as being from the same era as visuals I had spent so many hours watching. Near the door was a long bar, where women were sitting. Many, like Stephanie, wore their hair short and had little facepaint or jewelry. Stephanie bought herself and me drinks, and led me farther into the room. Near the bar was a number of small tables crowded together, all of them occupied. Beyond that was a large dance floor, crowded with women dancing in the strange, jerky way I had seen in the old 'visuals. And, barely visible at the other end of the club, was a stage on which the musicians were playing.

As we edged toward the stage, I realized that the musicians were...*men*. Seeing my reaction, Stephanie laughed.

"They can't be real," I gasped. "What are they?" I shouted over the music into Stephanie's ear.

She said something I couldn't catch. I turned my head, and she lowered her lips to my ear. "Holograms. They're really something, aren't they?" Stephanie said, her lips brushing my ear. "It's like they're almost alive."

I felt a peculiar exhilaration in my chest. I sensed that somehow she knew about me...about my secret. I lifted my head to speak into Stephanie's ear. "When I was in college, I spent a lot of time watching visuals from this time."

"What kind of visuals? What were your favorites about?" she asked, smiling an uninterpretable smile.

I must have blushed. "They were about...men and women. How they used to be together." I felt unable to explain, but Stephanie was nodding as if she understood. "Love stories."

Stephanie turned her head and put her lips to my ear again. "I have some very special visuals back at my place I think you'd really like. Want to see them?"

She lived in an ancient building that, centuries ago, must have been quite luxurious, but now was as decrepit as mine. Her room had been, apparently, one half of the apartment's great main room. She closed the door as I looked around. The most remarkable feature of her room was a set of shelves containing row after row of small rectangular boxes.

"What are those?" I asked, pointing at them.

"They're my collection of antique visuals, from before

the Cleansing," she said, crossing the room and taking one of the boxes.

"Like in the space?" I asked.

She opened the box and a black rectangular cartridge slipped out. "Oh, I don't think you ever saw anything like this in the space," she said with a smile. "I had to pay a lot of money for these."

"If they're not on the net, how do you view them?" I asked.

"Come over here," she said, walking over to her bed. "I have a player."

On a stand next to her bed was an antique device housed in a strange black metal. A set of eyephones was attached to the device by a narrow flexible connector.

"Are you sure you're ready for this?" she asked as I sat down on the edge of the bed and took the 'phones in my hands. "I'm sure they're much stronger than anything you've ever seen." She put the black cartridge into the playing device and pushed a button.

My hands were quivering. "Stronger how?" I asked.

"They show you…everything."

"Yes," I said quietly, putting on the 'phones. They were the opaque variety, and the earcups had no hear-through, so I waited for a moment in silent darkness.

After a few thousandthparts, the visual began. It had the same flat, grainy quality as the ancient visuals I'd seen when I was in school. After a few moments I saw a good-looking young man and young woman in an early-twenty-first-century bedroom. There was some conversation, and then they were embracing and kissing. I felt my heart pounding as I watched the man gradually undress the woman, caressing and kissing her as she did so.

The woman, now completely naked, undressed the man. I held my breath as I watched the woman unzip the man's pants and lower them to show me, for the very first time, a human penis in full erection.

My clitoris was throbbing, and my vagina was soaking my underclothes. I was so astounded and excited that I felt light-headed. I closed my eyes for a moment, trying to calm myself.

When I opened my eyes again, the man was lying on his back, and the woman was straddling him. She held his penis in her hand and rubbed it back and forth between her legs. My own labia glowed with sympathetic pleasure. She lowered herself onto his penis, sighing loudly into both my ears.

Without having touched myself, I had already almost reached climax. Without thinking, not knowing what to do, I tore the 'phones from my head.

Stephanie had opaqued the windows and dimmed the roomlight. I did not see her for a moment, and then she appeared from behind a tall screen. She was naked except for a loose-fitting top, which covered her small breasts. At her crotch, held by elastic bands around her waist and between her legs, was…an artificial penis. It looked just like what I had just seen in the visual.

"Shall we do what they're doing?" she asked, approaching me slowly.

She did not really look like a man, but she was close enough. I nodded. "Yes," I said, my voice choking me.

"Call me Stephen, then," she said, and reached for me.

SEX ON THE BEACH

Nature is inventive, and nature is ingenious, and nature is relentless. In the astonishingly profuse spectrum of life, there are dozens of instances of one species imitating another, to secure the services of pollination, to frighten potential predators, to camouflage themselves, and to lure prey. With humankind inhabiting virtually the entire planet, it was perhaps inevitable that somewhere on the globe would arise a species that mimicked it.

Jennifer walked along the beach with her feet in the surf, naked except for the briefest bikini bottoms, and watched the sun extinguish itself gloriously in the ocean. It was as extravagantly beautiful as the photographs in the brochure, but it did not make her happy. She had spent thousands of dollars for two weeks at this exclusive and exotic resort, so recently carved out of the South American jungle. Her friends had thought she was crazy—not only because the place was so new and so expensive, but because the beach was—as the brochure put it—clothing optional. She had never actually tried nudism before, but she had wanted to cut through the phoniness and the games of the singles bars and the dating services; she had wanted to meet men for whom sex was something other than manipulation and conquest, for whom sex was as natural and easy as breathing. But what she'd found, in the first week of her stay, were men as childish and neurotic as any she had ever known—and even more transparently obsessed and troubled by sex than most.

It turned out that clothing was not really optional at the beach at all. All the men went naked. All the women went topless, and about half of them went bottomless as well. The first morning Jennifer appeared on the beach, she had worn a bikini. Before she had even sat down, two men and—surprisingly—three women had made good-natured but pointed remarks: "You'll never get an even tan like that!" "Why the formal attire?" and so on.

She sat down on one of the beach chairs the resort provided and took off her top, and was immediately aware of heads—both male and female—turning all over the beach. Although she was comfortable with her body and knew that she had an attractive figure, she found the cold-blooded appraising stares of the men and the competitive looks of the women rude and discomfiting. Still hoping for the best, she took a bottle of suntan lotion from her beachbag. Within what seemed like only seconds, a man was standing next to her. It was disconcerting—to say the least—to turn and have a stranger's genitals all but in her face. "Can I help you with that?" the man asked. Jennifer looked up his tan body to his face. He was wearing opaque mirrored sunglasses and a pronounced leer.

"No, thanks," she replied, continuing to put the lotion on herself.

"I'm Dave," he said.

"I didn't ask your name," she said quietly.

"Hey," the man said in an aggrieved tone, "I was only trying to be friendly."

"Well, you weren't succeeding," she said.

"Lighten up, baby," the man said, angry now, as he retreated. "What'd you come here for, anyway?"

It was a good question, and one that Jennifer had asked herself several times since then.

Things had not improved from there. Except on the beach itself, the attire was like any other tropical resort, but the nudism of the beach seemed to set the tone everywhere. The women walked with out-thrust chests and swaying hips, and the men strutted and stared.

Each day, Jennifer found herself edging farther and farther away from the others on the beach, still hoping that her vacation would not prove a total disaster, that she would meet a man she could be comfortable with.

The beach was in a shallow bay perhaps a hundred yards wide. Jennifer decided to see what was beyond it, if the sand continued beyond where she could see. When she reached her destination, she was surprised to find several hundred more yards of sand, although it was entirely empty.

Entirely empty, that is, except for what appeared to be a dark-skinned man sitting by himself in the sand, close to the bushes, some fifty yards away.

Intrigued, Jennifer walked toward the figure.

In fact, the creature sitting naked on the beach was not a man. It was not even, properly speaking, a male—its species was one that changed its sex according to necessity. It was, actually, an amphibian—a distant relative of the frog—although its ancestors had largely given up life in water tens of millions of years earlier, when they had begun to prey upon the primates that had lately spread into their jungle.

As Jennifer approached the creature, she saw what appeared to be a naked man of about twenty-five. Its skin was quite dark—after all, the species had adapted to the indigenous humans, not the tourists—and unusually smooth. He—for she thought of the creature as *he*—had what looked like a full head of straight dark hair, and eyes of the most startling green, flecked with gold. He watched her walk toward him, his face impassive, his eyes unblinking. He kept his eyes on hers, rather than raking them down her body, as the other men at the resort did. She found him disturbingly attractive, and she felt a flush of optimism in her chest.

"Hello," she said. "Are you alone?"

"Yes," he said. He seemed to have a speech impediment, which made his S unusually hard. It came out "Yesss." His lips—which were unusually thin—seemed to curl into a slight smile.

"Are you a guest at the resort?" she asked. "I haven't seen you before."

"Yesss," he said.

"Would you like to be alone, or may I sit down?"

"Yesss."

"Thanks," she said, dropping onto the beach—not too near, about five feet away. Like him, she faced the ocean. She closed her eyes and felt the dying sun play on her eyelids. "I guess you don't like the company back there too much," she said with a nervous laugh. She was—she admitted to herself—excited.

"Yesss." He turned his head and met her eyes again. His stare was so intense it was hypnotic. She had never seen eyes so white with irises so dazzlingly colored. It would be easy, she said to herself, to get lost in eyes like those.

"Neither do I," she said, after a long moment, trying to remember the thread of conversation.

"Yesss."

With great difficulty, she looked away from him. "It's been a big disappointment," she said, with another nervous laugh. "I can't believe how much money I spent on this vacation. My girlfriends tried to talk me out of it, but I wouldn't listen. Now I feel like such a jerk!"

"Yesss."

"You, too, hunh?" He sure wasn't saying much, but she sensed that he wasn't at all like the others.

"Yesss."

"My name is Jennifer," she said, turning toward him, smiling, offering her hand.

"Yesss," he said, extending his own hand, smiling back, staring deeply into her eyes again.

"What's your name?" she asked, as their hands met. His hand was oddly smooth and cool to her touch, but she did not puzzle over it much, because he was drawing closer to her. He seemed completely self-assured. His eyes never left hers, and did not blink. Almost without her realizing it, he was beside her, smiling, staring deeply into her eyes. Where his hand had touched hers, her skin felt hot and tingly.

"Sssssssss," he hissed as he gently stroked her shoulder. Wherever he touched her, her skin seemed to glow. She heard it as "Shhhhhhhhh"—he was telling her that it was time to stop talking. But she had forgotten what she was saying. She felt light-headed and giddy. She lay back on the sand.

In her normal life, she would never have let things progress so quickly. But this was just the fantasy that had attracted her to the resort in the first place. Sex on the beach. She could feel her body already anticipating it. She attributed her giddiness and the glow of her flesh wherever he touched her to the excitement of the situation, not the poison that his skin exuded.

He ran his hand down her body. When he reached her bikini bottom, he snapped it off, roughly, with a quick, strong tug.

Back in the city, Jennifer would have been outraged by his roughness and his haste. But his impetuousness fit in well with the fantasy of the dark, silent stranger on the beach at sunset. He rolled between her upraised thighs, and she was already ready for him to enter her. She put her hands on the smooth, oddly cool skin at his hips to guide him. He must have just come out of the water, she decided. Her puzzlement was quickly swept aside by the thrill of the moment, and, with the toxins from his hands already circulating in her blood and reaching her brain, it did not occur to her that he did not show the slightest signs of wetness, even in his hair.

She felt his penis between her thighs. Like the rest of him, it was strangely cool.

In her real life, she would never make love without a condom, especially with a stranger. But it seemed a remote, theoretical concern. Her entire body was burning with—she thought—desire.

He entered her easily, at the same time wrapping his strong arms around her and putting his cool lips on hers, opening her mouth.

She realized something was terribly wrong when she felt his long, thin tongue snaking its way into her mouth and down her throat, but by then it was far too late. She was choking and gagging, but he kept his mouth locked to hers. She tried to free herself from his grip, but he was far too strong. The organ she had mistaken for a penis, which unfurled from within the creature's body cavity, forced its way through her uterus and into her viscera. She shrieked in agony, but his mouth muffled her cries. In a cruel parody of lovemaking, the creature used that penile organ to inject its venom into her. She felt the incomprehensible sensation of her innards dissolving, but only for the briefest moment. Her heart stopped. Her brain, disintegrating from pain and oxygen deprivation, flooded itself with endorphins, and her last moments of consciousness were filled with an hallucination of making love on the beach with a dark, silent stranger with hypnotically beautiful eyes. Her orgasm came almost instantly, and it was a pure white light of transcendental pleasure. After that, there was nothing.

†††

The creature withdrew its false penis, now covered with Jennifer's blood and other fluids, as it sucked Jennifer's liquefied tissues out through her mouth. When it was done, there was little left of her but a bag of skin, bones, and her skull. The creature, its belly grotesquely distended by the great quantity of protoplasm it had consumed, slithered back into the jungle. It would not have to feed again for at least a week.

The incoming tide lapped at Jennifer's remains, toying with the loose flesh. Once the ocean had her body within its grasp, the work the creature had begun would soon be finished.

VAMPIRE

After working as a male escort in Las Vegas for about three years, he'd decided to head east. He'd heard there were a lot of women in New York who were willing to pay for the safe, discreet, trouble-free attentions of a handsome young man. (How does someone become a male escort? The answer in his case was: by degrees. First he was a dancer in one of the nightclubs in one of the casinos. Then he was a dancer in a club for women where the dancers stripped. Then he started accepting invitations from women in the audience to go out. The women would take him to fancy restaurants and give him nice presents, and they would almost always end up in bed. In the mornings, the women would usually tip him. One of the other dancers told him about an escort service. It seemed like a small step from what he was already doing.)

The service he had worked for in Las Vegas took fifty percent of his fee (not including tips). In New York, he'd decided, he'd work for himself. After all, how much could a few small ads in a few weekly newspapers cost? To start off, as soon as he'd arrived, he'd written to a few of his old clients in Las Vegas, giving them his new location and letting them know he was interested in getting referrals.

When he'd been in New York only about a month, he got a call early one Saturday morning, waking him up. A woman with a polished voice—sounding twenty or thirty years younger than his usual clients—asked if he was available that same night. He pretended that he'd had a last-minute cancellation, and made arrangements to be picked up by her driver at eight o'clock that night.

When he came downstairs at eight o'clock, he was dressed in a dark, conservative suit, a button-down white cotton shirt with French cuffs, and a silk tie of a solid color. His shoes, which were Italian, were polished. The car that was waiting was a Rolls-Royce Silver Cloud limousine, and he regretted not quoting a higher fee. As he let himself into the passenger compartment, he wondered what his client would be like: Whether she would prove to be disabled, disfigured, or just plain ugly.

The trip took about an hour. The driver did not speak a word, and neither did he. After they crossed the bridge north out of Manhattan, he had no idea where they were, but not very long after that, the driver got off the parkway onto local streets. After a few blocks, the apartment buildings disappeared, and they might have been in a small village. A short distance after that, the street became more like a road, and they might have been in the country. They drove through a set of cast iron gates onto a circular driveway and stopped before what could only be described as a mansion, three stories high, with vaulted columns and wide stone steps.

The driver of the limousine spoke for the first time. "Just go up," he said. "It's open."

The front door was, as the chauffeur had said, open. He walked into a large entrance hall and closed the heavy door behind himself. On the wall to his left, between two doorways, was a large oil painting that looked as if it had just been finished. It was a full-length nude portrait of a woman as radiantly beautiful as any woman he had ever seen. She looked to be about twenty-five years old, and she was blonde, and the only flaw to her beauty—and it did not really detract at all—was a small beauty mark just above the right corner of her mouth. He wondered if this was the woman who had hired him, and he was as puzzled as ever.

Directly in front of him was a wide flight of dark wooden stairs. The hall had stone floors, and had a cold, uninhabited feeling. "Hello?" he called.

"Why, hello," came a thin, quavery voice from above. He looked up. At a railing overlooking the entrance hall stood an ancient-looking woman in a full-length yellow satin gown that seemed much too big for her. She might have been in her eighties; she might have been over a hundred. "Why, you're very handsome."

"Thank you," he said, puzzled. It was apparent that this woman was his client. But who had spoken to him that morning? Her granddaughter? Yet this woman had the same peculiar vocal mannerism of beginning sentences with *why*.

"Please come upstairs," she said.

He did, but slowly. Most of his clients in Las Vegas had been in their fifties or early sixties. This woman looked at least twenty years older, possibly twice that. Her face was completely etched with wrinkles, like the surface of a dried-out riverbed, and hung from the bones of her skull like a thin, lifeless rag.

When he reached her, he noticed that she had a beauty mark over her mouth in the same place as the woman in the portrait. Was the painting of her as a young woman? It must have been, but it looked too recent.

The old woman took his arm in her long, thin

fingers. "Would you care for a drink? I have wine in the bedroom."

"Yes, a glass of wine would be nice."

Gripping his arm for support, she slowly led him to a bedroom exquisitely appointed in silk and satin and crystal and porcelain and silver and mahogany. The room was lit only by the fire from a fireplace, which was almost large enough to stand in. Facing the fireplace were two high-backed upholstered chairs with matching footstools. Between them was a small round table with a carafe of wine and two glasses that had already been filled. Opposite the fireplace, behind the chairs, was an elaborately carved wooden bed with a mattress made up in yellow satin.

"Let's sit down," she said, gesturing with her free hand to the fireplace. He helped her to one of the chairs. It seemed to swallow her up. "If you'll hand me my wine," she said. He gave her one of the two glasses and then sat down in the other chair and took up the other glass.

"To youth," she toasted, raising her glass to him with a withered smile. He saw that she must have been quite beautiful when she was young.

"To youth," he echoed, and took a sip of the wine.

"You asked for half your fee in advance," she reminded him, and took a small envelope of cream-colored paper from the table. It was unsealed. She fanned the money inside it.

He saw ten crisp one-hundred-dollar bills. "That's my entire fee, not half."

"You'll get another envelope like that in the morning, if you prove satisfactory. I expect that will cover everything."

"Definitely. Whatever you want," he said, and reached for the envelope.

"A few points, then," she said casually, moving the envelope out of his reach, and he looked at her carefully. "I insist that you not simulate your orgasms. If you do, I'll know it. I want you to have as many orgasms as you can."

He had never encountered a client like her. She might just as easily have been talking about whether he had brushed his teeth. Usually, with most clients, he did exactly what she was insisting that he not do, so that he could service them as often as they wanted during the night. Only occasionally did a client insist on seeing him ejaculate, and that always cost extra. "Well, if you want me to last all night, I'll have to pace myself." He lifted his glass to his lips and drained the wine.

"Don't worry about that. Why, I'm going to give you more orgasms than you've had in one night since you were a teenager."

He smiled at her, although he could tell that she was serious.

"And you may not use a prophylactic," she said.

He shook his head as he put the wineglass back on

the table. "If we're going to have intercourse, I'm afraid I have to insist. It's as much for your protection as for mine."

She smiled sadly. "Why, then I'm afraid we can't continue." She took one of the bills out of the envelope and offered it too him, "I'll give you a hundred dollars for your trouble, and I'll call my driver."

He met her eyes. He could not seriously consider giving up nineteen hundred dollars for one night, and she knew it. "Well, perhaps I can make an exception, just this once. I'm sure you're in the best of health."

"Why, I knew you'd be reasonable," she said, returning the hundred-dollar bill to the envelope, and then handing the envelope to him.

"Thank you," he said, smoothly making the envelope disappear into an inside pocket of his suit jacket.

With great difficulty, she rose from her chair. "Help me to the bed, please." He came around to her side and gave her his arm.

Laboriously, with his help, she climbed onto the bed and arranged herself on the pillows, still dressed in her robe.

"There's a silent butler," she said, gesturing at a wooden clothing stand next to a chair beside the bed. "Please take your clothes off and come to me."

He undressed slowly and carefully, arranging his clothes on the silent butler as he went. When he was wearing only his bikini underpants, he approached the bed. Many of his clients seemed to prefer it that way. "Those, too," she said, pointing with a long, thin finger.

"As you like," he said, slipping them off and tossing them onto the clothing stand.

He lay down on the bed on his side, facing her. The bed was mostly in shadows, but he could still see how withered her face was.

"Lie on your back," she said, opening her robe but not taking it off.

He did so, and she turned her back toward him and straddled him, carefully settling her vulva down over his face. He closed his eyes as she put her mouth to his penis.

She was very good with her mouth and her hands, and he soon grew hard and forgot that she was as ancient and withered as she was. Her mouth was as warm and wet and soft as any he had ever felt, and it was all he could do to pay attention to what he was doing with his own mouth and tongue.

Without warning, she lifted herself up and crawled down the bed toward his waist, the silk of her gown brushing over his face and chest as she went. When she was straddling his hips, he felt her take hold of his penis with both hands and lower herself onto it. With her back to him and her gown still on, she might have been any woman. With both of them wet with each other's saliva, she felt like a woman forty or fifty years younger.

She hardly moved at all, but she still held the base

of his penis in one hand, and she stroked him rapidly.

"Come," she said urgently. "I want you to come."

Her fluttering fingers were very exciting. He closed his eyes and forgot about everything else and let himself go. His hips rose as if by themselves and he emptied himself in a light, effortless orgasm.

"Good, good," she said, as her fingers urged the last drops of pleasure from him.

She lifted her leg from across his body and turned around. It hadn't seemed that she had reached orgasm, or was even aroused at all, but she seemed completely satisfied with his performance. "Now rest," she whispered, almost tenderly, and drew the bedcovers over him. "I'll tell you when it's time again."

He closed his eyes, not really intending to fall asleep.

"Wake up," she was saying, gently stroking his face.

He opened his eyes. He had no idea how long he'd been sleeping, but he didn't think very long. The flickering light of the fireplace was not much different.

She was sitting at his side in her yellow robe, smiling down at him. She seemed to have more energy, as if the sex had revived her. Although she still looked ancient, he could almost see the beautiful young woman in the painting downstairs, if only in her eyes.

She reached under the covers and felt his penis, which was long but soft. She squeezed it rhythmically, and it started to stiffen.

"It would be better if I used the facilities first," he said.

"Of course. They're right there," she said, pointing to a door a few paces from the bed.

In the elegant old bathroom, he used the toilet and went to the mirror to wash his face. He was surprised at how haggard he looked. He wondered if he was getting sick, and whether he would have any problem satisfying this strange woman during the long night ahead. He splashed cold water on his face, dried himself off, and padded back into the bedroom.

She was waiting for him with a smile. "Now come lie down," she said, patting the bed beside her.

As soon as he lay down, she began to stroke him again. Her fingers seemed even softer and cleverer than the time before, and he rapidly became erect. She leaned over and took his penis in her mouth, but only long enough to wet it thoroughly. Then, once again, she turned her back and straddled him, and he had nothing to look at but her yellow robe.

It seemed she moved a little more vigorously this time. "Come on, come on," she urged, stroking the base of his penis and fondling his testicles. Her voice seemed more enthusiastic, "I want your come."

It took a little more time than the first, but he was surprised at how easily she brought him to the brink, and then to overflowing. He gasped as she squeezed his testicles as he ejaculated, as if milking them.

"What about you?" he asked as she lifted herself from him. "Don't you want to come?"

"Don't worry about me," she said, warmly. "My pleasure is in making you come." She turned around and gave him a small kiss on the cheek. "Now you rest again, and I'll come to you in a little while."

She got up from the bed and went to sit in her chair by the fireplace.

He had tried to stay awake, but once again she was stroking his face. "It's time again," she said softly. He opened his eyes. It seemed darker than before. He supposed the fire had died down. "Would you like to use the bathroom again?"

He yawned enormously. "I suppose I should," he said, and sat up. His back ached, and he felt tired. He was sure he was coming down with something, and he only hoped he would make it through the long night satisfactorily enough to earn that second envelope of a thousand dollars. With a groan, he stood up and walked toward the bathroom.

"Don't turn the light on. It's too bright. There's a small nightlight."

He hadn't noticed the nightlight on his previous visit to the bathroom. There was just enough light for him to find the toilet and the sink, although not enough to see himself in the mirror. It was just as well. He was sure he looked terrible. He felt as if he had aged twenty years.

†††

This third time they had sex, it took a while for her hands to make him hard, even though they seemed softer and warmer and more inventive than the times before. And this time, although she turned her robed back to him and straddled him without first using her mouth, she felt as wet and smooth and warm as any woman he had ever been with.

The third time, she was much more vigorous in her movements. Because he had already come twice that night, orgasm seemed like a remote possibility. But her hands moved down from the base of his penis, one to hold his testicles, the other down to his perineum, stroking and prodding. Suddenly his need to ejaculate was as urgent as ever. He raised his hips to meet her. Her fingers pressed and stroked and prodded, and he groaned and emptied himself into her once again.

"That's it, that's it," she said, her voice full of enthusiasm. "Come, come."

It was even darker when he opened his eyes to her fingers on his cheek again. He felt awful, and he was sure he was sick with something. But there was that second envelope to keep him from saying anything. "Would you like to use the bathroom first?" she asked.

He knew that he should, but he was too tired to move. His groin felt numb. "That's okay," he said. "I'm all right."

"Good," she said, with an easy laugh, and reached down under the covers again.

"How many more times?" he asked. His voice was plaintive and querulous.

"Why, don't worry," she said. "You're doing just fine," she assured him, her fingers stroking gently but insistently. "Just enjoy yourself. That's all I want."

He was surprised to find that her fingers were making him erect again, although he didn't feel as hard as he usually did. Still, after a few moments, she rose up and took the position she favored, her back to him, both hands guiding his penis inside her.

As if to make up for his increasing exhaustion, she moved with even more vigor and enthusiasm this time. Although he was more or less erect, he felt almost nothing, and he was sure that her efforts would be in vain. But, for the first time, he noticed that she was using the muscles of her vagina to grip his penis rhythmically as she rode it. She was as tight and as smooth and as hot as a young woman. He was puzzled, but he was freshly excited, too. He raised his hips to meet her pelvis, trying to increase the tempo, but he felt too tired, and he let himself fall back against the bed.

"Just relax," came her soothing voice. "Let me do all the work," she said, and reached down, past his perineum, and put a finger between his buttocks. She stroked and tickled, and he moaned and ejaculated, his muscles contracting almost violently. He felt his orgasm behind his eyes and in the base of his neck, like a terrible headache. "Good, good," she said, her voice warm and sweet.

As she rose from him and turned around, he caught a glimpse of her naked body silhouetted by the dying fire, and he knew that something was terribly wrong. Her body was that of a young woman.

She stood at the side of the bed and raised the covers over him. Even in the shadowy light, he could see that her face was no longer sagging and wrinkled.

"You're a witch, aren't you!?" he accused her, his voice sounding strange to himself. He raised himself up, but she put her hands on his shoulders and easily pushed him down again.

"It's too late," she said, her voice young and strong. "Don't try to fight me. I don't want to hurt you."

"Let me go!" he said. He sounded old and ineffectual.

"In the morning. When I'm through with you. As we agreed."

He felt tears well up in his eyes. He lifted one hand out of the covers and held it in front of his face. Even in the darkness, he could see that it was the hand of an old man.

"Go to sleep," she said softly. "You need your strength."

"What have you done to me?" he wailed.

"Go to sleep."

Despite himself, he found himself drifting off to sleep once again.

†††

He opened his eyes in confusion, certain that he had been dreaming. The first light of morning was sneaking in through the heavily curtained windows. The beautiful young woman he had seen in the portrait was sitting beside him, smiling. She was wearing the same yellow robe in which she had begun the evening, but now she wore it open carelessly. Her body was lavish, luscious, bountiful, flawless. It repelled him, and he tried to draw away from her, but he found that his wrists and ankles had been tied to the bed frame.

"Just one more time, and then I'll let you go," she said, her voice warm and sweet and tender. Standing, she shrugged off her robe and let it fall to the floor. She was even more beautiful than her portrait could convey. She reached under the covers and found his flaccid penis. It felt lifeless to him. Laughing, she swept the covers away, and he raised his head enough to look down at his own unfamiliar body. It was if he had been wracked by the most terrible of diseases. He had aged sixty—eighty—a hundred years in a single night.

"You're going to kill me!" he protested, his voice weak and quavering.

"Why, I don't think so," she said, laughing again, and turned to watch what her hands were doing.

Patiently, like a sculptress working a difficult piece of clay, she shaped his unwilling flesh into something resembling an erection. Gracefully, she threw one firm, muscular leg over his hips and lowered herself onto him. He watched her use both hands to guide his old man's penis into her beautiful young body. He hated her.

She rode him with the wild enthusiasm of a teenager. Her firm, beautifully round bottom bounced up and down. He closed his eyes and waited for the inevitable. Soon enough, he felt her reach down between his buttocks. A wet finger insinuated itself into him, pressing and stroking deep inside. His body spasmed without pleasure, more like a fit of coughing than an orgasm. "Yes, yes," she said, still fondling and stroking as she teased the last tremor from his failing body.

He settled against the bed, his heart pumping weakly but wildly. He felt drained and dry.

She all but sprang off the bed, full of energy and enthusiasm, and turned to face him.

"I'll let you rest for a few minutes, but then you'll have to get dressed and go. I have a lot of things to do today."

"What have you done to me? I'm going to die."

She smiled indulgently. "Not as soon as you think. If you're careful, you'll live to a ripe old age."

"I already have, thanks to you!"

"You just have to do what I just did to you. There are plenty of young, orgasmic girls in the world. At first, you'll only need one once a month or so. It'll be decades before you need someone every night, the way I do."

"I could never do this to someone else."

She shrugged. "That's what they all say. But you'll see."

arrived, none were more beautiful than the two sitting at the bar right then. Young and tall and slim, with big blue eyes and high cheekbones and full lips and blonde hair, they were like Norse goddesses, visions out of a folk legend. All the Norwegian girls looked alike to him, with their fair complexions and their long, straight blonde hair, but as he approached the bar he realized that these two were nearly twins. Watching with apparent interest and approval as he drew nearer, they leaned toward each other and murmured a few words.

"Good evening," Lester said as he put his hat on the bar a few empty stools away from the two. He addressed the remark generally, directing it as much to the bartender as to the other patrons, neither excluding nor specifically including the women.

"Good evening," said the closest woman, glancing at him with an amused smile. Her thick Norwegian accent was, to his ears, charming.

The bar was not very full; the other patrons glanced up at the big, loud American, nodded politely, and went back to their drinks and their conversations.

"Good evening, sir," said the bartender. "What can I get you?"

Lester ordered a whiskey, the best they had, and sat down. When his drink arrived, he lifted the glass toward the twins. "To the beauties of Norway!" he said, and drained it in one shot. "If you girls were old enough to drink, I'd buy a round for you."

The woman nearest him giggled. "We are old enough."

"How old are you? I'm surprised you're allowed to sit at the bar. The two of you don't look older than sixteen years old."

"We're over four hundred years old," said the other woman, her eyes twinkling.

Lester laughed at the absurdity of her remark.

"That's right," said the other, with a devilish smile. "We're witches."

"Really?" said Lester, smiling back. He waggled his finger at the bartender for another whiskey. "Why don't the two of you sit next to me and tell me all about it?"

The two slipped off their stools and sat down on either side of him.

"I'm Lester," he said, offering his hand to the one on his left. "Lester Ledbetter."

"I'm Astrid," she said, taking his hand. Hers was small and firm and warm, with long, delicately shaped fingers. "My friend is Ingrid."

"Pleased to meet you," he said, and then shook hands with the woman on his right. "I've never met a pair of witches before. I thought they were supposed to be old-looking and ugly," Lester said, looking at one and then the other, "not young and beautiful, like the two of you."

"Since we can take any form we like, why would we want to be old and ugly?" Ingrid asked, laughing.

"You have a point there. I declare the two of you look good enough to eat."

Astrid giggled. "What a remarkable coincidence! We were just saying the same thing about you!"

Lester had been feeling lucky all day, but he could not believe his good fortune. The fact was, he had never been to bed with two women at once, although he had often tried to arrange it.

"Here. Drink this," said Astrid as she handed him a glass, smiling invitingly. She sat down to his left on the leather couch in front of the fire. Their house was very old, in an old part of the city, but inside it was warm and comfortable.

"What is it?" he asked, smiling back.

"Something to make you feel good when we eat you up," said Ingrid, who was sitting on his other side, her thigh pressed against his as she played with his hair.

"And then we're going to love you as you've never been loved before," said Astrid, toying gently with his ear.

Lester smiled and took the glass from her. It contained a dark amber liquid that looked a little like whiskey. He sniffed it. Although it seemed to be alcoholic, it didn't smell anything like whiskey. "What's in it?"

"Oh, just the usual: eye of newt and blood of frog, certain mushrooms and roots and the bark of certain trees…that sort of thing," said Astrid, with a laugh.

Lester took a sip. "It tastes awful."

"You must drink it," said Ingrid, smiling but serious. "We cannot eat you up until you drink it all."

He laughed and, as quickly as he could, drained the glass. Immediately, Astrid took it from his hand and put it aside, and the two women moved closer toward him, one running her fingers through his hair, the other putting her hand on the back of his neck. They pressed themselves closer, and he could feel their soft, full breasts upon him. He turned from one beautiful, smiling face to the other and did not know where to begin. He kissed one and then the other. Their lips were sweet and hot and intoxicating.

"Come," said Astrid, laughing and smiling as she stood up. "It will be better in the bedroom."

When he stood, he felt dizzy, almost sick. "What was in that drink?" he asked, as the two women took him, stumbling, up the narrow wooden stairs. "My head is spinning." It occurred to him that he had been drugged, and that they were going to roll him, but he felt curiously indifferent to that possibility. He knew that he was not in his right mind, but he was indifferent to that, too.

"Don't worry," said one of the girls. He had lost track of which was which. "That will pass soon."

"It will all pass soon," said the other one, "but you will enjoy it."

He wanted to say, "I'm sure I will," but it was too much trouble to speak. He could barely walk.

At the top of the stairs, the girls took him into a small bedroom paneled in dark wood. One of the twins lit a few candles, and Lester saw that the only furniture was a large wooden bed with only a sheet and a few pillows on it. He stood passively, like a sleepy young child, as the two undressed him completely and then lay him down on the bed.

He watched the two women undress, laughing and playful. Their hands brushed lightly over each other's breasts and bellies, thighs and buttocks, as they helped each other shed their clothes into a heap on the floor until they were completely naked. Lester had never seen any one woman so beautiful, so desirable, much less two. The peculiar dizziness in his head had passed, and with it his concerns. Although his body still felt heavy and lethargic, he was eager for the two to join him on the bed.

They came to him on either side of him, their warm bodies enveloping him. "And now," said the one on the right into his ear, "we're going to eat you up." She kissed his ear and then began to nibble on the lobe.

"Just as we promised," said the other girl, and chewed on his left ear.

Although he felt barely able to raise his limbs, one part of him—at that moment, the most important part—seemed to be functioning properly, and rose eagerly. He felt two hands—one from each—caressing him as they tongued and licked and nibbled on his ears. Their hands were soft and warm and supple, and although he was feeling as strange as he had ever felt, he was also as aroused as he had ever been. Under their small fingers, he felt monstrously large, engorged to bursting. Their soft, full breasts brushed and pressed against him as they moved, the nipples like small hot fingers of pleasure.

The girls were licking and nuzzling his ears. Gradually, he realized that their love bites were growing harder. The sensation of the soft flesh of his earlobes trapped between their sharp, hard teeth ought to have reached the point of pain, but it did not. Instead, it lanced down his body, into his groin, raising his level of arousal. He thought he could hear his heart pounding. It seemed very far away.

He felt the lobe of his left ear resist the pressure of the teeth, and then, with a distinct crunch, give way. He felt a stab of what should have been pain, but was instead intense, exquisite pleasure. He felt a throbbing in two places at once. Something in the drink they had given him, his dulled mind managed to figure out, had transformed the pain into pleasure.

Nonetheless, it was inescapable that one of the girls had bitten off his earlobe. It seemed he should protest. He tried to speak, but all that came out was a low, inarticulate sound.

"Shhhhh," said the other one.

The one on his left sat up and met his eyes in the candlelight. She opened her mouth just enough to show him a bit of the top of his ear resting on her tongue. She closed her mouth, smiled, and swallowed.

Lester had no time to protest, because the girl on his right took what felt like an even larger piece of his other ear, tearing it as much as biting it. The sensation was almost unendurably strong but, once again, as pleasure rather than pain.

As he felt his ear being ripped from his head, he felt his blood well up from the wound and then, incomprehensibly, stop flowing, as if it had been cauterized. He realized that the drink had probably contained a drug for that, too.

Although much of his outer ear was gone, he could still hear the chilling sound of the girl chewing and swallowing. With his arms and legs apparently paralyzed, he knew he was doomed, but he still opened his mouth, only to find that he had no voice. "No," he mouthed silently. "No, please."

"Just relax," the one on his right whispered into what remained of his left ear, and then bit it off. The sensation raced down through his body into his groin. "Delicious," she whispered, and licked at the raw flesh.

The women moved down to his face, licking and nuzzling and kissing and nibbling. The mixture of delight and terror was almost unendurable, and yet he endured it. He knew that he was going to die, but at the same time he was more aroused than he had ever been, and he anticipated the inevitable climax with as much eagerness as dread.

Astrid on his left took a small bite of his left cheek.

The wound welled up with blood and then rapidly stopped bleeding, as if it had been seared. The ache of the bite amplified the ache in his penis. Ingrid nibbled at his chin, and then bit down and took off a small piece of flesh. Lester sighed at the pleasure of it.

She moved along his collarbone, taking nips as she went. When she reached Lester's upper arm, she took a very deep bite, reaching muscle for the first time. The sensation burned through Lester like anguish, making him shudder with pleasure.

Astrid sat up and lifted his right hand to her mouth. Fear welled up in his eyes. He watched helplessly as she licked and kissed and sucked on his fingers, taking each one at a time into her mouth. The sight of his fingers disappearing into that sweet, beautiful mouth was unbearably arousing, and the fear was overpowering.

She started with the smallest finger, biting it off just before the last joint. The sound of the bone cracking and splitting between her hard, sharp teeth was appalling, sickening. But it was as pleasurable as it should have been painful. The blood flowed quickly from the raw stump of his finger and a few drops fell, but then, with an astonishing rapidity, the wound stopped bleeding and scabbed over.

Holding it almost daintily by the tip, Astrid ate the meat of Lester's finger as if eating the drumstick of a very small bird. She stripped it of flesh and then popped it into her mouth. When she removed the fingernail and dropped it to the floor, Lester wanted to be sick, to express his revulsion by vomiting, but despite his terror, his stomach was calm.

Lester watched as the twin took the bare bone out of her mouth and tossed it across the room.

Lester lay immobilized, certain that he would lose his mind before he lost his life, and watched as the twin on his right bit off and ate the flesh of each of the remaining fingers of his right hand.

Although each of his wounds stopped bleeding almost as soon as it began, he still was covered in his own blood. There was blood, too, on the lips and faces and hands of the twins, who met his eyes from time to time, smiling dreamily, almost tenderly.

"You're delicious," one of them whispered.

"Just as we knew you'd be," the other murmured lovingly.

He could barely believe that he was still alive. They had bitten off and eaten most of both ears, both nipples, and all of his fingers and his toes, and had torn substantial pieces of skin and muscle out of his shoulders, arms, chest, thighs, and calves. Everywhere they had wounded him, Lester's body throbbed with every pulse, not in pain but in sexual arousal and desire. His terror was undiminished, and the certainty of his imminent death was no less; but only his craving for sexual release was completely real to him, although he was just as certain that his release would also be his death.

The women, their hair matted and their faces and their naked bodies streaked with his blood, looked like madwomen, like she-devils, like the witches they had told him they were, but they were still beautiful. They kneeled on either side of his waist, kissing each other as they fondled his penis with one hand and each other's breasts with the other.

Ingrid lifted a beautiful leg over his waist and straddled him. As Astrid caressed her, she slid herself over his body, smearing herself with his blood. Then, with a fluid motion, she raised herself slightly and impaled herself on his penis and settled herself deeply around him. She felt as slick and as hot and as tight as he had ever felt a woman, and despite the horror of the circumstances, it was profoundly pleasurable.

Astrid leaned forward and kissed him on the mouth for the first time, nibbling and biting on his lips, softly at first and then harder, until soon she had bitten most of them off. The sensation that should have been pain but inexplicably was pleasure coursed through him, down into his penis. He imagined his ruined face, his ruined body. For the first time that night, tears filled his eyes and he began to weep softly, as much from the exquisiteness of the experience as from the imminence of his death. The blood welled up at his new wounds, wetting her face and his, and then stopped flowing as the openings scarred over.

Ingrid rocked, ever so gently, up and down on his penis. His aching body, full to the point of bursting, longed to rise up and meet her, but could not.

With her hand on his cheeks, Astrid forced his mouth open. Sucking strongly, she drew his tongue into her mouth, and bit off the first several inches of his tongue.

She looked into his eyes as she swallowed. "Goodbye," she said. "You've been delicious."

She kissed his bloody mouth once again and then crawled down his body. After a moment he realized that she had positioned herself between his legs, behind Ingrid, and had crouched down to put her face between his thighs.

It was a configuration he had often imagined—but not like this, not like this! He felt her bloody, terrible lips at his scrotum, and felt her take his entire scrotal sac, testicles and all, into her mouth.

It was his last chance to reach orgasm—if she bit off his testicles, he would have nothing to ejaculate—and the realization triggered the reality.

Suddenly, finally, he felt the first spasm of ejaculation burst through him.

But not simply in his genitals. His entire body experienced orgasm. With that first spasm, every wound he had suffered that night—fingers, toes, ears, chin, tongue, shoulders, arms, nipples, chest, thighs—burst open, too, and blood began to flow. Still weeping, he was ejaculating blood from every gash, every rend they had made in the fabric of his skin. The pleasure was excruciating.

With every spasm of his orgasm, the wounds opened more completely. He tremored again and again, until his blood was running like water. His mind grew clouded; the room grew faint.

As the last shudder of pleasure rippled through him, he felt, inevitably, Astrid's teeth sever his scrotum, testicles and all, at the root. He was beyond both pleasure and pain as he felt his life seep away through this new wound. And, as the final surprise, a moment before his death, he felt the teeth of Ingrid's vagina as she used them to bite off his penis and consume it.

BLOODY MARY

When he first saw her at the bar, his heart stopped, and he knew that he had to have her. *These women,* he thought, shaking his head in mock disappointment with himself, *are going to be the death of me.* But it was a pantomime enacted only for his own amusement. He was, in truth, beguiled by his own weak- nesses, and as attached to his habits as a father to a beloved child.

She was the sort of woman one sees only in magazines or on the screen, a woman of such beauty and radiance and presence that she would be inevitably drawn into a life of glamour and wealth. She was as out of place in this ordinary restaurant as a unicorn in a barn. Not that the place was a dive: On the contrary, it catered to the professionals and white-collar workers from the many office buildings on the avenue it shared with them, and was carefully decorated and richly appointed in dark woods and etched glass. Still, in his many evenings there—he was one of the professionals from one of the nearby offices—although he had seen hundreds if not thousands of attractive women, he had never seen a woman like her.

Her profile was sharp and well defined and yet soft and delicate, every feature in harmony. Her hair, rich and full and deeply black, luminous in the colorful lights of the restaurant, set off her skin, which was almost dead white. Her body—as far as her elegant and expensive-looking dress, which was the same blood red as her lips, revealed it—was lush and full and yet firm and strong. She was smiling as she sipped her drink, and he could scarcely accept that she was sitting alone, that she was not surrounded by men as enraptured as he.

He had stopped, as he usually did, just inside the inner doors of the entranceway to survey the room. As usual at that hour, it was not too crowded. Over the next hour or so, it would grow gradually more boisterous, and then begin to empty out again as the men with families began their commutes home, as the women who were meeting their girlfriends before a night at the movies or shopping finished their drinks, as the single men made their connections or conceded defeat for another evening and left with their prize for the night or alone.

Usually, he'd take a seat at the bar near the door, where he could see down its length and keep an eye on the entrance. This was the process: Even if he'd immediately seen a woman he wanted to approach, he would have at least one drink before speaking to her. As he sipped his drink, he'd catch her eye a few times, letting her get used to him, letting her develop a sense of anticipation, letting her imagination do some of the work. Then, by the time he got off his stool and spoke to her, it was almost as if they knew each other. By that time, she would have met his eyes often enough that it was almost impossible for her not to exchange at least a few words of conversation.

But tonight, the woman at the bar turned and looked directly at him. The impact of her eyes—were they blue? gray? green?—upon his was like a blow to his viscera. Seen directly, her face was even more beautiful than in profile. She smiled, as if she knew him, as if she had been waiting for him all along, and then turned back to the bar. He could see her face in the mirror on the wall, but she was no longer looking at him.

Still, she had all but invited him over. He had no choice, it seemed, but to approach her immediately.

Usually, he was fearless in such situations: Confident of his good looks and his good luck, aware of the impression—accurate, as it happened—of success and affluence that his expensive clothing created, certain of his smile and his glib tongue. At thirty-six-years old, he was handsome, fit, and unattached—in his prime, and enjoying it completely. Even in this age of caution and distrust and suspicion, he was almost always successful. And when he *was* rebuffed, he always managed to reclaim his dignity and his self-esteem with a clever remark and, even more effective as an anodyne, a more attractive woman than the one who had turned him down. Tonight, such consolation was out of the question.

This woman was so beautiful he felt intimidated and uncertain of himself, a schoolboy with a college girl, a fan before his most adored star, an awkward teenager with a call girl. She was so beautiful she made the other women in the restaurant appear to be of an other, lesser species, and he almost wondered if she was, perhaps, not human at all, but a visitation.

He attributed his success with women to his sincerity, which he used adroitly, like a weapon. He prided himself on almost never lying to a woman, although he often omitted the truth. With this woman, too, he knew, honesty would be an effective ploy.

He walked toward her, approaching her from her left so that he could more easily look for a wedding ring. Not that one would stop him, but he had found that married women required somewhat different treatment. She wore no wedding band on her long, well-manicured hand. In the mirror behind the bar he saw that her dress had a scooped neckline that showed the slightest beginning of cleavage. Her breasts were full and apparently unconstrained by any undergarment.

"You're so beautiful I'm a little frightened," he said, sincerely, as he positioned himself at the bar beside her.

She turned and looked at him, smiling. Her teeth were like small white gems. "Thank you. You don't have to be afraid." Her voice was low and smooth and intimate and musical.

"You have the face of an angel," he said.

"Oh, I'm no angel, believe me," she replied, with a slight laugh that intoxicated him with its melodiousness.

"I'm astonished you're sitting alone," he said, continuing with his strategy of being honest.

"Why? I came here alone," she said.

"I can't understand why you're not surrounded by men as mesmerized as I am."

She laughed softly again. "Perhaps they're not as brave as you."

"Thank you." he replied. He waved his finger at the bartender—the usual one—and gestured at the woman's drink and at the empty spot on the bar in front of himself. The bartender nodded.

"I've never seen you here before," he told the woman.

"I've never been here before," she replied.

"Where are you from?"

"Out of town," she replied.

He noted her evasiveness but did not press her. "Here

on business or pleasure?" It was a question he often used, an invitation for flirtatious double entendre.

"Both," she answered easily, as if she had prepared herself for the question. "I've accomplished the former and now I'm looking for the latter."

He was surprised that she was so direct. "I'm sure you'll be successful," he replied, with his usual grin. "My name is Dave," he said, because it was true, and because it invited reciprocation. The exchange of names, he had found, was an important stage in the process.

"Hi, Dave," she said, smiling easily, obviously aware that she was not following form.

"What shall I call you?" he asked lightly.

She gave a short, quiet laugh. "It's not important. Anything you like."

"It's your choice," he replied.

The bartender placed his usual—a whiskey and soda—in front of him and replaced the woman's with a fresh one. She was, it appeared, drinking a Bloody Mary.

She lifted her glass. "Mary, then."

He smiled. "Bloody Mary? Should I be afraid?"

"I already told you not to be."

"Then I won't."

The maitre d' of the restaurant approached them. Dave knew him by name, but the maitre d' did not greet him. "Your table is ready now, ma'am," he murmured to the woman. "The waiter will bring your drink."

"Thank you," she said, putting her glass on the bar

and slipping off the bar stool as gracefully as Dave had ever seen done. He was surprised to see how tall she was. He was six feet tall, and she was almost eye to eye with him. "Care to join me for dinner?" she asked with an easy smile as she took her purse from the bar.

He felt unbalanced. She was making the moves he was used to making. But he knew, and he was sure that she knew, that he would let her. "I'd love to, but I insist that I be allowed to pay," he replied.

She laughed briefly. "If you like," she replied, following the maitre d'.

He put his drink down and let her get a few steps ahead of him. Her dress fit as if it were a natural part of her. He could see no trace of underclothing disturbing the lines of the cloth or compromising the suppleness of her body. Watching her walk was almost a spiritual experience. He followed her to the table.

They sat, as he preferred, at right angles to each other, on adjacent sides of their table, rather than opposite each other or side-by-side, and that was fortunate, because every time she turned to look directly at him he found himself dazzled and momentarily confused, disconcerted by her astonishing beauty. In the light of the candle at their table, her eyes were large and liquid and sparkling, and it was easy for him to lose himself in them.

The waiter brought their drinks and their menus at the same time.

"You've eaten here before?" she asked.

"Often," he conceded.

"Then order for me," she said, handing him her menu without having opened it.

"You trust me that much?" he asked, flirting.

"Completely," she replied, with mock gravity.

When the waiter returned after only a few moments, he ordered carefully, choosing for her an appetizer and a main dish that were sophisticated but not dangerously so. He wanted to flatter her without risking the chance that her tastes would actually be challenged. For himself he ordered an unusual appetizer and extremely ordinary main dish, to suggest daring and solidity at the same time. For wine he ordered the most expensive red they had. She seemed to approve of his all choices.

She said very little over dinner, but he was skillful at carrying a conversation without appearing to monopolize it, a technique he had polished over the years. The secret was always to suggest that you believed that the other person was already familiar with whatever you were telling her about, that she had already reached the opinion you were expressing, that she had the good taste to agree with you. He mentioned a recent movie he'd just seen. Had she seen it yet? No? Well, he was sure she'd have found it as disappointing as he did. She would have noticed how contrived it was. Didn't she dislike it, as he did, when movies manipulated the audience so transparently? How could they insult our intelligence like that? They just don't make movies for people like us anymore.

She ate, apparently as she did everything, gracefully and fastidiously, and he was for the first time in a great many years self-conscious at the table. He regarded dinner as a crucial stage in the process, and he prided himself on his table manners and his etiquette, but the woman calling herself Mary was so skillful and deft with her silverware that he felt, by contrast, almost clumsy and oafish. Once, when she had given him a particularly open smile, he had come close to knocking over his wineglass.

But she seemed pleased with him, and by the time the waiter came with their coffee and desserts, her knee was pressing softly against his leg.

With other women, at this stage of the process, he would not allow himself to become aroused, no matter how well everything was going. It threw off his rhythm, made him too eager, kept him from reading the woman as well as he might. But with this one, with Mary, he could not help himself. Her knee against his thigh was all it took to make him uncomfortably hard, to fill his gut with the familiar hunger. She was leaning forward a little, making the neckline of her dress gape open slightly, accentuating the cleavage of her breasts. His mind filled with imaginings of her naked body, her rich, white skin, his hands on those luscious, inviting breasts, his mouth on those luscious, inviting lips....

He realized that she had been speaking. "I'm so sorry," he said. "I'm afraid my mind wandered for a moment.

What did you say?"

She laughed. "It wasn't important. Where did it wander to?"

He met her languid, limpid eyes. Honesty was so often effective. With her knee still resting lightly against his leg, he judged that they were at the right stage of the process. "I was imagining making love with you," he said softly, and waited for her reaction.

She did not appear in the least bit surprised, or at all disconcerted. "Why settle for imagining?" she asked, and covered his hand, which was resting on the table, with her own. Under her fingers, his hand bloomed with sensation so intense it was almost like pain. "I'm ready to go," she murmured.

"My apartment is only a few blocks from here," he said, withdrawing his hand so that he could open the small leather folder that held the check for their dinner. "I have a wonderful view of the city," he said, almost automatically, as he quickly looked the bill over. It was something he often said, to give a woman the excuse—however transparent—she needed to come home with him. This woman clearly needed no such excuse.

"I'm sure it's beautiful," she replied, in a tone that implied they both knew they would not waste any time looking out windows.

He took out his wallet and quickly checked his cash. Fortunately, he had enough money with him that he did not have to wait the few extra minutes that using a card required. He counted out a few bills, rounding up to the next highest twenty to cover the tip. It was absurdly generous, and it might sow unfortunate expectations among the waiters there for the future, but he was impatient, and did not want to seem petty.

"Okay," he said, standing up. As he did, he took her purse from the back of her chair and handed it to her, a small familiarity he liked to take at this stage of the process.

Rising, she seemed amused at his gesture. "Thank you," she said, almost ironically, letting her hand brush his as she took her purse from him. Once again, his skin seemed to glow where she touched it, deepening his desire.

With a hand gently on her shoulder, he let her lead him out of the restaurant. The bar had reached its peak sometime during their dinner and was now beginning to empty out again.

"Good night, George," he said to the maitre d', for her benefit, determined to maintain his usual style although he felt as giddy and excited as a child.

"Good night, sir," the maitre d' replied. "Ma'am."

Dave pushed the inner door open just as she reached it, and did the same thing at the outer door. Outside, the street seemed abruptly dark and empty and quiet. The fall evening was cool. The office towers were all abandoned now; except for the restaurant, the shops were all closed, although most of them still had their window displays illuminated behind heavy metal gates. They were the only ones on the streets.

"It's really dead here tonight, isn't it?" she asked.

"It's always like this at this hour. Would you like to walk?" he asked, his usual line with other women, in other situations. It had a nice ambiguity to it. Did he mean, Would you like to walk as opposed to another means of transportation? Or only, Would you like to take a walk? The former, of course, implied that the destination had already been established, whereas the latter implied no destination at all. Depending on how the walk itself went, he could choose to interpret her assent either way, or allow her to claim she had understood his question either way. Of course, Mary had already made her intentions clear, so he asked the question only out of long practice.

"If it's not too far, we can walk," she said, confirming her intention. "I'm a little chilly."

He took her remark as an invitation, and put his arm around her shoulder. "It takes no time at all," he said as he turned in the right direction. She seemed to soften a little against him, conforming her body to his. She did not feel chilly at all to him. She felt hot.

The short walk to his apartment building had never seemed longer.

He could not get enough of her. He had slept only an hour or two, waking to remember with delight that she was still naked beside him, her face an inspiration, her bountiful body a miracle, her lovemaking a transport. Although they had already had sex twice that night, he wanted her yet again. He felt like an adolescent, drunk on her sight, her taste, her smell, the sensation of her skin against his skin, and most especially the hot liquid velvet glove of her sex. All his savoir faire seemed far away now, forgotten, irrelevant, a costume he had long since removed. He was only an ordinary man now, overwhelmed by the confusion of joy and gratitude and awe that comes when sex is perfect.

Among the hundreds of women he had slept with over the years, none had yielded him such intense pleasure. It was a paradox he could not trouble to examine that she satisfied him more deeply than any woman ever had, and yet he was feeling more hungry for satisfaction than before.

Although she seemed to be sleeping, he reached for her, unconcerned that he might appear to be inconsiderate or selfish. He needed to have her once again, and perhaps yet again after that, to burn the memory of her indelibly into his body and his mind, if not into his heart.

He moved against her, already aroused again, caressing her breasts with one hand. She murmured softly, apparently in pleasure rather than complaint, and he pressed himself harder against her.

Even in the dim light of his darkened bedroom, he

could tell that she was awake now. He rolled away from her and, with a deftness that came of his long experience, quickly took a fresh condom and fitted it onto himself. As he returned to her side, she opened her arms to him.

He rolled onto her, moving between her legs, which she parted immediately, unprotesting, unquestioning. He entered her smoothly; he seemed to fit even more perfectly than the time before.

She was letting him set the rhythm, as she had done the two previous times. She stroked his back almost consolingly as she lifted her hips to meet his.

He was as hungry as the first time, and she was as much a feast as ever, but he was not actually the adolescent he was behaving like, and he discovered that the goal he sought was evading him. His groin was filled with a dull, vague ache, like a cloudy lens over the burning brightness of his desire. As he moved—a little faster now, a little more effortfully—he realized that the sensations he was feeling no longer had anything to do with pleasure. He wanted only the relief, the release. Perhaps it had been a mistake to start this third time, but he could not imagine not finishing. He would even contemplate the shame of not completing the act, or the indignity of simulating his climax.

Although he prided himself on keeping himself fit and muscular, he was aware that his heart was racing. His body felt full to the point of bursting, but infuriatingly numb. It was suddenly a matter of desperation. He moved yet a little more vigorously, and felt an encouraging tickle. It seemed he could get there with just a little more effort.

He was moving as quickly as he could now. Beneath him, Mary followed his lead easily, as if it was effortless for her.

Her lush mouth opened and she cried out with pleasure, still following his rhythm as she reached her climax. Although he usually took great pleasure in a woman's orgasm—regarding it as his own accomplishment—the ease with which Mary reached hers seemed to mock him, making him even more desperate.

Somewhere, he found the strength to move even more strenuously and, at last, felt the inevitability that presages release. With a final stroke, he felt his body gather its energy and discharge itself violently, almost painfully.

Even as he groaned with relief, he realized that something was terribly wrong. He felt a strange, disorienting dizziness, as if his head was spinning and rising up.

Suddenly he knew that it was not his head rising up but his mind. He was having, he realized, one of those out-of-body experiences he had heard about.

As his mind rose up toward the ceiling, he felt the greatest terror he had ever known. *You don't have to be afraid,* he remembered the woman telling him, but he *was* afraid. He wanted more than anything else to come back to his body, but he had no idea how.

Seeing with his mind rather than his eyes, the room was as bright as in the daylight, and even in these unique circumstances he could not help but notice how beautiful she was. He saw that his body was still now, as if resting after the orgasm. She stroked his back comfortingly with her long, graceful hand.

As he reached the ceiling, matters grew a great deal worse. Suddenly he felt himself rushing upward through a long, dark tunnel. He heard voices murmuring to him sweetly, lovingly, but without words he recognized. He seemed to reach the end of the tunnel, and saw before him an ineffably beautiful white light beckoning him.

He was no believer, but he had read about this, too. This was the experience of death, according to those who had nearly died and had come back to life. *Oh, no! I don't want to die!* he said, without a body to speak. The white light seemed to call to him, urging him closer, luring him more seductively than any woman.

No! I'm not ready! Somehow he turned from the light and found his way back to the tunnel, down again to the ceiling of his room.

Things had changed. His body was on its back. His penis seemed limp and small and wet and pathetic, like a sea animal washed up onto the beach. The woman he had called Mary was sitting up, crying out, beating his chest ineffectually. It was obvious that she did not know how to revive him, or was too hysterical to do so.

He rushed back down to his body like a surfer riding a wave, expecting to find himself back inside himself as if back on the shore. But as he reached the surface of his body, he could sense that it would not work. His brain was already boiling with the chaos of oxygen starvation, its energy fading like a glowing coal in a pool of water.

He beat against his skull as if he were knocking on a locked door, but no one was home to let him in. His eyes were staring up at him, blind and stupid and without life. It was too late.

He had no choice now but to abandon his body. He raced back up toward the ceiling, eager now to get away from his own death. He readied himself for the dark tunnel that would bring him to the bright light again.

But when he reached the ceiling, to his shock, he went no farther. There was no longer any tunnel. It was too late for that, as well. The boundaries of the room were suddenly solid to him, as if he were nothing more than a moth or a bat.

He was trapped, he realized. He knew that his body was truly dead, and that he had missed his chance for whatever transcendence the white light had promised him. He regretted not going to the light when it had invited him. He regretted trying that third and last time with the woman. He regretted not having married and having a family. He regretted his selfishness, his shallowness. He regretted everything.

He sensed that it would all be over in only a moment

or two. Already the unnatural brightness of his bedroom was fading back into darkness.

As his vision dimmed, he looked down again at the scene on his bed. Was is it only the confusion of his consciousness as it flickered and disappeared, or had the woman changed? He felt stupid and sleepy, like a child woken after a long trip, but it seemed that she was laughing rather than weeping, grinning rather than grimacing, beating his chest in triumph rather than desperation. He could no longer trust his vision, but she appeared no longer to be the young and beautiful woman he had slept with.

She was now ugly and old, her body withered and parched. In these final moments, she seemed to look up at him. Her sunken eyes were red, her cheeks were sagging hollows, her mouth was a gaping hole, her long teeth were yellow streaked with black. What sort of hellish creature had he taken to bed? No—what sort of demon had taken *him* to bed?

With his final shreds of consciousness, he watched her use her bony, taloned hands to rip at his groin. He could no longer feel any pain, but the sight of his body so violated filled his dissolving mind with the profoundest anguish he had ever known. The last thing he saw was her triumphant smile as she lifted his lifeless, dripping organs to her mouth. *Bloody Mary*...was his very last thought.

FIRST LOOKS: THE MINDCAP DELUXE VERSION 1

As loyal readers of this magazine already know, once past the standard complement of earphones, eyephones, and optional datagloves, the road to true virtual reality is not an easy one. In earlier issues, your intrepid reporter has written about his experiences with such devices as the all-body glove [July, 1998] and the attachable organ stimulators [August, 1999]. I've also written extensively about the various ill-fated neural datajack implants [September, 2000; February, 2001; and October, 2001], although this magazine was unwilling to pay the several hundred thousand dollars for the operation and, frankly, I was unwilling to risk infection, disease, and death to have a parallel port protruding from the base of my skull. I was scheduled for a demonstration of the somewhat more promising automated intracranial neuropuncture, but I will have to wait until Acusex Corporation emerges from the bankruptcy precipitated by the many lawsuits filed by the families of the early volunteers.

Despite the difficulties and risks, however, I'm tireless and almost completely fearless in my quest for the latest and best in virtual pleasure on behalf of my readers.

Simucorp has finally unveiled its long-promised and long-awaited entry into the field, the Mindcap Deluxe Version 1. The Mindcap is entirely non-invasive, and yet it overcomes the limitations inherent in the usual eyephones-earphones-datagloves combination. I was privileged to be invited to examine and test a prototype model, and based on my experience I can say that Simucorp is a real winner, with one minor and I assume, easily corrected glitch.

Experienced virtual realists will be at first surprised at how bulky and old-fashioned the Mindcap appears to be. Unlike most recent hyperminiaturized offerings, the Mindcap looks like a football helmet for Blind Man's Bluff, covering not only the eyes and ears but most of the entire head. This complete cranial coverage, however, permits Mindcap's remarkable breakthrough: Using focused extremely low-energy microwaves, Mindcap actually selectively stimulates areas of the brain directly.

As usual, the Mindcap is attached by fiber optical

cable to a Cray (in this case, a Cray XCN III). In the configuration I tested, the unit came with a recliner—reminiscent of an old-fashioned dentist's chair—especially designed to accommodate a person wearing the otherwise awkward headgear.

"It has to be especially comfortable," Dr. Melissa Stanton, Simucorp's director of product development, explained to me, "because once the Mindcap is in operation, you're unable to move. The Mindcap actually inhibits your motor centers, as if you were sleeping. This allows you to act freely in virtual reality without having to be strapped into a simulator. It also means that you're going to be sitting in the same position for a long time."

"What if I want to get out?" I asked. "If I'm paralyzed, how do I hit the OFF switch?"

"We don't like to use the word 'paralyzed,'" Dr. Stanton replied. "We prefer to say that you're motor-inhibited. But, to answer your question, the Mindcap constantly monitors your emotional state, and if the anxiety level rises above a preset level, the system automatically quiesces and returns you to normal reality. Also, your eyelids are not inhibited. All you do is close your eyes for five seconds and you come back to Earth, so to speak."

My anxieties allayed, I indicated that I was ready to begin, and I lay down on the recliner as Dr. Stanton powered up the Cray. Once the system had booted, Dr. Stanton fit the Mindcap to my head, and then helped me settle comfortably into position. "I'll just be in the next room," she said, and then apparently flicked a switch. I say *apparently* because I could no longer hear any sounds from the room I was in.

"Just relax as the system calibrates itself," came a woman's soothing voice, seeming to be to my left, but actually originating from the Dolby-Lucas headphones built into the cap. All around me, barely audible music played. Before my eyes, a series of abstract, apparently three-dimensional imagery played on the super-high-resolution stereoscopic whole-field eyephones. (Simucorp claims the highest resolution displays of any eyephone, thanks to its patented foveal enhancement technology, which increases the density of the pixels in center of the visual field.) I could barely tell that I was not actually looking at a tranquil sylvan setting, so perfect was the simulation.

"You may feel slight discomfort during the next phase," the soothing voice said, "as you are introduced into the dream-safe state. Do not be alarmed. This is perfectly normal."

The fact is, I was somewhat alarmed. The sensation was one of falling through unending space, although the imagery I was seeing did not suggest that experience. I felt as if I was entering a dream, although my mind seemed to be completely lucid. After several seconds of this, the sensation stopped, and I realized I could no longer feel myself sitting on the recliner;

rather, I felt as if I were standing in the meadow I had been looking at.

"You are now dream-safe," the soothing voice said. "You may move about freely in the virtual space."

To test this, I tried walking forward. Let me say that my experience of virtual walking was incomparably better than even the best treadmill-and-harness arrangement used in the arcade reality games. It was more like walking in a dream. The visuals were uncannily accurate, with true stereoscopic depth, although I lacked a convincing feeling of weight. Nonetheless, I could actually bend my head and look down at my virtual body (usually a problem for most reality simulators).

"In normal reality, your body is not moving at all. If you wish to return to normal reality, close your eyes for five seconds. To access a display of choices, look at the icon at the extreme upper right of your peripheral vision for two seconds."

I had subliminally noticed something floating above me and to the right. When I looked there, I saw a very convincing-looking black leatherette menu—the sort you get in a Chinese menu. It even said MENU on it in gold embossed script.

I was admiring how the light seemed to play off the gold lettering when, with a disconcerting suddenness, I was standing in a corridor of some kind, looking at a colorful diagram rather like a floor plan of an office building. The choices included Sports, Arts, Heaven,

Celebrities, Traveling, Space, Underwater, Abstract, Adventure, Danger, Crime, and, of course, Adult. I noted where Adult was on the diagram and began to walk in its direction.

Abruptly, I was suddenly standing in front of a door labeled ADULT.

As most readers of this magazine know, the problem with virtual reality sex is in going beyond mere looking and listening. Unless you can convincingly participate in the action, virtual reality is just an expensive, high-fidelity, stereophonic porno movie—not that I have anything against expensive, high-fidelity, stereophonic porno movies, you understand, it's just that they're not virtual anything. But as many now-bankrupt companies have found, very few people are willing actually to trust their sexual organs to any electronic device more complicated than a good, old-fashioned vibrator.

But there I was, walking around in a convincing virtual space, with no stimulators attached to any of my important organs—except my brain, of course. I opened the virtual door and walked through.

A beautiful young woman—in fact, as beautiful a woman as I'd ever seen—was standing just inside the door. She had honey blonde hair, and brown eyes, and the sort of lush, generous lips that some men—me, for example—find extremely attractive. She was wearing an inviting smile and a simple black dress that suggested but did not reveal a lush, generous body underneath.

"Welcome to the Adult Space," she said, in a voice as smooth as melted chocolate.

"What are you?" I asked. "Are you real, or simulated?"

"I'm computer-generated in real-time, but I'm modeled on and licensed from Sarah McCullum. You may have seen her in some recent men's magazines. You can call me Sarah, or any other name you prefer."

"Sarah would be fine."

I'd met—if that's the right term—some other computer-generated women, but it's one thing to stare into a pair of eyephones and issue commands at a virtual woman, and it's entirely another thing to be in the same space with her. I felt a little shy.

"Why don't you sit down?" she said, gesturing to her right at what I saw was a comfortable-looking chair—more like a chaise longue, actually. I sat.

"Mind if I get comfortable, too?" she asked, smiling suggestively.

I started to mull over the philosophical question of whether the computer-generated simulation of a person could experience comfort—could experience anything, actually—but she took my silence as assent, and she began moving slowly to the music that I only just then realized was playing.

This is difficult to describe. She did a kind of virtual strip, although she never actually did anything to remove her clothes. As she swayed to the music, they just slowly and gracefully disappeared, without any of the awkwardness or abruptness that real women in real reality have to overcome or disguise. One moment she was in her black dress, and the next moment she was in a set of black panties and brassiere, and several moments later the brassiere had vanished, and then, a bit later, the panties were gone. And her body was as beautiful and alluring as any I had seen. She reclined on the chaise longue opposite mine, which I had only noticed that moment, and with a sweet smile opened her legs and showed me her pussy.

I had, of course, grown aroused, and glancing down at my virtual body I suddenly noticed that I, too, was naked. I was a bit surprised, and a trifle embarrassed, but I reminded myself that this was not real—although I supposed that, as during an erotic dream, I was having a real erection, too. To explore how good a simulation it was, I reached down with my virtual hand and grasped my virtual penis.

And gasped. It was, if anything, better than reality. My erection felt bigger and harder and hotter and more pleasurable than I remembered from the last time I'd done that—which was not so long ago that I could have forgotten what it was like.

"Would you like to tell me what to do?" the virtual woman opposite asked me. "Would you like someone to join us? Or would you like to join me here?"

I elected the latter. I got up and took a step toward her, and we were together.

There's no need for me to go into the details. If you're old enough to be reading this magazine, you know what having sex is like. I had sex with a computer-generated woman in virtual space. It was wonderful. It was like a dream. It was better than a dream. In fact, it was better than any real sex I'd ever experienced. Just as my erection was better than any I'd had in reality, so was everything about the woman and the sex we had.

There was only one small technical problem. One moment I was coming in the arms and the pussy of the most beautiful woman I'd ever been with, and the next moment I was sitting in the recliner, back in normal, real reality. staring at the blank black screen of the Mindcap, with a wet, uncomfortable feeling in my pants. I realized that I ought to have made better preparations for my journey into virtual reality. I reached up —a little relieved to find that I could really move—and managed to extricate myself from the headgear just as Dr. Stanton walked into the room.

"Is everything all right?" she asked, looking a little flushed. "I was monitoring…"

I blushed to realize that she had been peeking at my experience. I sat up on the recliner, casually arranging my arm across my crotch to hide the wet spot I knew was there. "Everything is fine," I said, "but I think you're going to have to find a different escape signal than closing the eyes. Sometimes you just can't help doing that."

Dr. Stanton looked at me blankly a moment and then suddenly smiled and nodded. "We'll have to work on that," she said. She promised to let me know when it's fixed, and I'll be sure to file an update.

Simucorp promises that the Mindcap Deluxe Version 1—with a better escape signal—will be installed in leading virtuality parlors in the fall of '03. Prices for a half-hour session are expected to be in the $300 to $400 range. A networked home version is planned for the spring of '05. The price for the home unit is not yet established, but expect it to be around $120,000. Start saving your nickels.

THE ART LESSON

Andrea was just finishing her coffee when she noticed that someone had approached her table. Looking up, she saw a man in his late forties with intense gray eyes and a gray goatee. "Andrea?" he asked, with a strange accent.

"What do you want?" she asked.

Unasked, the man sat down opposite Andrea. "I would like you to come with me." Andrea tried to place his accent. She decided that the man was trying to sound British.

"Come with you where?" she asked.

"I teach a life drawing class. I would like you to be the model for today."

Andrea made a face. "Why me?" she asked, pushing her tray into the center of the table and leaning back in her chair. Without looking, she gestured at the dining room. "There must be dozens women right here who are at least as good-looking as me, if not better-looking."

"Perhaps, but no one who looks just like you," the man replied, smiling knowingly.

Andrea shook her head skeptically. "I'm not in the mood for flattery right now."

"But it's true," the man said, meeting her eyes steadily. "You are very beautiful. I have seen your photographs."

Andrea flushed and looked down. "Oh."

"You are very beautiful, Andrea," he said in a quieter, more persuasive tone. "I would be most pleased if you posed for my class."

Still looking down, Andrea asked, "And if I declined?"

The man coughed. "Well," he said in a disappointed tone, "of course Carl would be most disappointed to hear of it."

Andrea looked up, resigned. "I see," she said. "All right, let's go."

The man smiled and stood up. "I am Charles," he said. He offered Andrea his arm in the European manner. She ignored it.

Charles took Andrea to a large studio in the north wing of the top floor. The ceiling contained a series of north-facing skylights. The natural morning light gave the room a pure, even glow. Seven easels and stools had been set up around a small platform, on which Andrea assumed she would pose. The easels each held a large drawing tablet, as well as a tray of pastels. Odds and ends of unmatched furniture were scattered through the large, open space.

"My students will be here in a minute or two. If you will, go behind that screen and remove your clothing," he said, indicating a standing bamboo screen at the far end of the room.

"You'll find a robe to wear," he told her as she walked across the room. "I'll call you when we're ready."

Behind the screen was a plain wooden chair. Hanging from a hook on the screen was a short silk robe. Andrea took off her slippers and her jumpsuit and put on the robe, and sat down in the chair and waited.

Echoing through the room, Andrea heard the door opening, footsteps, desultory words, the sound of wood moved against wood. She paid no attention to what was said. Eventually the noises settled down. "Andrea! We're ready for you!" came Charles's voice, quite loud.

Andrea rose and stepped out from behind the screen. She looked down toward the other side of the room, where the easels had been arranged. Now a man sat at each easel. Barefoot, Andrea walked toward the easels, aware of how intently the men were regarding her. *What now?* she asked herself.

She looked over the men quickly. They all seemed

to be in their late twenties or early thirties. Although they were all looking at her, none met her eyes.

Andrea stepped onto the raised platform at the center of the circle of easels and stood there for a moment. Since she had been brought to the center, she had been naked in front of so many strangers in so many different situations, but she still felt self-conscious and uncomfortable.

"Well, Andrea?" Charles said.

Andrea unfastened the belt and let the robe fall from her shoulders. She was, once again, naked. She found a spot on the shiny wooden floor between two of the students on which to rest her eyes.

"Please, Andrea," Charles said sarcastically. "You're not waiting for a bus. Show a little bearing."

Andrea stiffened under his rebuke and then changed her posture to stand a little taller.

"And you're not posing for a girlie magazine, either," Charles said. Some of the men laughed discreetly.

Andrea blushed. She had certainly not intended to strike a suggestive pose.

"All right, class," Charles said chastising the men for the laughter he himself had invited. "That's enough. Our model is inexperienced." Charles stepped onto the platform and stood directly in front of Andrea.

"Just relax a little," he said in a friendlier tone.

Andrea no longer had a good idea of what the man wanted. She tried to find another posture.

"That's better." Charles took hold of both her wrists and turned them so that her palms faced out in an unnatural way. "Good." He walked around to her back and placed his hands on both shoulders, pushing them back and down. "Just relax," he repeated. Still behind her, he put his foot between her legs just above her ankles and pushed her right leg to widen her stance. "Not too much."

Moving to one side, Charles put one hand on Andrea's stomach and the other on her spine. Using both hands, he pushed quite hard to bend her forward and then bend her backward. Then he pressed against her stomach. "Keep it in," he said.

He stepped off the platform and walked around it, studying her, one hand caressing his goatee pensively. "Beautiful," he pronounced. "Just hold it like that. Students, you may begin!"

Andrea could hear the faint sounds of pastel on paper.

Almost immediately Charles, who was now orbiting the circle of students, began speaking again, this time in a loud, authoritative voice.

"Remember to draw what you see, not what you think you see. We've all been exposed to so many nudes, in life and in photographs and in art, that it takes great discipline to see what is really there. You look and you see the naked woman, you see your own fantasies and memories and ideas rather than the particular female body before you. It is like seeing the word 'breast' and being able to notice the letters, the typeface, the spacing, the ink, rather than responding automatically to the meaning of the word.

"After all, why do we have a nude woman standing before us today, instead, for example, of a cow?" Some of the men laughed. Andrea blushed at the comparison. "Is it because, as some would have it, the nude woman is the pinnacle of creation? To a bull, I assure you, a cow is the pinnacle of creation, not a woman." There was more laughter. "The nude woman is the perennially favorite subject matter of artists for a simple reason: To men, there is no more fascinating and compelling sight. It is not abstract aesthetics, although, as with virtually every of human activity, we have developed an aesthetic for it.

"We have seen nudes a million times, and yet we wish to see the million-and-first. The challenge is to see this one before us as if we are seeing our first nude, rather than the pale shadow of the million ones we have seen before, and to capture what we are seeing on paper. Then, when people look at what we have drawn or painted, they, too, will see our nude with new eyes, and they will be made to feel as naked as the woman before us.

"That is art."

Andrea heard a sharp sound, and, without changing her posture, moved her eyes toward the source. Charles was holding a wooden pointer and tapping it against an anatomical diagram of a female body hung on the wall.

"The key to this is anatomy. A woman is not, as the Bible would have it, a lump of clay. Underneath her skin is muscle. You must see the muscle through the skin. Underneath the muscle is the skeleton. You must feel the bone."

Abruptly, he strode over to one of the easels, and rapped the man's work with his pointer. "These are lovely breasts you've drawn, but where are the model's ribs?"

Without pausing for a reply, Charles walked up to Andrea on the platform and put his hand just under her breasts. "Ribs." He turned to the man whose work he had criticized. "Come here."

Andrea's heart beat warningly as the man approached. She kept her eyes fixed to the spot she had chosen on the floor.

"Give me your hand," Charles was saying to the student. Andrea felt Charles press the man's hand against her. The man's thumb touched the underside of her breast, but it meant nothing. "Do you feel the bones there? There are bones there."

"Yes," the man said. He had a deep, resonant voice.

"Go back to your easel," Charles said dismissively.

Charles and the student stepped off the platform.

"Your eye has intelligence," Charles was saying, circling his students again. "But intelligence without education is useless. You must educate your eye to use its intelligence." He stopped at one of the student's easels and rapped it with his pointer. "What do you call that?"

"Her neck," said the student timidly.

"That is not a neck. That is a lump of pizza dough." The class laughed. "That could not possibly hold her up head."

Posing reminded Andrea of meditating. Time stretched and slowed. It seemed she had been standing for hours. She was continually fearful that a muscle was about to twitch uncontrollably. She focused her attention on her breathing, no longer listening to Charles's philosophizing or his criticism of his students, and silently begged to be told she could move.

"All right, Andrea," Charles finally said. "You can take a five-minute break. Put on your robe and wait behind the screen."

Sighing, Andrea quickly dropped to her knees and wrapped herself in her robe. Moving too quickly to see any of the men or the work they had done, she padded barefoot back to her place behind the bamboo screen. She sat down gratefully on the chair, stretching her legs and rotating her head in a great circle.

Andrea could hear the murmur of voices and furniture scraping along the floor. The sounds subsided and after a moment Andrea heard Charles call her name again.

Still in her robe, Andrea stepped out from behind the screen and looked down length of the room. The easels had been rearranged into a semicircle facing away from her. The men were all seated at their easels, facing fresh sheets of paper. Charles stood to one side, facing both the men and Andrea.

As she approached, she saw that the men all faced an upholstered wooden chair with claw feet and arms. The dark lacquer on the wood was worn and chipped. The upholstery was a threadbare green brocade. *This will be easier,* Andrea thought as she sat down.

"Andrea!" Charles said, tapping the floor with the rubber tip of his pointer. Andrea looked up at him quizzically. "Your robe," he said in a patronizing voice. Some of the men laughed softly.

Blushing, Andrea quickly stood up, removed the robe, and sat down again. She felt as self-conscious as ever, as if these men had not already seen her naked.

"This isn't the electric chair, Andrea," Charles said, provoking more laughter. "Try to relax." Andrea let out a breath and settled into the chair. "Better," Charles said. "Let me see. Let's try this—put one leg on the seat of the chair. Hold the shin with your hand."

Andrea did so, aware that this posture brought her genitals into view. "Good," Charles said. "Put your other elbow on the arm of the chair and let your hand touch your shoulder." Andrea did as she was told. "Spread your fingers out. Good. Move your hand down slightly. Good."

Her hands made it seem that she was calling attention to her breast, as if she was about to touch it. "Yes," he said. "That's fine. Lower your head a little. Look down. Good. Hold it just like that."

Andrea found a spot on the floor to study and took a breath.

"We may begin again," Charles told the class.

"Those are not mounds of mashed potatoes on her chest!" Charles said, poking at someone's easel with his pointer. The class laughed. Charles approached Andrea. "This is flesh," he said, running his forefinger along the curve of her left breast. Andrea felt her nipple harden and blushed, but was grateful Charles was not using his pointer. "It has weight and mass. It is mostly water, like all tissue. Gravity acts upon it. Look." He put three fingers below her breast and lifted it slightly. "Come here."

The student rose and joined him in front of Andrea. "You draw as if you have no idea what is inside a breast. Feel her breast," Charles said.

Andrea blushed deeply. The student reached out and took her right breast in her hand and held it. Now both her nipples were erect.

"Lift it," Charles said, doing so with Andrea's left breast. "Feel its weight?"

"Yes, sir," the man said quietly.

"All right. Go back to your easel and draw it that way."

They let go of her and stepped away, and Andrea sighed.

"If you've already done her nipples," Charles said casually, "don't change them. Just leave them unerect." Andrea blushed again.

"Five minutes, Andrea!"

She snatched her robe from the floor and threw it over herself as she walked back the screen. Her body pulsed with nervous expectancy. *Something is going to happen here,* she thought.

"We're ready, Andrea!"

She stepped back out from behind the screen. The easels and chairs were arranged as they had been before. As Andrea approached, she saw that they now faced a couch. Its low back and its seat were both upholstered in the same fabric as the chair, as were two cylindrical side pillows. A few square pillows in a dark floral print were scattered on it. Andrea took off her robe and sat down on the couch.

"Lie on your side. You can arrange the pillows behind yourself so as to be comfortable. Prop your head on your hand."

Andrea arranged herself on the couch facing the students. "That's good, but bend your upper leg at the knee and bring it up. Put that foot behind the other knee. Rest that hand on your thigh."

Andrea raised her leg. *Something is going to happen here,* she thought again.

"Good. Let us begin."

"Students! Students!" Charles cried, pacing back and forth behind the men. "This woman is lying on her side. Her breasts cannot possibly sit on her chest the way you are showing them." He stepped between two easels and walked over to Andrea. "Look," he said, putting his hand on her right breast, in her current position the lower of the two. He lifted it. "It has weight. It responds to gravity. Can you all see? Get up. All of you," he said impatiently. Seven men clustered around Charles as he lifted Andrea's breast in the palm of her hand.

"In this position," Charles said, "her left breast rests entirely on her rib cage." Dropping his pointer, Charles put his left hand over Andrea's left breast. "It is almost entirely flattened by gravity. It spreads evenly, like a liquid."

Andrea held her position, staring at a spot on the floor.

"Breasts are soft," Charles said, his hands moving in demonstration. "They are always changing shape and position. You must understand this." Charles took his hands away. Andrea's nipples were throbbing. "Students, feel her breasts," Charles said quietly, stepping back.

Andrea gasped as many hands reached for her

breasts at once. *Seven men,* Andrea thought, flooded with that familiar mixture of fear and excitement she had learned by now to find so intoxicating. Her vagina awakened, growing warm and moist, readying itself. Her clitoris pulsed and stirred, emerging from its sheath.

The men were touching her everywhere now, stroking her breasts and thighs and neck and arms. One man bent to kiss her left breast, and another leaned over the back of the couch to kiss her right breast. She felt lips and hands on her thighs, at her feet. She closed her eyes. *Seven men,* Andrea thought giddily.

They lifted her and laid her on her back. Her eyes still closed, Andrea heard the scratchy sound of the seams of their jumpsuits opening, and the rustling of the soft clothing.

Andrea opened her eyes. All seven men were naked, their penises already erect. She looked up into their faces, meeting their eyes for the first time. They were handsome in the rich morning light. They looked at her with an eager incredulity, like children on Christmas morning, that delighted her. Laughing, she reached out with both hands and fondled one penis and then another. They bobbed and danced before her like toys on springs. The men sighed when she touched them.

She sat up, and the men clustered around her. Lowering her head, she kissed and licked and suckled penis after penis, choosing one and then another on impulse, so the men would be surprised. Soon all seven penises were glistening with her saliva. The men made small sounds of pleasure.

Drunk with her power over the men, Andrea lay back and raised her knees, spreading her thighs wide in silent invitation. She looked up at the seven excited faces. She ran her hands down her breasts and into her crotch.

Hesitantly, one of the men dropped to his knees and, using both hands, positioned the head of his penis at the mouth of her vagina. Andrea put her legs around his waist and, with her heels in his back, pulled him into her. Staring at her, he moved his penis in and out in the rhythm Andrea set with her heels. The sense of power she felt made Andrea wildly aroused, and she knew she could reach orgasm any time.

The other men clustered around. Andrea reached out and pulled two of the men closer, tugging on their penises until they, too, climbed onto the couch. She drew them closer, bringing their penises to her breasts, and made them rub their penises against her. Her nipples rose and swelled. Andrea laughed with the pleasure of it.

Andrea threw her arms out again. She caught hold of another man by the penis and pulled him toward her. Leading him by the penis, she drew him to one side of the couch and had him lean over her until she could take his penis into her mouth.

Blindly reaching out, she found two more penises. She stroked and tickled and fondled.

She had one man in her vagina, one in her mouth, one in each hand, and one on each breast. But there were seven men.

Pushing all six away, Andrea stood up. Choosing at random, she took one of the men by the waist and pushed him down onto the couch. Kneeling before him, she took his penis into her mouth and soaked it with her saliva. When it was dripping wet, she took her mouth away, turned her back to him, and sat down in his lap, reaching between her legs to guide him into her anus. She had never felt more open, and he entered her smoothly, easily, naturally.

Pausing a moment to forestall the orgasm that was threatening her, Andrea took her hands from the penis and then sat down upon it completely. It seemed the penis filled her up to her breasts, that it touched her very heart. For a moment, Andrea held her breath. Then she raised her legs and opened her arms in invitation. Another man dropped to his knees before her. She locked her legs around his waist and pulled him into her. The two penises pressed against the thin wall between them. Her chest ached. She took another deep breath and waited for the level of stimulation to subside.

Beckoning with her arms, two more men climbed back onto the couch and brought their penises to her breasts, and another climbed up and pointed his penis at her face. She turned her head and opened her mouth to the waiting penis.

Reaching out again, she found the last two men and took their penises into her hands. Seven men, she thought, delighted.

Using her heels, she set the rhythm for the man in her vagina, and this was her rhythm as she rode so slightly up and down on the penis in her rectum, and the rhythm with which she sucked and licked the penis in her mouth, and the rhythm with which she stroked and caressed the penises in her hands, and the rhythm with which the men rubbed their penises on her breasts.

She wanted to prolong it forever, but she knew that she was close to overstimulating herself. Her orgasm would be so intense it would be her only one for some time. In the meantime, she husbanded her pleasure carefully.

One of the men groaned loudly, and the penis in her left hand twitched. She ran her hand up to its tip, catching the semen in her palm.

The man's orgasm was contagious. A moment later, the man beneath her shuddered and jerked and groaned and filled her rectum with his hot fluid. The next moment, the penis in her mouth stiffened and shook and discharged its semen.

The men at her breasts groaned, one after the other, and their penises spat onto her nipples.

The penis in her right hand ejaculated. Letting go of both penises, Andrea put her wet hands on the back of the man in her vagina.

He grunted, his body shivering, and thrust into her violently.

Her orgasm was everywhere, in her vagina and her clitoris and her anus and her rectum and her breasts and her back and her hands and her feet and her tongue and her mouth and her throat. Every part of her body was filled with pulsing, dizzying pleasure. Behind closed lids, she saw sparks of light in every color imaginable, and then blackness.

The men disentangled themselves from her. She lay back on the couch. Semen was leaking from her anus and her vagina, on her lips and her chin and her breasts and her hands. Her body felt soft and wet and warm. The men looked down at her with expressions of awe and tenderness. One by one, they leaned down and kissed her on the lips.

"Very good, Andrea!" said Charles. The crowd of men before her parted and she looked past them. Still dressed, Charles was perched on one of the stools, his penis in his fist, semen covering his fingers.

Andrea picked her robe up from the floor and rose from the couch. The men fell back, making a passageway for her. She walked across the room and went behind the bamboo screen. She put on her jumpsuit. The semen on her skin made the cloth stick in spots, but she did not care.

When she came out from behind the screen, all the

students were gone, and Charles had put his penis back into his clothing.

"Thank you, Andrea," Charles said.

Andrea looked at him momentarily. Saying nothing, she left quickly.

MASQUERADE BOOKS

MASQUERADE

CLAIRE BAEDER, ED.

LA DOMME:
A Dominatrix Anthology
$6.95/649-9
A steamy smorgasbord of female domination! Erotic literature has long been filled with heart-stopping portraits of domineering women, and now Claire Baeder has assembled the most memorable in one beautifully brutal volume. No fan of real woman-power can afford to miss this ultimate compendium of dominatrix fiction.

P. N. DEDEAUX

THE NOTHING THINGS
$6.95/653-7
Another classic sorority blowout! Beta Beta Rho—highly exclusive and widely honored—has taken on a new group of pledges. Five women elect to put themselves through the most grueling of ordeals, during which all their defenses will be stripped away—much to the delight of their stern pledgemistresses! The pleasure mounts as these young women leave behind the lowly status of nothing things....

THE TERRITORY WITHIN
$6.95/640-5
A fantastical tale of pleasure! Dedeaux sets his tale within the boundaries of "The Territory," the ultimate fantasy patriarchy. While residing there, all women are strongly encouraged to live by its unusual system. As they discover, it's hard to tell what's more enjoyable: strict obedience or thrilling chastisement!

J. P. KANSAS

THE HOUSE GUEST AND OTHER STORIES
$6.95/638-3
A collection of stories from the author of the best-selling *Andrea at the Center.* From the tale of one woman's stay with an unusually welcoming—and horny—young couple to an encounter with a pair of identical women possessed by decidedly carnal desires, the tales of J. P. Kansas will set your senses aflame!

STEVE RICHARDSON, EDITOR

THE SWEET SPOT
$6.95/628-6
A collection of red-hot stories from C. F. Publications, today's foremost publisher of spanking fiction. A dozen titillating scenarios designed to appeal to devotees of this popular fetish, the stories in *The Sweet Spot* will please all readers of erotica.

CLAIRE THOMPSON

SARAH'S SURRENDER
$6.95/620-0
Lovely Sarah denies her true desires for many years, hoping to find happiness with the pallid men who court her. Unable to hide her true feelings anymore, Sarah explores the SM scene—and tastes fulfillment for the first time. Gradually, her desires lead her to Lawrence, a discriminating man whose course of erotic training bring Sarah to a fuller realization of her submissive nature—and a deeper love—than she had ever imagined possible....

S. CRABB

CHATS ON OLD PEWTER
$6.95/611-1
A compendium of tales dedicated to dominant women. From domineering check-out girls to merciless flirts on the prowl, these women know what men like—and are highly skilled at reducing men to putty in their hands.

PAT CALIFIA

SENSUOUS MAGIC
$7.95/610-3
"*Sensuous Magic* is clear, succinct and engaging.... Califia is the Dr. Ruth of the alternative sexuality set...."
—*Lambda Book Report*

Erotic pioneer Pat Califia provides this unpretentious peek behind the mask of dominant/submissive sexuality. With her trademark wit and insight, Califia demystifies "the scene" for the novice, explaining the terms and techniques behind many misunderstood sexual practices. One of today's bestselling erotic manuals—a must-read for novices and long-time players alike.

ANAÏS NIN AND FRIENDS

WHITE STAINS
$6.95/609-X
Written by Anaïs Nin, Virginia Admiral, Caresse Crosby, and others for a dollar per page, this breathtaking volume was printed privately and soon became an underground legend. After more than fifty years, this collection of explicit but sophisticated musings is back in print.

DENISE HALL

JUDGMENT
$6.95/590-5
Judgment—a forbidding edifice where unfortunate young women find themselves subject to the wiles of their masters. Abandoned to the whims of Judgment's thrilling masters, Callie descends into the depths of this prison, discovering a new capacity for sensuality....

MASQUERADE BOOKS

LONDON GIRLS
$6.50/531-X
In 1875, Samuel Brown arrives in London, determined to take the glorious city by storm. Randy Samuel quickly distinguishes himself as one of the city's most notorious rakehells. Young Mr. Brown knows well the many ways of making a lady weak at the knees—and uses them not only to his delight, but to his enormous profit!

ATAULLAH MARDAAN

KAMA HOURI/DEVA DASI
$7.95/512-3
"Mardaan excels in crowding her pages with the sights and smells of India, and her erotic descriptions are convincingly realistic." —Michael Perkins, *The Secret Record: Modern Erotic Literature*

Kama Houri details the life of a sheltered Western woman who finds herself living within the confines of a harem. *Deva Dasi* is a tale dedicated to the sacred women of India who devoted their lives to the fulfillment of the senses.

ERICA BRONTE

LUST, INC.
$6.50/467-4
Explore the extremes of passion that lurk beneath even the most businesslike exteriors. Join in the sexy escapades of a group of professionals whose idea of office decorum is like nothing you've ever encountered!

VISCOUNT LADYWOOD

GYNECOCRACY
$9.95/511-5
Julian is sent to a private school, and discovers that his program of study has been devised by stern Mademoiselle de Chambonnard. In no time, Julian is learning the many ways of pleasure and pain—under the firm hand of this beautifully demanding headmistress.

N. T. MORLEY

THE APPOINTMENT
$6.95/667-7
Vanya Garrison is married to a wealthy man, but she's beautiful enough to have plenty of fun on her own. Vanya knows just how to please a lover, and she practices her skills with almost any man who crosses her path! It takes a firm hand to control this pampered nymphomaniac; luckily, Dr. Rachel Quarry—Vanya's favorite shrink—provides a type of restraint and guidance unmatched in contemporary psychology. Dr. Quarry makes certain that all of Vanya's deep-seated issues are thoroughly explored!

THE CIRCLE
$6.95/627-8
Gina, a high-class "working girl," encounters a mysterious woman who pays her to indulge her kinky whims. Gina finds herself increasingly aroused by her encounters with Miranda, expanding her limits further than she could ever have imagined. Gradually, additional partners join in the fun, creating a circle of friends who just couldn't be closer!

THE OFFICE
$6.95/616-2
Lovely Suzette interviews for a desirable new position on the staff of a bondage magazine. Once hired, she discovers that her new employer's interest in dominance and submission extends beyond the printed page. Soon, Suzette is putting in plenty of overtime—as the bound sextoy of her demanding superior.

THE CONTRACT
$6.95/575-1
Beautiful Sarah is experiencing some difficulty in training her current submissive. Carlton proposes an unusual wager: if Carlton is unsuccessful in bringing Tina to a full appreciation of Sarah's domination, Carlton himself will become Sarah's devoted slave....

THE LIMOUSINE
$6.95/555-7
Brenda was enthralled with her roommate Kristi's desire to be dominated. Brenda decides to embark on a trip into submission, beginning in the long, white limousine where Kristi first met the Master.

THE CASTLE
$6.95/530-1
Tess Roberts is held captive by a crew of disciplinarians intent on making all her dreams come true—even those she'd never admitted to herself. While anyone can arrange for a stay at the Castle, Tess proves herself one of the most gifted applicants yet....

THE PARLOR
$6.50/496-8
The mysterious John and Sarah ask Kathryn to be their slave—an idea that turns her on so much that she can't refuse! Little by little, Kathryn not only learns to serve, but comes to know the inner secrets of her keepers.

VANESSA DURIÈS

THE TIES THAT BIND
$6.50/510-7
This best-selling account of real-life dominance and submission will keep you gasping with its vivid depictions of sensual abandon. At the hand of Masters Georges, Patrick, Pierre and others, this submissive seductress experiences pleasures she never knew existed....

MASQUERADE BOOKS

M. S. VALENTINE

THE GOVERNESS

$6.95/562-X

Lovely Miss Hunnicut eagerly embarks upon her new career as a governess. Little does the virtuous young woman know that Crawleigh Manor is far from the upstanding household it appears. The handsome and unrelenting Mr. Crawleigh, in particular, devotes himself to Miss Hunnicut's thorough defiling. In no time, the beautiful governess distinguishes herself as a fitting resident of perverse Crawleigh Manor.

AMANDA WARE

BOUND TO THE PAST

$6.50/452-6

Doing research in an old Tudor mansion, beautiful Anne finds herself aroused by James, a descendant of the property's owners. Together they uncover the perverse desires of the mansion's long-dead master—desires that bind Anne inexorably to the past—not to mention the bedpost!

SACHI MIZUNO

SHINJUKU NIGHTS

$6.50/493-3

Using Tokyo's infamous red light district as his backdrop, Sachi Mizuno weaves an intricate web of sensual desire, wherein many characters are ensnared by the demands of their carnal natures.

PASSION IN TOKYO

$6.50/454-2

Tokyo—one of Asia's most historic and seductive cities. Come behind the closed doors of its citizens, and witness the many pleasures that await intrepid explorers. Men and women from every stratum of society free themselves of all inhibitions in this thrilling tour through the libidinous East.

MARTINE GLOWINSKI

POINT OF VIEW

$6.50/433-X

The story of one woman's erotic awakening. After her divorce, a lonely woman decides to expand her sexual horizons. With the assistance of a new, unexpectedly kinky lover, she discovers and explores her exhibitionist tendencies—until there is virtually nothing she won't do before the horny audiences her man arranges. Soon she is infamous for her unabashed sexual performances. An exhibitionist run wild!

RICHARD McGOWAN

A HARLOT OF VENUS

$6.50/425-9

A highly fanciful, epic tale of lust on Mars! Cavortia—the most famous and sought-after courtesan in the cosmopolitan city of Venus—finds love and much more during her adventures with some cosmic characters. A sexy, sci-fi fairytale.

M. ORLANDO

THE SLEEPING PALACE

$6.95/582-4

Another thrilling volume of erotic reveries from the author of *The Architecture of Desire*. *Maison Bizarre* is the scene of unspeakable erotic cruelty; the *Lust Akademie* holds captive only the most luscious students of the sensual arts; *Baden-Eros* is the luxurious retreat of one's nastiest dreams.

CHET ROTHWELL

KISS ME, KATHERINE

$5.95/410-0

Beautiful Katherine can hardly believe her luck. Not only is she married to the charming Nelson, she's free to live out all her erotic fantasies with other men. Katherine's desires are more than any one man can handle—and plenty of men wait to fulfill her needs!

MARCO VASSI

THE STONED APOCALYPSE

$5.95/401-1/Mass market

"Marco Vassi is our champion sexual energist." —*VLS*

During his lifetime, Marco Vassi's reputation as a champion of sexual experimentation was worldwide. Funded by his groundbreaking erotic writing, *The Stoned Apocalypse* is Vassi's autobiography; chronicling a cross-country trip on America's erotic byways.

THE SALINE SOLUTION

$6.95/568-9/Mass market

"I've always read Marco's work with interest and I have the highest opinion not only of his talent but his intellectual boldness." —Norman Mailer

During the Sexual Revolution, Vassi established himself as an explorer of an uncharted sexual landscape. Through this story of one couple's brief affair and the events that lead them to desperately reassess their lives, Vassi examines the dangers of intimacy in an age of extraordinary freedom.

BUY ANY 4 BOOKS & CHOOSE 1 ADDITIONAL BOOK, OF EQUAL OR LESSER VALUE, AS YOUR FREE GIFT

ROBIN WILDE

TABITHA'S TEASE

$6.95/597-2

When poor Robin arrives at The Valentine Academy, he finds himself subject to the torturous teasing of Tabitha—the Academy's most notoriously domineering co-ed. Adding to Robin's delicious suffering is the fact that Tabitha is pledge-mistress of a secret sorority dedicated to enslaving young men. Men suffer deliciously at the hands of Tabitha and her wicked beauties.

TABITHA'S TICKLE

$6.50/468-2

Tabitha's back! Once again, men fall under the spell of scrumptious co-eds and find themselves enslaved to demands and desires they never dreamed existed. Think it's a man's world? Guess again. With Tabitha around, no man gets what he wants until she's satisfied—and maybe not even then....

CHARLES G. WOOD

HELLFIRE

$5.95/358-9

A vicious murderer is running amok in New York's sexual underground—and Nick O'Shay, a virile detective with the NYPD, plunges into the case. He soon becomes embroiled in the Big Apple's notorious nightworld of dungeons and sex clubs, hunting a relentless madman seeking to purge America with fire and blood sacrifices.

CHARISSE VAN DER LYN

SEX ON THE NET

$5.95/399-6

Electrifying sex tales from one of the Internet's hottest authors. Encounters of all kinds—straight, lesbian, dominant/submissive and all sorts of extreme passions—are explored in thrilling detail. Discover the scintillating cyber-erotica that's turning on horny hackers the world over!

STANLEY CARTEN

NAUGHTY MESSAGE

$5.95/333-3

Innocent and unsuspecting Wesley Arthur discovers a lascivious message on his answering machine. Aroused beyond his wildest dreams by the kinky acts described, he becomes obsessed with tracking down the woman behind the seductive voice. His search takes him through strip clubs, sex parlors and no-tell motels—before finally leading him to his randy reward....

CAROLE REMY

FANTASY IMPROMPTU

$6.50/513-1

Kidnapped to a remote island retreat, Chantal finds herself catering to every sexual whim of the mysterious Bran. Bran is determined to bring Chantal to a full embracing of her sensual nature, even while revealing himself to be something far more than human....

BEAUTY OF THE BEAST

$5.95/332-5

A shocking tell-all, written from the point-of-view of a prize-winning reporter. Endowed with a restless curiosity and tireless libido, she stops at nothing in her quest to reveal the inside story—and spares no details in the reporting.

ANONYMOUS

LADY F.

$6.95/642-1

It is the age of Queen Victoria and the moral price of pleasure is high. Master Kidrodstock—full as he is of wicked and uncontrollable impulses and urges—soon discovers just how high the price is when he encounters Lady F. Stunningly cruel and sensuous, this haughty lady leaves all men gasping—for more!

THE YELLOW ROOM

$6.95/631-6

The "yellow room" holds the secrets of lust, lechery, and the lash. There, demure Alice Darvell soon experiences a variety of extraordinary experiences. Another story follows the perversions of a sadistic heiress and her two lusty ladies.

DANIELLE: DIARY OF A SLAVE GIRL

$6.95/591-3

At the age of 19, Danielle Appleton vanishes. The frantic efforts of her family notwithstanding, she is never seen by them again. After her disappearance, Danielle finds herself doomed to a life of sexual slavery, obliged to become the ultimate instrument of pleasure to the man—or men—who own her and dictate her every move and desire.

ROMANCE OF LUST

$9.95/604-9

"Truly remarkable...all the pleasure of fine historical fiction combined with the most intimate descriptions of explicit love-making." —*The Times*

One of the most famous erotic novels of the century! This collaborative work of sexual awakening in Victorian England was repeatedly been banned for its "immorality"—and much sought after for its vivid portrayals of sodomy, sexual initiation, and flagellation. A look at the many possibilities of sexual love.

MASQUERADE BOOKS

SUBURBAN SOULS

$9.95/563-8

One of American erotica's first classics. Focusing on the May–December sexual relationship of nubile Lillian and the more experienced Jack, all three volumes of *Suburban Souls* now appear in one special edition—guaranteed to enrapture modern readers with its lurid detail.

THE MISFORTUNES OF COLETTE

$7.95/564-6

The tale of one woman's erotic suffering at the hands of a sadistic man and woman. Beautiful Colette is the victim of an obscene plot guaranteed to keep her in erotic servitude. Passed from one lustful tormentor to another, Colette wonders whether she is destined to find her greatest pleasures in punishment!

LOVE'S ILLUSION

$6.95/549-2

Elizabeth Renard yearned for the body of rich and successful Dan Harrington. Then she discovered Harrington's secret weakness: a need to be humiliated and punished. She makes him her slave, and together they commence a thrilling journey into depravity that leaves nothing to the imagination!

NADIA

$5.95/267-1

Follow the delicious but neglected Nadia as she works to wring every drop of pleasure out of life—despite an unhappy marriage. With the help of some very eager men, Nadia soon experiences the erotic pleasures she had always dreamed of....

TITIAN BERESFORD

CINDERELLA

$6.95/606-5

An exploration of the erotic potential of this famous fairy tale. Beresford triumphs again with castle dungeons and tightly corseted ladies-in-waiting, naughty viscounts and cruel masturbatrixes—nearly every conceivable method of kinky arousal is explored and described in lush, vivid detail. A fetishist's dream and a masochist's delight!

CHIDEWELL HOUSE AND OTHER STORIES

$6.95/554-9

What keeps Cecil a virtual, if willing, prisoner of Chidewell House? One man has been sent to investigate the sexy situation—and reports back with tales of such depravity that no expense is spared in attempting Cecil's rescue. But what man would possibly desire release from the breathtakingly corrupt Elizabeth?

JUDITH BOSTON

$6.50/525-5

A bestselling chronicle of female domination. Edward would have been lucky to get the stodgy companion he thought his parents had hired for him. But an exquisite woman arrives at his door, and Edward finds—to his increasing delight—that his lewd behavior never goes unpunished by the unflinchingly severe Judith Boston!

AKBAR DEL PIOMBO

THE FETISH CROWD

$6.95/556-5

An infamous trilogy presented in one volume guaranteed to appeal to the modern sophisticate. Separately, *Paula the Piquôse*, the infamous *Duke Cosimo*, and *The Double-Bellied Companion* are rightly considered individual masterpieces—together they make an unforgettable volume.

TINY ALICE

THE GEEK

$5.95/341-4

An offbeat classic of modern erotica, *The Geek* is told from the point of view of, well, a chicken who reports on the various perversities he witnesses as part of a traveling carnival. When a gang of renegade lesbians kidnaps Chicken and his geek, all hell breaks loose. A strange but highly arousing tale, filled with outrageous erotic oddities, that finally returns to print after years of infamy.

LYN DAVENPORT

THE GUARDIAN II

$6.50/505-0

The tale of submissive Felicia Brookes continues. No sooner has Felicia come to love Rodney than she discovers that she has been sold—and must now accustom herself to the guardianship of the debauched Duke of Smithton. Surely Rodney will rescue her from the domination of this depraved stranger. *Won't he?*

GWYNETH JAMES

DREAM CRUISE

$4.95/3045-8

Angelia has it all—exciting career and breathtaking beauty. But she longs to kick up her high heels and have some fun, so she takes an island vacation and vows to leave her inhibitions behind. From the moment her plane takes off, she finds herself in one steamy encounter after another—and wishes her horny holiday would never end!

BUY ANY 4 BOOKS & CHOOSE 1 ADDITIONAL BOOK, OF EQUAL OR LESSER VALUE, AS YOUR FREE GIFT

MASQUERADE BOOKS

LIZBETH DUSSEAU

TRINKETS
$6.95/668-5
A luscious woman toys with the idea of complete erotic submission, never thinking her lascivious dream might come true. But it does, and Tessa finds herself gleefully subordinate to an eccentric artist's every whim. In no time, the domineering Miles fashions her into the ultimate erotic bauble—to be shown off in public, but fully enjoyed in private....

THE BEST OF LIZBETH DUSSEAU
$6.95/630-8
Dusseau's explorations of male-dominant lust have made her a favorite with fans of contemporary erotica. This volume is full of heroines who are unafraid to put everything on the line in order to experience pleasure at the hands of a virile man...

MEMBER OF THE CLUB
$6.95/608-1
A restless woman yearns to realize her most secret, licentious desires. There is a club that exists for the fulfillment of such fantasies—a club devoted to the pleasures of the flesh, and the gratification of every hunger. When its members call she is compelled to answer—and serve each in an endless quest for satisfaction.... A thrilling tale of the ultimate sex club.

SPANISH HOLIDAY
$4.95/185-3
Lauren didn't mean to fall in love with the enigmatic Sam, but a once-in-a-lifetime European vacation gives her all the evidence she needs that this hot, insatiable man might be the one for her....Soon, both irrepressible lovers are exploring the furthest reaches of their desires.

JOCELYN JOYCE

PRIVATE LIVES
$4.95/309-0
The dirty habits of the illustrious make for a sizzling tale of French erotic life. A widow has a craving for a young busboy; he's sleeping with a rich businessman's wife; her husband is minding his sex business elsewhere!

SABINE
$4.95/3046-6
There is no one who can refuse her once she casts her spell; no lover can do anything less than give up his whole life for her. Great men and empires fall at her feet; but she is haughty, distracted, impervious. It is the eve of WW II, and Sabine must find a new lover equal to her talents and her tastes. A legendary seductress.

SARA H. FRENCH

MASTER OF TIMBERLAND
$6.95/595-6
A tale of sexual slavery at the ultimate paradise resort—where sizzling submissives serve their masters without question. One of our bestselling titles, this trek to Timberland has ignited passions the world over.

MARY LOVE

ANGELA
$6.95/545-X
Angela's game is "look but don't touch," and she drives everyone mad with desire, dancing for their pleasure but never allowing a single caress. Soon her sensual spell is cast, and she's the only one who can break it!

MASTERING MARY SUE
$6.95/660-X
Mary Sue is a rich nymphomaniac whose husband is determined to declare her mentally incompetent and gain control of her fortune. He brings her to a castle where, to Mary Sue's delight, she is unleashed for a veritable sex-fest!

AMARANTHA KNIGHT

The Darker Passions: THE PIT AND THE PENDULUM
$6.95/639-1
The mistress of erotic horror takes on Edgar Allen Poe—and produces her most stimulating volume yet! Poe's deadly pit is transformed into the site of a thousand unbearable pleasures, a carnal playground frequented by the perverse members of a secret society devoted to sensual experimentation. One young woman, herself blessed with extraordinary talents, is about to discover what has made the Pit of Delights a legend....

The Darker Passions: FRANKENSTEIN
$6.95/617-0
The mistress of erotic horror sets her sights on Mary Shelley's darkest creation. What if you could create a living, breathing human? What shocking acts could it be taught to perform, to desire, to love? Find out what pleasures await those who play God in another breathtaking journey through the Darker Passions.

The Darker Passions: CARMILLA
$6.95/578-6
Captivated by the portrait of a beautiful woman, a young man finds himself becoming obsessed with her remarkable story. Little by little, he uncovers the many blasphemies and debaucheries with which the beauteous Laura filled her hours—even as an otherworldly presence began feasting upon her....

MASQUERADE BOOKS

THE END OF INNOCENCE
$6.95/546-8
The days of Women's Emancipation are the setting for this story. These women were willing to go to any lengths to fight for their sexual freedom, and willing to endure any punishment in their desire for liberation.

THE BEST OF PAUL LITTLE
$6.50/469-0
Known for his portrayals of punishment and pleasure, Little never fails to push readers over the edge of sensual excitement. His best scenes are now collected in one volume.

CAPTIVE MAIDENS
$5.95/440-2
The story of three independent and beautiful young women who find themselves powerless against the debauched landowners of 1824 England. The unlucky lovelies find themselves banished to a sex colony, where they are subjected to unspeakable perversions.

THE PRISONER
$5.95/330-9
Judge Black has built a secret room below a penitentiary, where he sentences his female prisoners to hours of exhibition while his friends watch. Judge Black's justice keeps his captives on the brink of utter pleasure!

DOUBLE NOVEL
$6.95/86-6
The Metamorphosis of Lisette Joyaux tells the story of a young woman initiated into an incredible world world of lesbian lusts. *The Story of Monique* reveals the twisted sexual rituals that beckon the willing Monique.

ALIZARIN LAKE

THE INSTRUMENTS OF THE PASSION
$6.95/659-6
All that remains is the diary of a young initiate, detailing the rituals of a mysterious cult institution known only as "Rossiter." Behind sinister walls, a beautiful woman performs an unending drama of desire and submission.

MISS HIGH HEELS
$6.95/632-4
Forced by his wicked sisters to dress and behave like a proper lady, Dennis Beryl finds he enjoys life as Denise much more! Petticoats and punishments make for one kinky romp!

CLARA
$6.95/548-4
The mysterious death of a beautiful woman leads her old boyfriend on a harrowing journey of discovery. His search uncovers an unimaginably sensuous woman embarked on a quest for deeper and more unusual sensations, each more shocking than the one before!

SEX ON DOCTOR'S ORDERS
$5.95/402-X
Naughty nurse Beth uses her considerable skills to further medical science by offering insatiable assistance in the gathering of specimens. Soon she's involved everyone in her horny work—and no one leaves without surrendering what Beth wants!

THE EROTIC ADVENTURES OF HARRY TEMPLE
$4.95/127-6
Harry Temple's memoirs chronicle his incredibly amorous adventures—from his initiation at the hands of insatiable sirens, through his stay at a house of hot repute, to his encounters with a chastity-belted nympho, and much more!

LUSCIDIA WALLACE

THE ICE MAIDEN
$6.95/613-8
Edward Canton has everything he wants in life, with one exception: Rebecca Esterbrook. He whisks her away to his remote island compound, where she learns to shed her inhibitions. Fully aroused for the first time in her life, she becomes a slave to desire!

JOHN NORMAN

MARAUDERS OF GOR
$6.95/662-6
Tarl Cabot has struggled to free himself from the control of Gor's powerful Priest-Kings, but to no avail. Now he finds that mission challenged by a threat emanating from the planet's forbidding northern lands. There, a menacing alien force waits for Tarl, who faces an awesome choice: protect his own position as a rich merchant-slaver, or risk everything to defend the freedom of his world....

HUNTERS OF GOR
$6.95/592-1
Tarl Cabot ventures into the wilderness of Gor, pitting his skill against brutal outlaws and sly warriors. His life on Gor been complicated by three beautiful, very different women: Talena, Tarl's one-time queen; Elizabeth, his fearless comrade; and Verna, chief of the feral panther women. In this installment of Norman's million-selling sci-fi phenomenon, the fates of these uncommon women are finally revealed....

CAPTIVE OF GOR
$6.95/581-6
On Earth, Elinor Brinton was accustomed to having it all—wealth, beauty, and a host of men wrapped around her little finger. But Elinor is now a pleasure slave of Gor, a world whose society insists on her subservience, and Elinor finds herself succumbing—with pleasure—to her powerful Master....

MASQUERADE BOOKS

RAIDERS OF GOR
$6.95/558-1
Tarl Cabot descends into the depths of Port Kar—the most degenerate port city of the Counter-Earth. There Cabot learns the ways of Kar, whose residents are renowned for the grip in which they hold their voluptuous slaves....

ASSASSIN OF GOR
$6.95/538-7
The chronicles of Counter-Earth continue with this examination of Gorean society. Here is the brutal caste system of Gor: from the Assassin Kuurus, on a mission of vengeance, to Pleasure Slaves, trained in the ways of personal ecstasy.

NOMADS OF GOR
$6.95/527-1
Cabot finds his way across Gor, pledged to serve the Priest-Kings. Unfortunately for Cabot, his mission leads him to the savage Wagon People—nomads who may very well kill before surrendering any secrets....

PRIEST-KINGS OF GOR
$6.95/488-7
Tarl Cabot searches for his lovely wife Talena. Does she live, or was she destroyed by the all-powerful Priest-Kings? Cabot is determined to find out—though no one who has approached the mountain stronghold of the Priest-Kings has ever returned alive....

OUTLAW OF GOR
$6.95/487-9
Tarl Cabot returns to Gor. Upon arriving, he discovers that his name, his city and the names of those he loves have become unspeakable. Once a respected Tarnsman, Cabot has become an outlaw, and must discover his new purpose on this strange planet, where even simple answers have their price....

TARNSMAN OF GOR
$6.95/486-0
This controversial series returns! Tarl Cabot is transported to Gor. He must quickly accustom himself to the ways of this world, including the caste system which exalts some as Warriors, and debases others as slaves.

SYDNEY ST. JAMES

RIVE GAUCHE
$5.95/317-1
The Latin Quarter, Paris, circa 1920. Expatriate bohemians couple wildly—before eventually abandoning their ambitions amidst the temptations waiting to be indulged in every bedroom.

DON WINSLOW

THE MANY PLEASURES OF IRONWOOD
$6.95/661-8
Welcome to the Ironwood Sportsmen's Club, specifically designed for the erotic entertainment of gentlemen. Charli, Robin, Kitteridge, Nikki, Annie, Diane and Meredith—seven lovely young women who, employed by the small and exclusive club, consider it their vocation to provide the members of Ironwood with the time of their lives. But even these dedicated pros could not have imagined the outrageous orgies the randy membership would dream up....

THE BEST OF DON WINSLOW
$6.95/607-3
Internationally best-selling fetish author Don Winslow personally selected his hottest passages for this special collection. Sizzling excerpts are woven together to make this an extraordinary overview of Winslow's work.

SLAVE GIRLS OF ROME
$6.95/577-8
Never were women so relentlessly used as were ancient Rome's voluptuous slaves! With no choice but to serve their lustful masters, these captive beauties learn to perform their duties with the passion of Venus herself.

PRIVATE PLEASURES
$6.50/504-2
Frantic voyeurs and licentious exhibitionists are here displayed in all their wanton glory—laid bare by the perverse and probing eye of Don Winslow.

THE INSATIABLE MISTRESS OF ROSEDALE
$6.50/494-1
Edward and Lady Penelope reside in Rosedale manor. While Edward is a connoisseur of sexual perversion, it is Lady Penelope whose mastery of complete sensual pleasure makes their home infamous. Indulging one another's bizarre whims is a way of life for this wicked couple....

N. WHALLEN

THE EDUCATION OF SITA MANSOOR
$6.95/567-0
On the eve of her wedding, Sita Mansoor is left without a bridegroom. Sita travels to America, where she hopes to become educated in the ways of a permissive society. She could never have imagined the wide variety of tutors—both male and female—who would be waiting to take on so beautiful a pupil.

BUY ANY 4 BOOKS & CHOOSE 1 ADDITIONAL BOOK, OF EQUAL OR LESSER VALUE, AS YOUR FREE GIFT

MASQUERADE BOOKS

THE CLASSIC COLLECTION

THE ENGLISH GOVERNESS

$6.95/622-7

When Lord Lovell's son was expelled from his prep school for masturbation, he hired a very proper governess to tutor the boy—giving her strict instructions not to spare the rod to break him of his bad habits. Upon her arrival in Lord Lovell's home, governess Harriet Marwood reveals herself a force to be reckoned with—particularly by her randy charge. In no time, Master Lovell's onanism is under control—as are all other aspects of his life.

MAN WITH A MAID

$4.95/307-4

The adventures of Jack and Alice have delighted readers for eight decades! *Man with a Maid* tells a tale of desire and submission. Join Jack in the Snuggery, where many lovely women learn the ways of pleasure.

MASQUERADE READERS

THE 50 BEST PLAYGIRL FANTASIES

$7.95/648-0

A steamy selection of women's fantasies straight from the pages of *PLAYGIRL*—the leading magazine of sexy entertainment for women. Contemporary heroines pursue liaisons with horny men from every walk of life in these tales of modern lust.

INTIMATE PLEASURES

$4.95/38-6

Indulge your most private penchants with this specially chosen selection of Masquerade's hottest moments.

RHINOCEROS

CHRISTA FAUST

CONTROL FREAK

$7.95/633-2

"Christa Faust is a Veronica in a world of Betties."

—Quentin Tarantino

"Takes the reader on an odyssey of the spirit leading to places that most of us have neither the imagination nor the courage to envision." —John Pelan

Caitlin McCullough, an author of cheap detective novels who has a nose for the sensational, is fascinated by the grisly particulars of a brutal murder. As Caitlin's investigation into Eva's wild life and brutal death draws her deeper into the labyrinth of New York's infamous sexual playground, she finds herself perversely attracted to the killing's prime suspect—a notorious SM club owner.

M. CHRISTIAN, ED.

EROS EX MACHINA: Eroticizing the Mechanical

$7.95/593-X

As the millennium approaches, technology is not only an inevitable, but a desirable addition to daily life. *Eros Ex Machina* explores the thrill and danger of machines—our literal and literary love of technology. Join over 25 of today's hottest writers as they explore erotic relationships with all kinds of gadgets, and devices.

LEOPOLD VON SACHER-MASOCH

VENUS IN FURS

$7.95/589-1

The alliance of Severin and Wanda epitomizes Sacher-Masoch's obsession with a cruel goddess and the urges that drive the man held in her thrall. Exclusive to this edition are letters exchanged between Sacher-Masoch and Emilie Mataja—an aspiring writer he sought as the avatar of his desires.

JOHN NORMAN

IMAGINATIVE SEX

$7.95/561-1

The author of the Gor novels outlines his philosophy on relations between the sexes, and presents fifty-three scenarios designed to reintroduce fantasy to the bedroom.

THOMAS S. ROCHE

NOIROTICA 2: Pulp Friction (Ed.)

$7.95/584-0

Another volume of criminally seductive stories set in the murky terrain of the erotic and noir genres. Thomas Roche has gathered the darkest jewels from today's edgiest writers to create this provocative collection.

NOIROTICA: An Anthology of Erotic Crime Stories (Ed.)

$6.95/390-2

A collection of darkly sexy tales, taking place at the crossroads of the crime and erotic genres. Here are some of today's finest writers, all of whom explore the extraordinary and arousing terrain where desire runs irrevocably afoul of the law. A groundbreaking collection of contemporary erotica.

DARK MATTER

$6.95/484-4

"*Dark Matter* is sure to please gender outlaws, bodymod junkies, goth vampires, boys who wish they were dykes, and anybody who's not to sure where the fine line should be drawn between pleasure and pain. It's a handful."—Pat Califia

"Here is the erotica of the cumming millennium.... You will be deliciously disturbed, but never disappointed."

—Poppy Z. Brite

MASQUERADE BOOKS

DAVID MELTZER

UNDER

$6.95/290-6

The story of a 21st century sex professional living at the bottom of the social heap. After surgeries designed to increase his physical allure, corrupt government forces drive the cyber-gigolo underground, where even more bizarre cultures await....

KATHLEEN K.

SWEET TALKERS

$6.95/516-6

"If you enjoy eavesdropping on explicit conversations about sex... this book is for you." —*Spectator*

A explicit look at the burgeoning phenomenon of phone sex. Kathleen K. ran a phone-sex company in the late 80s, and she opens up her diary for a peek at the life of a phone-sex operator. Transcripts of actual conversations are included.

Trade /$12.95/192-6

LAURA ANTONIOU, ED.

SOME WOMEN

$7.95/573-5

Introduction by Pat Califia

"Makes the reader think about the wide range of SM experiences, beyond the glamour of fiction and fantasy, or the clever-clever prose of the perverati." —*SKIN TWO*

Over forty essays written by women actively involved in consensual dominance and submission. Professional mistresses, lifestyle leatherdykes, whipmakers, titleholders—women from every conceivable walk of life lay bare their true feelings about issues as explosive as feminism, abuse, pleasure and public image.

NO OTHER TRIBUTE

$7.95/603-0

A volume sure to challenge Political Correctness in a way that few others have. Tales of women kept in bondage to their lovers by their deepest passions. Love pushes these women beyond acceptable limits, rendering them helpless to deny anything to the men and women they adore.

BY HER SUBDUED

$6.95/281-7

These tales all involve women in control—of their lives and their lovers. So much in control that they can remorselessly break rules to become powerful goddesses of those who sacrifice all to worship at their feet.

AMELIA G, ED.

BACKSTAGE PASSES: Rock n' Roll Erotica from the Pages of *Blue Blood* Magazine

$6.95/438-0

Amelia G, editor of the goth-sex journal *Blue Blood*, has brought together some of today's most irreverent writers, each of whom has outdone themselves with an edgy, antic tale of modern lust.

ROMY ROSEN

SPUNK

$6.95/492-5

Casey, a lovely model poised upon the verge of super-celebrity, falls for an insatiable young rock singer—not suspecting that his sexual appetite has led him to experiment with a dangerous new aphrodisiac. Soon, Casey becomes addicted to the drug, and her craving plunges her into a strange underworld.... A knowing tour through the world of the hip and beautiful.

MOLLY WEATHERFIELD

SAFE WORD: CARRIE'S STORY II

$7.95/665-0

The sequel to Molly Weatherfield's best-selling look at contemporary dominance and submission, *Carrie's Story*. Carrie leaves behind her life with Jonathan, intent on proving herself with the demanding gentleman who has chosen her as his own. Whisked away to Greece, Carrie learns new, more rigorous methods of sexual satisfaction. When her year of training is complete, Carrie faces a decision—life on her own, or in the embrace of her beloved but estranged Jonathan....

CARRIE'S STORY

$7.95/652-9

"I was stunned by how well it was written and how intensely foreign I found its sexual world.... And, since this is a world I don't frequent... I thoroughly enjoyed the National Geo tour." —*bOING bOING*

"Hilarious and harrowing... just when you think things can't get any wilder, they do." —*Black Sheets*

Weatherfield's bestselling examination of dominance and submission. "I had been Jonathan's slave for about a year when he told me he wanted to sell me at an auction...." A rare piece of erotica, both thoughtful and hot!

BUY ANY 4 BOOKS & CHOOSE 1 ADDITIONAL BOOK, OF EQUAL OR LESSER VALUE, AS YOUR FREE GIFT

MASQUERADE BOOKS

CYBERSEX CONSORTIUM

CYBERSEX: The Perv's Guide to Finding Sex on the Internet

$6.95/471-2

You've heard the objections: cyberspace is soaked with sex, mired in immorality. Okay—so where is it!? Tracking down the good stuff—the real good stuff—can waste an awful lot of expensive time, and frequently leave you high and dry. An easy-to-use guide for those intrepid adults who know what they want.

TAMMY JO ECKHART

AMAZONS: Erotic Explorations of Ancient Myths

$7.95/534-4

The Amazon—the fierce woman warrior—appears in the traditions of many cultures, but never before has the erotic potential of this archetype been explored with such energy and imagination. Powerful pleasures await anyone lucky enough to encounter Eckhart's legendary spitfires.

PUNISHMENT FOR THE CRIME

$6.95/427-5

Stories that explore dominance and submission. From an encounter between two of society's most despised individuals, to the explorations of longtime friends, these tales take you where few others have ever dared....

LAURA ANTONIOU ("Sara Adamson")

"Ms. Adamson creates a wonderfully diverse world of lesbian, gay, straight, bi and transgendered characters, all mixing delightfully in the melting pot of sadomasochism and planting the genre more firmly in the culture at large. I for one am cheering her on!" —Kate Bornstein

THE MARKETPLACE

$7.95/602-2

The first title in Antoniou's thrilling Marketplace Trilogy, following the lives an lusts of those who have been deemed worthy to participate in the Marketplace—the ultimate BD/SM arena.

THE SLAVE

$7.95/601-4

The Slave covers the experience of one submissive who longs to join the ranks of those who have proven themselves worthy of entry into the Marketplace. But the price of admission, while delicious, is staggeringly high....

THE TRAINER

$6.95/249-3

The Marketplace Trilogy concludes with the story of the trainers, and the desires and paths that led them to become the ultimate figures of authority.

THE CATALYST

$6.95/621-9

A kinky art movie inspires the audience members—het and queer—to try some SM play of their own. Different from a lot of SM smut in that it depicts actual consensual SM scenes between just plain folks rather than wild impossible fantasies, *The Catalyst* is both sweet-natured and nastily perverse. The "why don't we give this kinky stuff a try" tone is a true delight.
—*Blowfish*

After viewing an explicitly kinky film full of images of bondage and submission, several audience members find themselves deeply moved by the erotic suggestions they've seen on the screen. A modern BD/SM classic, and this popular author's debut.

GERI NETTICK WITH BETH ELLIOT

MIRRORS: Portrait of a Lesbian Transsexual

$6.95/435-6

Born a male, Geri Nettick knew something just didn't fit. Even after coming to terms with her own gender dysphoria, and taking steps to correct it, she still fought to be accepted by the lesbian feminist community to which she felt she belonged. An inspiring true story of self-discover and acceptance.

TRISTAN TAORMINO & DAVID AARON CLARK, EDS.

RITUAL SEX

$6.95/391-0

The contributors to *Ritual Sex* know that body and soul share more common ground than society feels comfortable acknowledging. From memoirs of ecstatic revelation, to quests to reconcile sex and spirit, *Ritual Sex* provides an unprecedented look at private ritual.

AMARANTHA KNIGHT, ED.

DEMON SEX

$7.95/594-8

Examining the dark forces of humankind's oldest stories, the contributors to *Demon Sex* reveal the strange symbiosis of dread and desire. Stories include a streetwalker's deal with the devil; a visit with the stripper from Hell; the secrets behind an aging rocker's timeless appeal; and many more guaranteed to shatter preconceptions about modern lust.

SEDUCTIVE SPECTRES

$6.95/464-X

Tours through the erotic supernatural via the imaginations of today's best writers. Never have ghostly encounters been so alluring, thanks to otherworldly characters well-acquainted with the pleasures of the flesh.

MASQUERADE BOOKS

SEX MACABRE
$6.95/392-9
Horror tales designed for dark and sexy nights—sure to make your skin crawl, and heart beat faster. A cast of stellar talents makes this a compelling volume, and an important title in the emerging genre of erotic horror.

FLESH FANTASTIC
$6.95/352-X
Humans have long toyed with the idea of "playing God": creating life from nothingness, bringing life to the inanimate. Now Amarantha Knight collects stories exploring not only the act of Creation, but the lust that follows.

GARY BOWEN

DIARY OF A VAMPIRE
$6.95/331-7
"Gifted with a darkly sensual vision and a fresh voice, [Bowen] is a writer to watch out for." —Cecilia Tan

Rafael, a red-blooded male with an insatiable hunger for the same, is the perfect antidote to the effete malcontents haunting bookstores today. The emergence of a bold and brilliant vision, rooted in past and present.

GRANT ANTREWS

LEGACIES
$7.95/605-7
Kathi Lawton discovers that she has inherited the troubling secret of her late mother's scandalous sexuality. In an effort to understand what motivated her mother's desires, Kathi embarks on an exploration of SM that leads her into the arms of Horace Moore, a mysterious man who seems to see into her very soul. As she begins falling for her new master, Kathi finds herself wondering just how far she'll go to prove her love....

SUBMISSIONS
$7.95/618-9
Suddenly finding himself a millionaire, Kevin Donovan thinks his worries are over—until his restless soul tires of the high life. He turns to the icy Maitresse Genevieve, hoping that her ministrations will guide him to some deeper peace....

ROGUES GALLERY
$6.95/522-0
A stirring evocation of dominant/submissive love. Two doctors meet and slowly fall in love. Once lovely Beth reveals her hidden, kinky desires to Jim, the two explore the forbidden acts that will come to define their affair.

MY DARLING DOMINATRIX
$7.95/566-2
When a man and a woman fall in love, it's supposed to be simple, uncomplicated, easy—unless that woman happens to be a dominatrix. One couple exlores the outer limits and inner depths of desire in this unpretentious love story that captures the richness of this special kind of love without leering or smirking.

JEAN STINE

THRILL CITY
$6.95/411-9
Thrill City is the seat of the world's increasing depravity, and this classic novel transports you there with a vivid style you'd be hard pressed to ignore. No writer is better suited to describe the extremes of this modern Babylon.

JOHN WARREN

THE TORQUEMADA KILLER
$6.95/367-8
Detective Eva Hernandez gets her first "big case": a string of murders taking place within New York's SM community. Eva assembles the evidence, revealing a picture of a world misunderstood and under attack—and gradually comes to face her own hidden longings. An edge-of-the-seat thriller from this popular fetish author.

THE LOVING DOMINANT
$7.95/600-6
Everything you need to know about an infamous sexual variation, and an unspoken type of love. Warren, a scene veteran, guides readers through this rarely seen world, and offers clear-eyed advice guaranteed to enlighten the novice and seasoned erotic explorer alike.

DAVID AARON CLARK

SISTER RADIANCE
$6.95/215-9
A meditation on love, sex, devotion and death. The vicissitudes of lust and romance are examined against a backdrop of urban decay and postmodern kink, in this testament to the allure— and inevitability—of the forbidden.

THE WET FOREVER
$6.95/117-9
The chilling story of Janus and Madchen—a small-time hood and a beautiful sex worker on the run—examines themes of loyalty, sacrifice, redemption and obsession amidst Manhattan's sex parlors and underground S/M clubs.

BUY ANY 4 BOOKS & CHOOSE 1 ADDITIONAL BOOK, OF EQUAL OR LESSER VALUE, AS YOUR FREE GIFT

MASQUERADE BOOKS

MICHAEL PERKINS

EVIL COMPANIONS

$6.95/3067-9

Evil Companions has been hailed as "a frightening classic." A young couple explores the nether reaches of the erotic unconscious in a confrontation with the extremes of passion.

THE SECRET RECORD: Modern Erotic Literature

$6.95/3039-3

Michael Perkins surveys the field with authority and unique insight. Updated and revised to include the latest trends, tastes, and developments in this misunderstood genre.

AN ANTHOLOGY OF CLASSIC ANONYMOUS EROTIC WRITING

$6.95/140-3

The best passages from the world's erotic writing. "Anonymous" is one of the most infamous bylines in publishing history—and these excerpts show why!

PHILIP JOSÉ FARMER

A FEAST UNKNOWN

$6.95/276-0

"Sprawling, brawling, shocking, suspenseful, hilarious..."

—Theodore Sturgeon

Lord Grandrith—armed with the belief that he is the son of Jack the Ripper—tells the story of his remarkable life. His story progresses to encompass the furthest extremes of human behavior.

FLESH

$6.95/303-1

Stagg explored the galaxies for 800 years. Upon his return, the hero Stagg is made the centerpiece of an incredible public ritual—one that will take him to the heights of ecstasy, and drag him toward the depths of hell.

HELEN HENLEY

ENTER WITH TRUMPETS

$6.95/197-7

Helen Henley was told that women just don't write about sex. So Henley did it alone, flying in the face of "tradition" by writing this touching tale of arousal and devotion in one couple's kinky relationship.

ALICE JOANOU

THE BEST OF ALICE JOANOU

$7.95/623-5

"Outstanding erotic fiction." —*Susie Bright*

The best from this major name in the renaissance of American erotica. This volume includes excerpts from *Cannibal Flower*, *Tourniquet* and *Black Tongue*—the titles that announced her talent to the world.

BLACK TONGUE

$6.95/258-2

"Joanou has created a series of sumptuous, brooding, dark visions of sexual obsession, and is undoubtedly a name to look out for in the future." —*Redeemer*

Exploring lust at its most florid and unsparing, *Black Tongue* is redolent of forbidden passions.

TUPPY OWENS

SENSATIONS

$6.95/3081-4

Tuppy Owens takes a rare peek behind the scenes of *Sensations*—the first big-budget sex flick. Originally commissioned to appear in book form after the release of the film in 1975, *Sensations* is finally available to fans of modern erotica.

SAMUEL R. DELANY

THE MAD MAN

$8.99/408-9/Mass market

"Delany develops an insightful dichotomy between [his protagonist]'s two worlds: the one of cerebral philosophy and dry academia, the other of heedless, 'impersonal' obsessive sexual extremism. When these worlds finally collide...the novel achieves a surprisingly satisfying resolution...."

—*Publishers Weekly*

Graduate student John Marr researches the life of Timothy Hasler: a philosopher whose career was cut tragically short over a decade earlier. Marr begins to find himself increasingly drawn toward shocking sexual encounters with the homeless men, until it begins to seem that Hasler's death might hold some key to his own life as a gay man in the age of AIDS. Surely this legendary writer's most mind-blowing and explicit novel.

DANIEL VIAN

ILLUSIONS

$6.95/3074-1

Two tales of danger and desire in Berlin on the eve of WWII. From private homes to lurid cafés, passion is exposed in stark contrast to the brutal violence of the time, as desperate people explore their darkest sexual desires.

PERSUASIONS

$4.95/183-7

"The stockings are drawn tight by the suspender belt, tight enough to be stretched to the limit just above the middle part of her thighs, tight enough so that her calves glow through the sheer silk..." A double novel, including the classics *Adagio* and *Gabriela and the General*, this volume traces lust around the globe.